I0627621

Open Pollinated Productions LLC
ISBN (ebook) 978-1-988759-11-1
ISBN (paperback) 978-1-988759-12-8

www.mskaminsky.com
Receive a free book and learn more about the author!

<u>Special Thanks</u>

Dedicated to all the truth-seekers, daring souls, and bold rufflers of societal feathers.

Hey, my awesome beta-readers! I wanted to give a big shoutout to each and every one of you for your keen eye and incredible attention to detail. Seriously, you're all lifesavers, and I couldn't do this without you.

I also want to give a special thanks to the Brooklyn Speculative Fiction Writers group for their helpful feedback and for keeping me connected to the writing community. You guys rock!

And, of course, a huge thank you to my husband and the Kaminsky family for all of their love and support. Not to mention the delicious meals we've shared together that have fueled my creativity and helped me power through my writing sessions.

You guys are the best, and I am so grateful for all of you. Thank you for being a part of this journey with me, and I can't wait for you to read the finished product!

CHAPTER ONE

I LAY PARALYZED in the suffocating darkness. My heart throbbed in my chest like a frantic drumbeat. The Fright had taken over, and I was drowning in my fear. I pounded my fists against the door of the infusion pod. My voice was hoarse from screaming. When I tried to call for help again, the only sound that emerged was a feral yelp.

Lister sat on the hatch door above me, holding it shut. This time I was going to die—I knew it. The ward nurse would not help me. Piper was away on a mission, and my sister was powerless against the loathsome man.

My hearing faded out like the last chords of a dying song. Consciousness slipped away, but you know what? I was okay with it. Better to be knocked out than to keep dealing with The Fright. This cramped, airless coffin of a space was too much to handle. Just when I thought I'd reached the end of the line, *BAM!* The hatch door exploded open, and there was Piper, my brother, looking furious. Myhhris cowered in the corner, tears streaming down her face.

"What were you doing to her?" Piper demanded. He raised his safety gun and pointed it at Lister's garland. Lister waggled his finger.

"Uh uh, I don't think you want to be doing that unless—?"

To my surprise, Piper lowered the safety gun. The warning bell for our first shift sounded. Lister exited, a satisfied smirk on his face. I was too shattered to speak, my body still trembling.

"The ward nurse allowed this? She should have scanned him!" Piper said, turning to Myhhris.

Myhhris's eyes met mine, tears streaming down her face. "The nurse won't help us, Piper," she whispered.

Piper's eyes hardened. "Enough is enough. In two weeks, I'll gain enough points to upgrade, not just me, but all of us. I'll get us away from that psychopath soon. I'll get us away from all of this."

At the time, I didn't understand his choice of words. *Get us away from all of what?* We lived in the Hive, one of the last habitable places on earth. Getting away from Lister would be more than enough for me.

Piper massaged the back of his neck and then cracked his back. "Can you hang on just a couple more weeks? Both of you."

With a brave nod, I mirrored Myhhris's confident gesture, but deep down, I couldn't shake the gnawing fear that Lister would snuff me out before I saw the end of this hopeless situation.

CHAPTER TWO

JUST TWO WEEKS later, a chocolate cupcake changed my life. Back then, I had no idea that such a wonderful thing existed. The Hive was the only life I knew.

"Where's Piper?" I mouthed to Myrrhis. We stood in our assigned places in the Great Hall—a vast dome of white that soared over polished floors as white as bone. Massive ventilation fans hummed sending a continual rush of clean, cool sterile air. Myrrhis stood on my left, and Piper should have been on my right. He was not.

Myrrhis glanced around the Great Hall crowded with several hundred other Free Citizens, blinked twice, and turned to the raised altar in the center, face impassive. "Piper is being Piper," she whispered.

The weekly dance of the First Nurses was the event I looked forward to the most. Attendance was not mandatory—we were Free Citizens. However, non-participation was uncommunal behavior, and he'd never missed a gathering.

"Will he lose points?"

"Shush!" Myrrhis said. "He has plenty to spare. You'll lose what's left of yours if you don't keep quiet."

"Sorry."

Usually, Myrrhis would have been as worried as me, but, she'd changed. I patted down my unruly mane and, not for the first time, envied her flat, dark hair. My auburn hair erupted from my head like a burst of electricity. "Yeah, perhaps you're right."

She shushed me again, and my face reddened. As hard as I tried, I always seemed to break the rules without meaning to. My garland had the fewest points in our ward. We'd still live with Lister in Zone One if not for Piper. If not for Myrrhis' help, I'd never have had the opportunity to train to be a Sanitary Clerk. Just once, I wanted to be the one who helped them. If I got selected to become a First Nurse, Myrrhis and Piper would be so proud, and I would earn more than enough points for us all.

A fantasy flickered through my head as the First Nurses glided onto the raised center stage in their blues. I imagined I stood with them, arms at my side, as I gazed straight ahead, calm and poised. Citizens such as myself wore white. Ward nurses wore green. First Nurses and all others above Zone Three wore blue.

I was uncertain what purposes the colors served, but I'd made up my own story. Ward nurses in their greens were like the plants that no longer grew. They provided nourishment. Free Citizens such as myself wore white—sanitation for an unclean world. And First Nurses? They were like the sky that was no longer blue—they provided hope and inspiration.

It was hard to see the First Nurses' faces through the sanitary shields that buzzed around their faces like silvery flies. But I imagined they wore knowing smiles and that their cheeks were rosy. My hands clutched my breast. The room grew silent as they descended from the stage and circulated through the enchanted crowd.

Eyes taking in every minute detail, I adjusted my stance, attempting to emulate their stillness. Arms floating at their sides like feathers, they balanced on the balls of feet wrapped in soft slippers. How did they manage such grace? Would my clumsy feet ever do the same? It filled me with determination.

Soon the First Nurses stopped and stood in a solemn line. Lights rose, and stage illumination blinded me. Dr. Whisper's glimmering digital avatar descended a spiral silver staircase. He reached the bottom and stepped onto the platform that overlooked the room.

When he gazed out, I felt he only had eyes for me. He smiled at his

First Nurses, perfect, white teeth accenting silver hair. His eyes emanated such compassion that I felt my heart might burst with gratitude.

Opening his palms toward us, he spoke. "May health be with you!"

"And also with you!" I shouted so loud my throat burned. We owed him everything. Our lives. Our community. But I was perhaps most grateful for the opportunity to witness the First Nurses.

One day, I will dance with them. I vowed. *One day I will make their movements my own.*

"In a few days, it will be time for another Selection!"

Cheering filled the room. "On that day, one of you, should you be worthy, will join our First Nurses—dancers of grace and beauty here on stage. Will it be you?" He pointed to the left in the audience. Or you? He gestured in my direction, and I waved my hand in what I hoped was a graceful yet eager manner. "Earn your points, be model Citizens. This is key." I clutched my Garland wishing that I had more points.

Then Dr. Whisper closed his eyes and nodded his head. The First Nurses continued, the front row moving in perfect unison, their arms floating overhead as they undulated in larger and larger arcs, transforming the stage with their graceful dance. I swayed back and forth, mimicking their rhythm, but something felt different today. Something felt wrong.

When the dance ended, I stamped my feet so hard that my bones ached, my heart overflowing with determination. One day, I vowed I would dance with them. One day, I would make their movements my own.

Myrrhis walked ahead on the way back to our ward. I attempted to copy their movements when we reached a corridor with no one else around. Hands above the head, feet pointed inward, head arched. It hurt my back, and I nearly fell.

My sister turned and frowned. "Whatever are you doing? I'm certain that you will never be selected as First Nurse, and you may hurt yourself."

Not long ago, Myrrhis indulged my fantasy, silly as it was. But lately, Myrrhis hadn't quite been herself.

"Perhaps it's unlikely I'll be selected First Nurse, but still—"

Myrrhis nodded. "Dr. Whisper warns against idle fantasy. We each exist to fulfill our purpose and contribute to the community in our own ways."

"Of course, but Piper said it's healthy to dream from time to time, and during the Selection, anyone can—"

Myrrhis shook her head. "Piper speaks rubbish half the time, and I'll scan him if I hear him repeat such nonsense. Think about the past Selections. Whom did Dr. Whisper pick? Not anyone from our Zone, that's for sure. Zone 3 and higher or people whose garlands were full of points."

Having reached the door to our ward, I slid it open along its well-oiled casing. Many years ago, these doors opened automatically, but sufficient electricity no longer existed to provide such wasteful luxury.

We entered the two compartments that made up our ward. Three infuser pods, about six feet by three feet each, sat well apart so the ward nurses had room to move. The second room contained the disinfecting shower we used each night and morning.

Our brother, Piper, lay in his pod, a scowl furrowing his brow and sweat dampening his face. He looked as if he had exerted himself. "Piper! You missed the dance," I said.

"Yeah, so what?"

Why would anyone want to miss something so beautiful?

Myrrhis sprayed her pod with disinfectant. "A drone malfunctioned, remember? Piper probably had extra maintenance work, didn't you, Piper?" In the dim light, the circles beneath her eyes appeared more pronounced.

Piper mumbled something. He had been cranky recently, but I didn't have time to brood. Once we had our showers and settled into our pods, it was only a few minutes before our ward nurse came to insert needles and tubes into various parts of my body. When she finished, the nurse left my pod hatch open with just a slight gap.

"Health be with you," Myrrhis' voice sounded muffled from inside her pod several feet away.

"And also with you," I said.

"Persi, I'm sorry I snapped at your earlier. Maybe you will be selected First Nurse someday." Her words were already slurred as the potent recipe took effect. My eyes misted up.

Meanwhile, Piper's laughter echoed from his pod. "Why would anyone even *want* to be selected?"

His words shocked me, and I meant to reply, but I drifted off. In the faint light that seeped through the crack, I noticed a fresh bruise on my left arm, a yellowish-brown hue. I gazed at the bruise, sometimes imagining faces in the interplay of brown, yellow, and blue markings that appeared and disappeared on my body. My thoughts returned to the First Nurses.

Before the last scrap of consciousness left me, I realized what bothered me. I knew their movements by heart—nothing wrong there. However, the three most recently selected First Nurses were missing.

CHAPTER THREE

I JOLTED AWAKE to the blaring morning music, disoriented and frightened. However, the slight gap that let in a sliver of light comforted me. My left arm pulsed with pain from a needle that got jammed in the wrong spot. My nose itched like crazy, but I lay still. The pain lessened, but the itch grew maddening.

A ward nurse arrived and lifted my hatch. Her precise movements mesmerized me as she removed the needles and tubes from my body.

"How are we this morning?" she asked, face obscured behind a buzzing sanitary shield. I could make out that she had frizzy red hair and kind blue eyes.

"The sores around my mouth hurt less. My nose is itchy. " I didn't mention the needle pain. That was expected. All other symptoms were to be reported.

"Gently scratch it." The nurse moved on to my brother's pod before heading to Myrrhis', who had a list of symptoms, including a crick in her neck, feet burning more than usual, dry eyes, and a headache. My eyes were dry too, and I felt terrible not to have mentioned it. What if I got docked points? Too late. The nurse left to complete her rounds.

Sitting up, I scratched my nose but disappointedly found it was no longer itchy. The cold tile floor sent shivers up my legs as I tried to mimic the grace of the First Nurses, but ended up stubbing my toe on my pod's metal corner.

Myrrhis went into the sanitation cube, leaving my brother and me alone. He stood at his pod, his body at an awkward angle, making me uneasy.

"What's wrong?" I asked, surprised he'd reported no symptoms.

Piper glanced at the sanitation chamber, turned, and removed a roundish brown object from beneath his pod. I stepped closer, but not too close. "What is that?"

"Liberation, or at least its seed." He held it up to the bright light. "It's called a cupcake."

I stared at the object in disbelief, its rough surface making me uneasy. "Is that one of the thingamawhatits that makes the drones fly?"

"Nah." His chuckle caught me off guard. I missed the old, light-hearted Piper.

I folded my arms. "Okay, I give up. What does it do?"

"It's food," he said, a dreamy look in his eyes.

"Food!" The word caught in my throat like a clump of hair as I thought of the consequences of possession.

"Shh! Pipe down," he whispered. Piper jutted his chin toward me. "You must wonder what it would be like to—"

"Don't you dare say it!"

"Eat?" Piper gazed at the object, and the look in his eyes startled me. "Would ya scan me if I ate it right now? Or maybe you'd like to try it?"

The garland embedded in Piper's neck was fully lit up. Unlike me, he could afford to lose a stone or two. He could be late for a shift, forget to report a symptom, or miss a First Nurse ceremony. But eating? No way. Lights out.

"Possession is a mortal threat to community safety. Eating is a primitive, narcissistic custom that breeds—"

Piper raised his hand. "Spare me Doc's speech, sis."

I reached into the storage slot beneath my pod and pointed my brand-new safety gun at his garland. A wistful smile flitted across his face. "Myrrhis might. You won't."

Tears stung my eyes. My brother knew me well. "This is wrong."

I lowered the gun. "You'll end up banished to Zone Zero if you get caught. Myrrhis and I don't earn enough to stay here. We'd wind up back with Lister!"

"No. You'll both leave The Hive with me. But I'll need your help to convince Myrrhis."

"Leave? No healthy person wants that!" I spat. "Where in the heck did you get that thing?"

"Let's just say a friend. I'm in love, and I've learned a lot since I met them."

"In love, what are you talking about?"

The sanitation cube stopped hissing. In a moment, Myrrhis' cycle would be complete.

Piper walked to me, standing closer than the acceptable four feet. His sad hazel eyes bored into mine. His expression confused me; it was only later that I learned about hunger.

"We're being lied to. Eating…it's not—"

"Stop!" My fingers trembled against the cool metal of my safety gun. "I'm not so weak. You think you know me, but—"

"Weak? No. *You* still have a shred of sanity. I need your help. Keep your eye on the North window during the next big moon. I'll be sending you a message. When you get it, bring it to Carum."

"Crazy Carum? No—"

But the cube door slid open just then, and Myrrhis stepped out bright and clean in her sanitary suit. The sweet tang of disinfectant filled the air, and I yearned for yesterday or the day before. I'd take any day other than the one where Piper brandished his hideous cupcake.

Myrrhis folded her arms. "Persi, you know how flustered I get when I have to rush. Piper, where were you yesterday?"

Piper offered her a sly smile, dropping his hand by his side. "I'll explain later—just a bit delayed. Whatever you do, make sure you head to the North window at the end of the first shift. Remember," he looked at me and winked. "I'll see you later. Think about what I said." Before I could stop him, he left.

Myrrhis turned to me, mortified. "Piper didn't sanitize!"

While the disinfectant spray washed over me, burning my skin, I thought about what Piper had said and what he had shown me. The entire event must have discombobulated me because soon Myrrhis pounded at the door.

"We're late!" Myrrhis said. Chemicals still dampened my skin as I hurried to dress.

* * *
* * *

The busiest travel time had begun, and we had far to walk. Plus, Myrrhis, with her feet, was slow. After the last scourge, red sores appeared around my lips. For Myrrhis, they'd sprouted on her feet. Yet without Dr. Whisper's infusions, we'd be dead, so I had no cause for complaint.

"Are you still pretending to be a First Nurse?" Myrrhis asked. "Please, not this morning?"

Sighing, I settled into my regular, lopping stride. I walked much more like my clumsy brother than a First Nurse.

We entered Zone Two's central corridor and fell into step with several hundred others heading in the same direction. Dressed in pristine sanitary whites, we walked the long halls toward our stations in neat lines. A group of women merged left ahead of us while we continued in the slow lane on the far left.

A Sanitary Supervisor approached in the opposite direction, spraying a delicate blue mist from his wand. As we grew closer, I saw it was Lister. A few days ago, I spotted him working in Zone Two, which made me very nervous. I looked away, hoping he wouldn't notice us.

Germicidal disinfectant filled my nostrils, and I breathed deeply, savoring the slight burn in my nose. A sting of excitement ran through me at the thought of soon being a part of the team responsible for sanitizing these endless halls.

"Take the fast lane! My feet are burning," Myrrhis waved me onward. "I will make it on time. I'll be fine."

Not on graduation day," I replied, clutching her hand. The pressure of the day showed on her face, her nerves frayed by the fear of tardiness. It broke my heart to see her struggle. "Besides, I'm the one to blame. Piper distracted me."

"Yes, but—" she glanced at the garland embedded at the base of my neck—only one-quarter of my stones were lit. The rest lay dormant and black. "You can't afford to lose another stone."

My right hand covered my garland as if I could force points into them through sheer want and wish. But, nope, it didn't work that way.

As we approached our destination, Myrrhis froze. "Persi, your safety gun! Where is it?"

Panic gripped me as I realized the gun was missing from my waist. We'd only been issued them two days ago, and it wasn't yet second nature to carry them.

"Go without me," I told her. "I may not be good at much, but I am fast."

"Don't you dare run!" Myrrhis called after me. I walked at a brisk pace until I rounded the corner...and then I ran.

CHAPTER FOUR

A FEW MINUTES farther down the endless, pristine hallway, I heard a noise and slowed to a walk. Around the next corner, I was surprised to encounter Lister again. His eyes narrowed to slits as I approached.

Before Piper got us our upgrades, Lister had been our supervisor. He started by gaining points through pure sneakiness—scanning me even when I made small honest mistakes. Then he learned about my issue—The Frights. The more he tortured me, the more I messed up, and the more points he harvested.

I experienced constant anxiety. Finally, our upgrade allowed us to escape him. Ever since, I felt a burning resentment emanating from him whenever our eyes met. I slowed to a health-minded walk as I navigated the labyrinth of corridors. I reached the familiar confines of our empty ward, and there it was—my safety gun had fallen at the foot of my pod.

Back in the hall, Lister was gone. The corridor lay empty, glistening with disinfectant. I raised my arms and soared down it, imagining I was a First Nurse. The blisters around my lips stung from the exertion, and my breath burned in my lungs, but I didn't care.

"Aha! Gotcha! Endangering community safety." Lister stepped from around the corner, safety gun in hand. It blinked and chimed as it scanned. *Infraction recorded.* A tinny female voice stated. A green stone on my garland winked out and became amber.

"But, I was just—"

A satisfied grin spread across his face, and he lifted it again.

Swallowing, I stopped the words from leaving my mouth. "Thank you for the correction, Citizen. Health be with you."

Lister grinned. "Obliged. And also with you. If you'll excuse me, I need to get to the assembly line. We miss you and hope you'll be back soon. " He lifted his spray wand and continued down the corridor while I walked the rest of the way, aware that I was late and had lost immunity. Dread collected in my gut. I'd never faced punishment without exemption.

* * *

The students stood spaced in five rows in the training room. A bleak view of The Desolation was visible through two small windows at the far end. My shoe squeaked on the disinfected floor, and I stumbled.

Angelica, our instructor, paused in her speech and turned to me, her piercing blue eyes blazing. Then, with a menacing stride in my direction, she aimed her safety gun at my neck. I had made the mistake of correcting her during a history lesson, and she'd held a grudge ever since.

She sneered, addressing the rest of the cadets. "Today, we have a live demonstration of what happens to those who do not comply with protocols. Watch closely."

I braced for the worst as she pulled the trigger. A bright green flash lit my garland, and electric jolts coursed through my body. I crumpled to the ground, convulsing, my head slamming against the hard floor.

Behind me stood a statue of Dr. Whisper, our revered leader, and I felt ashamed for my misdeeds. Through the pain, I gazed at his compassionate face and wished I were a better citizen. Eventually, the seizures subsided, leaving my head throbbing and my mouth stinging.

"Stand!" Angelica commanded.

I struggled to my feet, legs shaking. "Thank you for the teaching."

Angelica tensed her jaw. "Pleased. Now you all see this safety gun taught an important lesson to our fellow Citizen. Tardiness is unacceptable, especially for those with such privilege. It harms the community, which, by extension, harms health. I will strip you of your privileges if you lose another stone."

Ferula, a bald boy with beady eyes, raised his hand. "Will the safety gun kill her if she loses all her stones?"

Angelica frowned. "No. Citizens deserve correction. Even our unhealthiest, least promising members. The health of one is the health of all." She looked over at me. I looked away.

"I should have gone back myself," Myrrhis whispered. "Were you trying to dance again?"

I shook my head, too ashamed to tell her that my stupidity got me in trouble.

Angelica gave us our assignments. Tomorrow would be our first day working on our own. My eyes misted with tears. I'd been near the top of our group during our first training days. Myrrhis was right; my obsession with The First Nurses had to end.

The notion that the doctor might select me as a First Nurse had only occurred to me recently. But when we upgraded zones, I couldn't help but hope. People in Zone One were eligible but unlikely to be selected. But now we were in Zone Two, which raised our chances.

On the other hand, how would I ever catch Dr. Whisper's eye with my meager points and clumsiness? Laid out in my head, the idea of making it all that way seemed absurd.

I gazed at the gray horizon through the grime-covered window. Had Piper left The Hive and gone out there? A barren desert filled with disease and death? And then there was the poisonous thing he called a cupcake. Food. A bio-toxin and an abomination that would remove even the slightest chance of me being selected as First Nurse and send me right back to Lister or worse.

We were not prisoners. If I chose to, I could leave and walk outside. Living in The Hive was a privilege. At any time, I could take the long metal stairways down to Zone Zero, walk to the Final Door, open one, then two airlock seals, and step out and leave just as my parents did when they abandoned us. And now Piper too?

Far in the distance, a remote-controlled drone hovered near the horizon. Suddenly, an emergency alarm blared, interrupting my thoughts. "Attention all citizens. A grade four community health advisory is in effect. Proceed to your infusion pods and enter safe mode." Dr. Whisper's voice boomed over the loudspeaker.

I pointed as we hurried past the large North window that looked out onto the barren terrain. "Myrrhis! Over there."

She put her hand to her forehead and gazed at the horizon. "Where are they going?" We paused and stared out into the darkness.

Two drones chased a third, weaving in and out of the moonlit terrain farther than I'd ever seen them travel. We watched, transfixed, as one drone shot at the other.

Piper had given us the lowdown: keep your eyes glued to the North window when the big moon shows up. You see, it's one of the rare moments we get a peek at the world beyond The Hive. And that's something worth looking forward to, especially since our poor old sun decided to call it quits ages ago. But what were the drones doing?

* * *

That night, Piper did not return to his pod. Just before the infusion kicked in, something strange happened. A knocking sound echoed in my brain like someone was banging on a far-off door. Answering felt like the worst idea in the world. My world seemed to be falling apart, and I pointed the finger at Piper. It all started with that freakin' cupcake.

CHAPTER FIVE

TODAY OUR TRIAL period as sanitary clerks started. I should have felt excited. But instead, I felt unprepared for my duties and anxious about Piper. As Myrrhis and I walked down the long, white hall that led to the training room, I couldn't stop worrying.

"Something's wrong, Myrrhis. I can feel it."

"Relax, Persi," Myrrhis whispered as we headed to our morning duties. "Piper will be back."

Free Citizens kept three lines three feet apart between them when we walked. We were not soldiers. No one expected us to keep a marching pace, but out of consideration for those in front, behind, and to the side, we kept the same pace. Slower people kept to the right side, and those faster passed on the left two lanes. Citizens who walked too slow or fast would be scanned and lose points as they deserved.

Not only did I care for Piper, but he also held the key to our future. As a skilled drone electrician, he earned enough points to keep us in Zone Two. If he didn't return, Myrrhis and I would have to work twice as hard to make up the difference, or it was right back to Lister, the assembly line, and little for Selection.

I thought of the cupcake. "This time feels different. He told us to look through the window, and we saw those drones."

Myrrhis sighed with exasperation. "They were flying a training mission, and Piper has to maintain them. He probably worked overnight."

"If we get demoted back to Zone One, Lister will make our lives miserable."

Myrris shot me a sympathetic look. "Well, maybe you're right. But I still don't see how worrying changes anything."

At the next juncture, we separated and went to our designated starting areas.

My loop didn't take long to sanitize, so I went over it again, ensuring I sprayed every corner. The Hive was built during the final scourge that sickened and killed most of the world's population. Dr. Whisper was one of the original survivors of that period. His foresight ensured our comfort, but pathogens were a constant concern. Several hundred of us lived here now. We had plenty of space, which did not even count the abandoned, unused areas where the maglevs entered and left.

My assignment lay in one of our zone's outlying areas. The corridors were narrow here. There were few citizens around. When I had the halls to myself, I practiced the dance of the First Nurse, careful not to walk faster than the proper speed or threaten public safety. I had my reputation to uphold, after all.

A man appeared ahead, walking head down, and I fell back into a slow walk. He stopped when he saw me. Picking up my pace, I lifted my safety gun and scanned his garland to identify him.

Location authorized. No violation was detected. Five points, Persi.

"Thank you. Health above all." The man flashed a grateful smile and continued. It felt strange to be on the other side. Several others passed, and I scanned each of them. No one ventured out of their designated zones. No one ran or committed any other infraction. Part of me felt disappointed. Every person I scanned allotted me a few points, but I'd earn points faster if I recorded infractions. I wanted to accrue as many points as possible before Selection Day.

What I needed was to catch a full-on rule-breaker. Then I would pull the trigger and need to do nothing from that moment on—another beautiful aspect of our system. The safety guns rewarded or debited points and doled appropriate punishments. Most often, it would be a deduction of points. However, if the person lacked immunity…well, I knew firsthand what happened. Rebooting the brain, Dr. Whisper called it. The idea of doing that to someone left me queasy. But I had deserved it.

Soon, I reached an area with small windows looking out onto The Desolation. The Big Moon lit the world with its cold, blue light. Nothing to see but a patch of barren, sandy soil that ended at a spiny ridge of gnarly cliffs. Did Piper's body lie in that barren land? Tendrils of moisture crept along the window like gray tears. I sprayed my disinfecting wand down the hall and continued, trying to quiet my mind.

Back in our ward, Myrrhis and I showered and prepared ourselves for infusion. Myrrhis' eyes were dull, and she didn't seem keen on discussing her day. "I earned fifty-two points," she said when I asked.

"Better than me. Thirty-eight. At this rate, we'll end up back with Lister in no time."

"Whatever happens, happens," she said.

"How can you be so calm about this?"

Myrrhis shrugged and lay down in her pod, waiting. Each night, the doctor customized our infusions according to the community's needs. Nutrient deficiencies were rectified. Every cell, corpuscle, glob of hemoglobin, and white blood cell was lovingly scanned for pathogens and evidence of cellular disruption.

After analysis by the central AI, Dr. Whisper reviewed and tweaked his recipe to create the perfect health-giving elixir that kept us alive. His recipes held the key to our incredible longevity. Recipe X would allow us to become the first immortals in history if all went well.

I stared at Piper's empty pod. A shiny object caught my eye. Piper's safety gun sat in the storage rack beneath his pod. I picked it up.

"Why didn't he take this with him?" I went to Myrrhis' pod and showed it to her. She already lay, eyes closed, and appeared annoyed.

Myrrhis frowned. "Lie down. Let it go."

"He said he was in love. Maybe he did fly?" I said before I could take the words back.

Myrrhis' eyes focused on me. "He *did say* something to you, didn't he?"

"I don't know, and yes, I should have told them, but—"

"Another word, and I'll be duty-bound to scan *you*."

My brother's safety gun felt cool in my hand. Made of a stronger metallic substance than mine, it also had a heft. The holograph screen activated at my touch.

Tiny characters scrolled across the screen, and the safety gun chimed.

Hopper 902

Tears stung my eyes. Piper left that information for me. Myrrhis sat up.

"What was that? A message?"

I released my grip, and the message disappeared. There was no need to get Myrrhis involved in this.

"Hand that to our proctor."

"To Angelica?"

"Yes. Just because you don't like her doesn't mean we stop following the rules. Health above all."

"The message is for me, not Angelica!"

Myrrhis glared at me. "For you? Piper's safety gun is not yours to keep."

"But...he wanted me to have it. I promised—"

"That is not community-minded thinking. Have you forgotten our lessons already?"

"I will hand it in," I promised. "After tomorrow."

"Why after tomorrow?"

"Carum." I could not lie to my sister.

"Crazy Carum?"

"Oh, people call her that. She's quite wise. I found out she was a First Nurse once."

"Sure, and banished to Zone Zero for some crime. What did you promise her?"

I glanced at the scanner and then back at Myrrhis. "Piper asked me to give Carum a piece of information, and this must be it."

"When did you start keeping secrets? Now that you have the information, you don't need his safety gun anymore."

The infusion alarm went off, and I stashed Piper's safety gun under my pod. Then I climbed in, stretched out my arms, closed my eyes, and waited for the nurse to stick me with the needles that would take me on a journey to healing.

CHAPTER SIX

The following morning, Piper's pod still remained empty. The cupcake and all the prior events felt like a bizarre dream. Myrrhis was heading toward the sanitary spray cubicle when the door burst open. Angelica stormed in, accompanied by Nurse Sammon, his face red and blotchy.

"When did you last see your brother?" Nurse Sammon asked, his voice stern.

"Yesterday morning," Myrrhis' voice trembled.

"Is he okay?" I tried to hide my fear.

Angelica hesitated, glancing at Nurse Sammon before delivering the news that sent my world crashing down. "Free Citizen Piper 4089 has abandoned The Hive," she said, her voice cold.

Myrrhis' hand flew to her mouth. "No, he wouldn't do that," she said, disbelief etched on her face.

"He walked through the Final Door?" The memory of Piper's words about the cupcake and his desire to leave The Hive came flooding back. Had it driven him to madness?

Angelica's eyes narrowed. "How else would he leave? Did he say anything to you?"

Just as I was about to answer, I glanced over to where my brother had stood when I saw him last. On the floor, something caught my eye. Pieces of that object lay near his pod. *The cupcake.* Either they escaped sanitation, or he returned sometime when we weren't here.

I could've stopped everything if I had reported him when he showed me that poison! A burst of anger surged in my gut. Then I remembered he wanted Myrrhis and me to leave with him. But why?

If I told Angelica about our conversation, not only would I face punishment, but Myrrhis might also lose points—even her immunity depending on the severity of the penalty. The thought of being scanned again filled me with a sense of dread. No, I wouldn't risk Myrrhis being subjected to that. Myhrris had emotional grit, but I'd always been stronger physically. She might never be the same with her poor feet. I stepped over to the spot and stood on top of the particles.

"He was running late for his shift, but he seemed fine," I lied. Angelica glanced at the floor, and I froze, but then she turned back to Myrrhis.

Myrrhis nodded. "He was seldom late. That itself was odd. But what did he say to you, Persi? You told me you two spoke."

Angelica stepped closer. "Yes, tell me."

"I asked him why he was late, and he didn't give me a suitable answer," I said, realizing that my answer was not great either. Their faces remained neutral.

Nurse Sammon pursed his lips. "Well, you'll no longer be able to remain in Zone Two."

"Couldn't we have a little more time to regain points?" I asked.

Angelica smiled, seeming to gain satisfaction from this. "No. Against the rules. Back to Zone One as soon as we finish the arrangements. Unfortunately, you no longer have the luxury of your brother's points." Nurse Sammon nodded. "However, Myrrhis has enough points to remain in Zone Two in a collective ward."

Myrrhis looked at me, and I saw my fear reflected in hers. We'd never been separated.

"Can I still stay with Persi?" Myrrhis asked. "Zone One is fine."

"You don't have to do that, Myrrhis." But I didn't protest too much. The thought of not seeing her every day filled me with sadness.

"Fine. We'll assign you to a proctor there," Angelica said.

Every ward needed a point leader as its head. Piper had been our proctor.

"Lister has space in his ward," Nurse Sammon remarked. "They can live there. Will that be suitable, Nurse Angelica?"

"Oh, very acceptable. I was about to recommend the same."

* * *

After Angelica's visit, Myrrhis' face looked paler than usual. She turned to me. "Lister again? You were right."

"If you change your mind, I'll understand. You don't need to stay with me."

Myrrhis shook her head. "I won't leave you alone to face him." She shuddered. "Plus, what if you get The Fright again?" she asked.

"I won't. I'm over that now." The truth was, I did not know if I was over it. A crushing sense of claustrophobia overcame me when the pods were shut. Eventually, the infusion took hold, but it was sheer torture prior. Our current ward nurse knew this and took mercy. She left my hatch open, just a gap. That sliver of air and light made all the difference.

"We'll find a solution. But first, we need to earn more credits...." My mind ran through different scenarios. "But how will we earn enough to make up for Piper?"

"We'll work harder than anyone else, that's how," Myrrhis said, mouth a grim line.

"He was a drone mechanic. One of only four in The Hive. He was special. We're not. If I were selected First Nurse, I'd have enough credits for us to stay here," I said, voice lowered. "Perhaps Dr. Whisper will notice me if I practice hard. We wouldn't have to live with Lister. As First Nurse, I'd gain even *more* credits than Piper did. Then we could upgrade and—"

"Persi! Stop it right now!" Myrrhis shouted.

I shrunk back, startled. Not once in my entire life had I ever heard Myrrhis shout. "You are speaking like a crazy person. I've tried to be patient, but you must be realistic, or you'll end up in Zone Zero and die like Mom, Dad...or Piper."

"Piper is *not* dead! He's too smart to die." But not smart enough to avoid eating.

Myrrhis marched into the shower and slammed the door.

She was right. I'd never be selected. I had neither the poise nor the coordination. We'd live with Lister and go back to our old positions. We were lucky to be healthy and safe from The Desolation. Dreaming of being selected First Nurse was irrational. Anger burned my chest as I thought of Piper.

I leaned against my pod and looked at the cupcake remnants that lay where I'd crushed them beneath my foot. Things would get worse if someone found these.

Sighing, I bent to gather the foul substance and toss it down into the refuse shoot. On my hands and knees, the strange sweet smell rising from them grew stronger. My entire body trembled, and a peculiar sensation rose.

Eat it.

The idea caught me off guard. It sounded like me, yet the thoughts were unlike my own. Hand shaking, I raised several crumbs to my nose and sniffed. Then, without warning, a repulsive force overtook me. My finger popped into my mouth like a worm and fed me the crumbs.

A strange liquid exploded in my mouth. My cheeks burned, my eyes watered, and a moan escaped my lips. Tears streamed down my cheeks as new sensations flooded my body. Myrrhis emerged from the shower just as I finished licking the last crumbs from the floor.

Her shriek brought me back to my senses. "Oh gosh! What...?"

I hid my mouth with my hand as shame washed over me. Crumbs stuck to my lips. Huddled on the floor like a vile creature, a horrid eater, I was even worse than my brother. For all I knew, he'd never even tasted the cupcake but only threatened to. I gazed up at Myrrhis. "I—"

She backed away and grabbed her safety gun, pointing it at me. "I'm sorry, Persi!"

I stood. "No, please. I don't know what happened. I'll be downgraded to Zone Zero!"

Myrrhis clenched her finger, but tears glistened, and she leaned against her pod, eyes fixed on the ground. "Go. If you don't shower quickly, you'll lose points."

I scurried past her into the shower. As the disinfectant coated my body, strange feelings surged through me. A wild glow danced in my belly and crept to my face, which grew hot and prickly. Energy surged through my limbs, and I swayed in the disinfectant spray...more graceful than ever. Optimism bloomed in my chest. I'd made a mistake, that was true, but I would redeem myself! Deep inside, I knew I could become a First Nurse. I *would* prove Myrrhis wrong.

Humming, I spun, allowing the spray to sanitize every crevice of my body. Then I scoured my face and especially my lips and inside my mouth, washing away all traces of the cupcake. Soon my lips burned, my body stung, my face was chafed, and the feelings of elation diminished, replaced by a dull ache in my midsection. The pain increased until I doubled over and lay on the floor while the finishing spray misted me.

My gut twisted and convulsed as I experienced something shocking. A sickening liquid spewed from my mouth and hit the floor with a splat. The room spun as bright lights and jets of water pounded me, washing away all evidence of my wrongdoing.

"I'm sorry," I whispered. I felt cleansed and resolved never to make such a horrible mistake again. "I will not let Lister beat us, Myrrhis," I said, just as the warning bell echoed throughout the room.

I rinsed my mouth again, slipped into my uniform, and entered our ward. Myrrhis had left without me! Adrenaline pumped through my veins as I stepped out into the hall, frightened of the difficulties that lay ahead.

CHAPTER SEVEN

THE TRAINING ROOM loomed as I approached, heart pounding in my chest. Myrrhis was on the other side, deep in conversation with Angelica. My sister's gaze flicked toward me, and she glanced away. My face flushed with embarrassment, realizing the irony of my position. Here I was, a junior Sanitary Clerk, barely a day into my new role, and I'd committed the worst infraction possible.

Myrrhis left to begin her shift. The tension left my body. She would not betray me. As I watched her exit into the hallway, a flush of love and gratitude filled my heart.

"I will make it right," I whispered to myself. "I won't let you down."

I knew it would take a monumental effort to implement my plan, but it was the only way forward. Myrrhis had always called me stubborn, but for once, I'd use that trait to my advantage. I knew it wouldn't be easy, but I had to try. The first step was to get to Carum. She might know why Piper left or have a message from him.

Each week, we have two periods of unallocated time to take care of personal business. We used most of this time for basic tasks such as laundering clothes. Still, there was time for recreation, like visiting the seven statues of Dr. W or sitting and watching the night sky over the dusty plain and reminding ourselves how lucky we are not to be in The Desolation.

After completing my sanitary duties that afternoon, I left for Zone Zero. A single, dank stairway connects Zone One to Zone Zero. Crudely painted signs on the walls greeted me as I walked down long flights of metal stairs. *Freedom is our greatest gift. One body, one health, one mind.* It smelled of rust and decay.

After several minutes, I burst into a long, dimly lit hall. A rumble from deep underground tickled my feet. Perhaps a maglev passed, taking our exports to Free Cities to the east or west. Maybe one of our signature handmade toy bears sat in the cargo on its way to sick children? It cheered me to think of the bears despite the dismal surroundings.

Zone Zero is dark and full of shadows. It is here where The Final Door is located. It scared me to think that if I chose, I could walk out that door to my death. Like Piper did, cupcake in hand? *Eater.* Shame and sourness rose in my throat, reminding me of the cupcake's revenge.

The area around the Final Door area lay deserted—a few footprints on the dusty floor. Sanitation Clerks seldom came here. After the power disruptions, we no longer had the resources. It made me uneasy. Pathogens might lurk. Forcing away my fear, I continued.

"Looking for your brother? Or me?" a gravely female voice said behind me.

"What?" I spun around. "Oh, Carum, you scared me. Piper? Did you see him?"

"The boy who stole the drone." Dark yellowish circles the same color as the rind of Myrrhis' calloused heel lay beneath her eyes. Zone Zero was home to those who couldn't—well, make that wouldn't—contribute to the healthy functioning of The Free City. They received the lowest grade infusions and no health upgrades. Most died or walked through the Final Door and entered The Desolation. Survival here was difficult.

Myrrhis was right. No one in their right mind would exchange First Nurse for life here. Something *was* wrong with Carum. And yet still....she had once danced on the stage for Dr. Whisper. She had been one of his First Nurses. Piper confirmed it, and he had access to information we did not. Perhaps she knew something that would help me.

"I have the information you wanted."

"Good, good. They'll be delighted."

"Who will be delighted?"

"No one and everyone." She winked. Crazy Carum lived up to her nickname.

"What's the number? Tell me. Gimme, gimme." I gave her the hopper number I'd seen on Piper's screen, and she grunted, unimpressed.

"Your brother left you behind?"

"No. Maybe. I don't know what happened. Have you heard from him?"

"Is that him there?" she pointed through a grimy window that looked out into the dark of The Desolation.

"What?" My heart hammered. She took a few steps closer and pointed again.

I walked to the window and cupped my hands to see better. Far in the distance, barely visible in the starlight, lay a pile of human bones in a patch of sand and rock. This forlorn individual had died a long time ago.

"You are crazy." I looked away, tears in my eyes. Even though I knew it could not be Piper, my heart pounded.

"No, I'm not crazy," the woman smiled and inclined her head toward me. "My name is Carum, remember?"

"Is that all you do all day? Hang around here and bother people?" I was still shaken from seeing the bones. I'd never seen a body before in real life. "When did you last see Piper?"

"Three days ago."

I stepped toward her. She smelled odd. The odor prompted me to tap my garland. It showed that there was one hour before our infusion, and already I felt tired and spent. "Did he leave through the Final Door?"

Carum shrugged and gave me a sympathetic look that terrified me more than anything she'd done so far.

"Why did you give it all up? You were a First Nurse and…"

Carum snorted. "There are always some who don't fit in, and that's why the good doctor put those doors there—an escape hatch to release the pressure. If only I had the guts to leave, I'd go too. God bless him."

"How did you become a First Nurse? Is there a secret that might help me during Selection Day?"

"You must have thought about it once or twice? Wondered what it was like out there?" Carum grinned, ignoring my question.

"No! You seem to feel that it's okay to say whatever you like. Show me a pile of someone else's bones...lie about my brother."

"I've told you no lies. But there can be no freedom without truth. Go out there and look if you like."

"Into the Desolation? You are crazy."

"No," she laughed, "My name is Carum, and—"

I spun on my heel and marched away.

"Wait, girl!" Carum laughed. "I'm just amusing myself. Come and talk...I'll tell you what I know about Piper and why he left."

"I won't listen anymore!" Soon it would be infusion time, and I didn't want to rush up the stairs, which I knew would be tiring.

As I turned the corner, I looked back. Carum gave a backhanded wave of dismissal and shrugged. Instead of heading the way she'd come, she walked in the other direction. What if she knew something about my brother?

With no time to spare, I followed, feet silent on the smooth, plasticized walkway. She walked faster than expected. If she continued much farther, I'd have to turn back. I glanced at my safety gun, and when I looked up again, she'd disappeared. I crept forward, cautious. The hall lay shrouded in darkness and I could barely see my hand in front of my face. A few dusty lightbulbs, many burnt out, were the only source of illumination.

An open door led to an abandoned ward. I entered, but it lay empty. A strange-looking bed so old it was nothing but springs sat in the corner. I was turning to leave when a sliver of light caught my eye. It came from a one-inch gap between the floor. I walked over to it and tugged. What looked like a solid wall lifted to reveal a long metal staircase leading down.

My garland pulsed and vibrated, tickling my collarbone—no more time. Not only could I not afford to lose points by being late, but I'd also been looking forward to the infusion all day. Unfortunately, after all the excitement, I felt lightheaded and weak. I'd return after I'd regained my strength.

As I turned to leave, a strange odor hit my nose. It was not the cupcake smell. But, despite that, it was odd and unfamiliar. *Food?* It might be nothing, but it also might be a violation that would offer a massive reward of points and the chance to redeem myself.

My mind raced as I weighed the options, but then I decided: this was my opportunity. When the moment was right, I'd return and investigate.

CHAPTER EIGHT

WHEN I MADE it back to our ward just in time, I was shocked to find it deserted. Where had Myrrhis gone? I disinfected and was about to settle into my pod when the door slid open. Supervisor Angelica and Nurse Sammon stood there, looking like they meant business.

"Hold up, don't get too comfy!" Angelica announced. "You're being transferred back to Zone One, remember?"

"What? Right now? But we thought..." I stammered, caught off guard.

"There's no 'we' in this situation. Your sister stayed in a communal ward in Zone Two as we offered," Angelica explained with a sly smile.

"She said she wouldn't!" I said, feeling betrayed.

Nurse Sammon grabbed my arm and led me out of the ward. Angelica just shrugged. "Let's say I convinced her to change her mind. We both want what's best for Myrrhis, after all."

The halls were eerily quiet, with most citizens already snug in their infusion pods. But I was anything but calm as Angelica and Sammon rushed me along.

"We're late for the infusion," I said, heart pounding with anxiety.

Angelica shot me a wicked grin. "Don't worry. Lister will wait."

Lister's ward lay silent, and the space was dark and full of shadows. Everyone lay in their pods. Then an oily figure slid from the gloom.

"Welcome back, my dear." Lister's eyes narrowed. "I knew you weren't fit for Zone Two."

My cheeks flushed with shame.

"You handle her from here," Angelica commanded. Lister's mouth split into a toothy grin, and they left.

"Guess your brother's luck wore off, huh?" He swung his arms open wide. "I missed you, and it'll be my pleasure to have you back. Tsk, so sad that face." He licked his lips. "Allow me to show you your new infusion pod. In *our* infusion chamber." He emphasized the word *our* with a leer.

My heart raced as he led me down the wide, white corridor. We rounded the corner and entered a small communal infusion ward.

"Aren't you going to thank me?" he asked. "I know how you like special treatment. It'll be cozier. Where is your sister, by the way?"

"She stayed in Zone Two," I choked.

"Ah well, even nicer. It'll just be you and I. Hop in. We're late."

The warning bell rang.

"Okay," I said, trying to control my voice as I stepped toward the pod. "Well..." I turned my head, avoiding his gaze and hiding the tears in my eyes. He grabbed my arm.

"Where did your brother go?" he demanded. "I know you know something." He stood over me, his fingers digging into my skin.

"I don't know!"

"If you don't tell me now, I'll find out. No one keeps a secret from Lister for very long."

Trembling, I climbed into the pod. Finally, the ward nurse arrived, and I asked her to open the hatch just a crack, hoping Lister wouldn't overhear.

"Shut her up tight!" he commanded.

I clenched my jaw, determined to endure The Fright for a brief time. The ward nurse, her expression hidden behind her sanitary mask, followed his instructions and closed the pod.

"No, please," I protested, acting impulsively and blocking the hatch with my arm. My left IV line came loose. After that, I only have a hazy memory of Lister coming to scan me and taking away more points.

* * *

* * *

Little brown eyes made of felt-like material, light brown whiskers, and a belly embroidered with the words *Huggable* passed by one by one.

Bam! My right hand slammed a stamp on the paper tag attached to the bear's ear. *Handmade With Love in the Southern Free City.*

"Four-point bonus to Persi 4091! Fastest on the line!" A digital voice announced.

If I'd lost focus and taken the precious few seconds away to look up, I'm sure I'd have spotted more than a few looks of envy. But right now, I focused on the task—sending toys to sick kids—and gaining as many points as possible.

These toys were destined for a children's ward in the Western Free Cities. I frequently glanced at the scoreboard screen when I first learned this task. Not anymore. That slowed me. Instead, I kept my eyes on the job. Nothing but the teddies, stamping, scanning, ignoring the pain in my wrists, and enjoying the chirp and chime as each one entered the shoot and hurried down to be transported by drone to kids in need.

I was so lost in the rhythm that when the stream of teddies stopped, I almost toppled over into the teddy shoot. Rotating my swollen wrist to ease the pain, I looked up at the leaderboard. A warning flashed.

Citizens—Special Announcement. A few seconds later, the image flickered, and Dr. Whisper's avatar appeared. Distinguished and handsome as always in his pristine blue uniform, his voice sent a thrill up my body.

"Living in the Free City comes with the many rewards you know well—health, freedom from the many illnesses that plague The Desolation, and of course, fun. We don't work here. We play."

We stomped our feet to show appreciation and gratitude.

"I must postpone my two hundred and sixtieth birthday celebration because of recent events. A new contagion was detected. The good news is that the genome has been sequenced, and your infusion recipe is being continually adjusted. Safety protocols are part of your basic health guarantee. No upgrades are required to receive this critical update, and we will clean your blood of all pathogens!"

I stomped my feet. It made me think of Myrrhis. I always stomped for her since she couldn't stomp very hard. Now it didn't seem worth the effort.

"However, I'll have to postpone my birthday celebration for later in the cycle," Dr. Whisper announced. "But don't worry. There's no need to panic. Free citizens, head to your pods and prepare for safety mode to start in half an hour. If you're in other zones, keep going about your daily routine. Infusions will start an hour earlier than usual in all zones. May health be with you!"

"And also with you!" we shouted in unison.

The thrill I had felt only moments before vanished as Lister sauntered past. The bright lights of the assembly room illuminated his greasy face, but a tiny speck on his uniform caught my eye. It looked like a crumb, similar to the one from Piper's cupcake.

I tried to look closer, but Lister turned away before I could examine it further. The sudden movement left me wondering what he was trying to hide. Maybe it was nothing, but if it were something...if Lister were an eater? This seemed less likely than my being chosen as the First Nurse, yet the reward would be nearly as significant.

From now on, I'd watch the loathsome man closely.

CHAPTER NINE

THE NEXT DAY during our break, Myrrhis came to see me. Silently, she whisked me down the corridor. I glanced toward the bear assembly line. Lister remained inside, chewing out one of the slower workers.

Myrrhis placed her hand on her heart and gazed at my garland. "I wish things were different," she said with a sigh.

"I miss you. But I understand.."

"So, how's it going with Lister?" she asked, raising an eyebrow.

"As horrible as ever, maybe even worse," I admitted, feeling my mouth sores burn. "He's got me assigned to a small ward with him, to intimidate me. And the Frights came back," I added, feeling ashamed. "But I'm determined to make up for it and earn enough points to join you again," I told her what I had learned after speaking to Carum, including my suspicions about Lister.

"Persi, if people are breaking Codes of Health and Wellness, you must inform your Proctor. Zone Zero is not somewhere you want to spend time!"

"Inform a Proctor? Do you mean Lister? I don't even have any proof yet."

"Well, maybe not, Lister."

"Plus, I have no proof yet. But I smelled something strange there, Myrrhis. Possibly food. Rule breakers. And I aim to scan them for the good of our community and to make up for my misdeeds."

"How would you scan them? You no longer have your safety gun. Unless you kept Piper's. You promised to return it."

My face reddened as I realized she'd caught me in a fib. "Right now, I can't think of anyone who needs points more than me, can you?"

"Your actions are not community-minded."

"All free citizens may visit Zone Zero!"

"Who in their right mind would want to?"

"My plan *will* work, Myrrhis. I promise. I can't spend the rest of my days with Lister. What kind of life would that be?"

Myrrhis folded her arms. "What if you don't find any rule breakers?"

That hadn't occurred to me. Would I know food when I saw it? I'd seen the cupcake and even tasted it. That was a start. But what if the strange odor I detected was not food but something else? All I could do was hope my instincts were correct.

* * *

Finding the entrance I'd seen Carum go through took me longer than expected. The silence unnerved me as I prowled the lonely corridors of Zone Zero. Passages in the upper zones were never crowded, but a steady stream of Citizens traveled for various shifts and duties. Here I saw no one.

This time, the door was closed when I arrived. I stumbled through four other abandoned rooms before finding the right area. I wedged my fingers under the gap and pushed the door up. The metal staircase beckoned me, extending to a landing and then turning. How far down did it go, and where did it lead? Nothing below Zone Zero except for the maglevs, at least not that I knew of. Zone Negative One? The idea made me chuckle.

Today was our day of rest, so I was in no hurry. I had time to complete my mission. But tomorrow was Selection Day, so I needed to make it happen. What struck me was the smell. It was unfamiliar but not unpleasant and may have been from the metal stairs or something further below. One thing was sure, though: these stairs had not been sanitized. The thought filled me with dread.

However, I thought of Lister's leering face and spending day after day with him. I had to turn a negative into a positive. I imagined Myrrhis's smile when I arrived, with my garland lit up and all my lost points restored. I hastened onward, step by step until I became dizzy and my heart was pounding. It was not just from the exertion. I was scared.

After what felt like hours, the stairs ended. To my right was a large steel door, locked. To my left was a long passage lit by lights as yellow as the moon.

"Hello?" I called out, taking a few steps down the corridor. I heard dripping water, but there was no response, no voices. For a moment, I thought about turning back and returning to the staircase. Our living quarters were pristine and sanitary, with white walls, whereas here, the walls were red and marred with what could be mold or unknown bacteria. My body shuddered with disgust.

"May health be with me," I whispered, voice trembling. Then I shut my mouth for fear I might inhale contamination. I breathed shallowly and through my nose as much as possible as I crept down the hallway. The passage ended a few minutes later, and I found myself in a strange space.

The light was dimmer here, but those strange yellow lights remained glowing in the ceiling. To my left, rows of giant rusting metal things sat squat and ugly. They each had four round, black circular wheels beneath them. Whatever they were, they were ancient. It didn't take much to figure out that these came from the time before. The scent I'd noticed earlier at the top of the stairs wafted in on a breeze, drawing me forward and warning me to be cautious.

Shrill laughter echoed through the damp walls as I approached, and the smell grew stronger. I spotted some people around the corner and recoiled. Carum appeared from a silver door and joined them, holding a large black pot. I wondered why they would want to spend time in such a terrible place. They were gathered around an orange glowing object, which I did not recognize.

It's called a fire. The idea jumped into my mind, but I wasn't sure from where.

Carum was chewing something, eating. My heart raced. Scanning one of them would restore my lost points and upgrade me to Myrrhis' zone. If I scanned all of them, I'd earn enough points to upgrade to Zone Three, and being selected First Nurse would be all but certain.

My hand trembled as I lifted my safety gun and turned it on, but the display read, *No signal.*

I tapped it—the same message. The green blinking light showed that the safety gun was ready. Perhaps it would correct itself after I'd scanned a target? I crept forward. Carum stood laughing and eating with three others. My stomach looped over itself, and nausea rose. They were drinking too! An acrid liquid that permeated the air with its stench.

Taking one, two, and three steps, I leaped forward and shone the green light at Carum's garland. She yelped. My safety gun beeped as it scanned her garland and stored it in its memory bank.

Scan stored. Transmission failed.

"Ah, for crying out loud, can't I enjoy my dinner in peace!" Carum shouted; particles from her mouth flew in the air, and I stumbled back.

"What the hell?" A man carrying a food tray emerged from a metal door hidden in the wall. I didn't need to see his face. I already recognized his voice. *Lister.*

"You?" he slammed the door shut and put down the tray. I lifted my safety gun and pulled the trigger.

Scan stored. Transmission failed.

"Don't worry. I'll grab her before she gets a signal. Bust the bloody thing." Lister lumbered toward me.

I lifted my safety gun. "I'll scan you again!"

"Go ahead, do what you want. You'll be lucky even to hold the scanner after I'm through with ya." He circled me around a giant, rusting metal contraption with four black wheels.

"Why isn't my safety gun working?" I asked no one in particular.

"Too far underground, that's why. Signal don't work here," Lister snarled. He seemed confident that he'd catch me. "C'mon, cutie-pie, hand it over, and I'll go easy on you."

I turned and ran. I didn't expect him to follow, but he did, and much faster than I expected. Soon the lights faded, and I slowed my pace.

"Watch out, or you're gonna get hurt. There's a good twenty-foot drop ahead," Lister said, trying to catch his breath. "Slow down. Let's work this out."

"You're an eater!" I shouted over my shoulder, pushing away the thought that I, too, had eaten.

"Yeah, yeah. But eating is not what you think. Dr. W tricked you."

Blood rushed to my face. Dr. Whisper was my hero, and we owed our lives to him. Adrenaline coursed through my body, but I forced myself to calm down.

"Yes, you're right." I stopped running and faced him.

Lister arrived seconds later. He stopped and shot me a wary glance through watery, bloodshot eyes. "Good, now hand me that."

I held it out. The moment he stepped closer, I ducked beneath his outstretched arm. As I scooted past him, I felt swift and agile as a First Nurse...until his foot jabbed out, and I tumbled to the ground.

Lister got me in a chokehold, cackling with glee. His giant hands were wrapped around my neck, cutting off my air supply. My vision was going black, and I struggled to breathe. The stench of his breath was overpowering, and I felt like I'd pass out any moment.

Suddenly, I glimpsed something from the corner of my eye. At first, I thought I imagined things, but then I saw them again. A boy I'd never seen before was staring in shock. But he didn't waste any time.

"Hey!" he shouted, catching Lister's attention. His grip on my neck loosened, and I gasped for air, sitting up.

Lister turned and punched the boy in the head. "Mind your own business, hominoid."

Hominoid?

"Run!" the boy shouted, and I didn't need to be told twice. I wriggled from beneath Lister and took off. However, I was running not only from Lister but also from the mysterious boy.

A hominoid? What did it all mean?

CHAPTER TEN

DEEPER AND DEEPER into the gloomy, underground realm, I ran. One bleak corridor resembled the other. I was disoriented and lost, but I didn't care. My legs were pumping, heart was racing as I pushed myself further than I ever had before. It was dangerous to run like this, but I felt like a rebel, breaking rule after rule in my desperate escape.

My mouth felt like it was on fire, blisters burning, and my whole body trembled with exhaustion. But had to find my way out. I checked my garland, but it was dead. No signal. Had I been banished already?

Health Above All.

What if I had contracted a disease? That might explain why I felt so sick and why my chest ached. Then, just as I was about to collapse from the dizziness, I caught a faint glimmer of light in the distance. A cool breeze brushed against my face. It grew stronger, faster, until it was a full-blown gale, whipping my hair and clothes. The comforting scent of disinfectant filled my nostrils, and I knew I was close. I raced towards the light, determined to find my way out of this hellish place.

The passage opened into a massive chamber. Three rows of single tracks disappeared into a tunnel on the other side. A robotic arm loaded crates into the hopper of a maglev that sat docked.

Hopper 902. Is this what Piper's note referred to?

The air felt warm and sticky, but the scent of disinfectant was strong, and it smelled like home. In the far corner was a pile of stuffing—bear stuffing. I settled into it to catch my breath like a bird in her nest.

I'd only seen a bird once—most died long ago—but one made her home outside in The Desolation on one of the contagion sniffer poles. It didn't take long before a drone flew down low and eliminated her for our safety. Until then, I enjoyed watching the doomed creature nest with her chicks whenever I passed that window.

All I could do was rest and hope I gained enough strength to move again. Nestled down and comfortable, my eyes grew heavy, and soon I fell asleep.

At some point, I dreamt of something strange. Liquid filled my mouth, and a taste...an indescribable taste—what a wonderful dream. As I realized what was happening, the dream turned into a nightmare. I was drinking.

Drinking?

My eyes fluttered open. The boy I'd spotted earlier kneeled over me, a concerned look on his face.

"Drink more." He smiled.

"What are you doing?" I shouted, spitting the liquid in his face. He sputtered and stumbled away.

I lay in a pile of stuffing, just like in my dream. A short distance away, crates continued to be loaded into their hoppers.

"Hey! Why did you do that? I'm trying to help you," his voice sounded different from others in the Free City. His vowels were longer, and his voice had a smooth quality that made the voices of the Free Citizens sound harsh in comparison.

"You're poisoning me."

"Tea. I'm trying to help you."

I fumbled for my safety gun, raised it, and pointed it at him. "You are in violation."

The boy looked frightened.

I'm unsure why I felt the urge to apologize, but I did. "I'm sorry." Then I pressed the trigger. A bolt shot from the safety gun.

Scan failed. Transmission failed.

Scan failed? I'd never seen that before. Then I noticed he had no garland.

I leaped to my feet. "You're a hominoid!"

The boy's broad brow crinkled. "I'm not sure what a hominoid is, so how could I be one?"

Perhaps he had a point, but on the other hand, a hominoid may resemble a human. "You have no garland," I said. My finger hovered over the trigger, but it felt useless. "Where did you come from?"

He wiped the tea from his forehead. "Out there. The place you call The Desolation."

"Lies. No one survives The Desolation. Everyone dies from disease or solar radiation."

The boy shrugged. "Yet, here I am."

"Why were you making me drink poison?"

"I found you, passed out. You needed healing."

"I need my infusion, and somehow, I got lost." The boy took a sip from his bottle. Watching his Adam's apple bob as he drank filled me with fascination and disgust.

"What? You look like you've never seen anyone drink before?"

I shook my head. "Not until recently. It's...an archaic, unhealthy, uncommunal way to get nutrition. It's also revolting."

His face reddened, and he put the canister away. "What's your name? I'm Noah." He stepped toward me and jutted his hand in my direction. I drew back, clutching my safety gun.

He raised his hand again. "Whoah, sorry. I was trying to shake your hand."

"Why would you want to shake me?"

"Not shake you...shake your hand." He paused and scratched the scruff on his chin. "Well, I guess your hand is part of you."

"Physical contact spreads disease." No one could be that stupid. This must be some test, this shaking. Whoever heard of wanting to shake someone's hand?

"My name is Persi. I came here to earn points and replenish my garland." I pointed down at my neck. All my stones remained dark. I'd never seen this happen before, and I stared at them in shock.

"Hey, you alright?" he asked. "You look like you're about to cry."

While still shaky, I felt better than I had before my rest. However, whatever the boy had given me caused my stomach to cramp. Groaning, I bent over. The cramp dissipated, and when I stood, my legs felt stronger.

"What did you give me?"

"Spirit root tea. A powerful medicine."

"I don't know what spirit root tea is, but I need to get back, or I'll miss my infusion." Then, a horrible thought occurred to me. "And the Selection!" I must not miss that with all the new points that I'd now gain.

I stumbled to my feet and headed toward the giant area with three rows of metal tracks. The maglev was gone. Perhaps I could follow the tunnel back to safety?

"You'll get crushed by a maglev walking those tracks. I know the way. Come on. I'll introduce you to Kendel."

* * *

A tall, beautiful girl exited the silver door that Lister and Carum had emerged from. "Noah? What trouble are you getting us into now? It's bad enough we have to cook for that asshole. Don't make things worse," she said as she touched Noah's bleeding forehead. "Oh, please, don't tell me...." The girl shook her head and let out a weary laugh. "Now you've been attacked by one of them?"

"Crane will be pissed." Kendel folded her arms. Her skin was a pleasant tanned shade, and I didn't see a single sore or blister. I covered my mouth to hide my own.

"They hurt her, Kendel! Plus, I promised Piper," Noah said.

"You know my brother?" I forgot my self-consciousness and stepped forward.

Noah started to answer, but Kendel swatted his chest, and he stopped. "It's complicated," he said.

We walked together, with Noah holding a metal cylinder that sprayed light out of its front. He was careful to shine it so I wouldn't trip.

"Is it true that you're afraid of food?" Kendel asked as we walked.

"I'm not afraid of food. It disgusts me," I replied.

"But the others...." Noah started.

"Rule-breakers. Deviants. *Eaters*," I spat. "I came to scan them, to punish them. I have enough points to upgrade and be selected as First Nurse. But I need to get back. It must be infusion time soon, right?"

Kendel and Noah looked at me, confused. "Points?" Kendel said.

"Yes. I lost all my points when my brother disappeared. Do you know him or not?"

Noah glanced at his sister.

"Noah, if you—"

"Kendel, it's okay. Trust me."

45

"Yes, we know your brother. He asked me to find you and your sister."

My legs kept moving, but I felt so overwhelmed with confusion that they might giveaway at any moment.

"Is Piper here?"

"No, he's back home."

"Home? Which zone are you from again?"

"I told you, we're not from a zone. We're from The Cliffs. He asked me to come and get you and your sister. Are you Persi or Myrrhis?"

"Persi."

"Ah. Well, that's good luck on my part. You look nothing like Piper said. You're quite pretty. Wouldn't you say, Kendel?"

Kendel said nothing, and I felt my face redden. That was Piper for you.

"I'm not so fond of Piper's looks either."

"You look nothing alike," Kendel said.

"My brother is in the Desolation? And alive? But that's not possible."

Kendel brushed her glossy hair back from her face. "I guarantee you. He's very much alive. Follow me. We want to show you something."

"No...I need my infusion. Please help me find my way out." My head throbbed and my back ached. My mouth was pasty, and my heart burned and pitter-pattered in my chest. How long would the prior infusion's recipe protect me?

What felt like days later, we reached a familiar area. We walked past the rusting hulks of the metal objects. "What were these things?"

Noah answered. "Cars. Trucks."

"I've never heard those words," I said.

Kendel glanced at Noah. "They are an old means of transportation."

The thought of it seemed familiar, but I couldn't quite place why.

"Wait, this isn't the way I came." I gasped as we stepped into a massive cavern with a soaring ceiling. A rickety ladder, rusted with age, was embedded in the rock wall and stretched as far as my eyes could see.

"What is this place?" I asked, filled with awe and a sense of foreboding.

"A detour," Kendel answered as she climbed the ladder. "And we have to take it. Senior told me you can help us."

"Help with what?"

"You'll see."

Noah hesitated for a moment. "Kendel, we don't have time."

But Kendel was already making her way up the ladder. "It won't take long. Trust me."

CHAPTER ELEVEN

AFTER A GRUELING climb up the ladder, we reached our destination. We entered a dark, dreary tunnel and crawled through it on our hands and knees.

"This isn't the way out!" I said, wondering why I was following them, but afraid to get lost.

"A shortcut, just a bit farther," Kendel reassured me while Noah grumbled.

Trapped between them, I didn't see any other option, so I kept crawling. We arrived at a hatch, and Kendel pushed it open.

We emerged into a cavernous room with rows of gleaming silver doors connected by narrow stairways. The air was frigid.

"Well, now, how do we find it?" Noah asked, looking around in wonder.

"By her name and number," Kendel answered, walking up to one of the silver doors. "What's your full name, girl?"

"Persi 4091," I answered.

"Look!" she pointed. Each door had a name and number etched on it. "We need to find hers."

Noah led the way, holding his light out like a beacon, and I struggled to keep up with their quick pace. "Kendel took the long way to avoid your friends and show you this," Noah explained.

"Lister is *not* my friend." The thought of his icy hands gripped tight around my neck sent spiders up my spine.

"Uh, yeah, I was being sarcastic."

The word sounded familiar, but I wasn't sure what he meant. I stopped and craned my neck. Metal staircases led to rusty ramparts that connected the pods. How many levels were there? After five, the higher levels disappeared into the darkness.

"We wanted to show you this, Persi 4091," Kendel said.

"What are these things for?" Noah asked.

"This is where he hatches them," Kendel said.

Noah and Kendel distracted me from the reality of my situation. "Soon, I'll be late for my infusion! I can't afford to lose more points!" I clutched at my darkened garland.

Noah looked at me with sympathy. "We're close to the exit. Yeah, let's go."

Kendel stopped him. "We will, but first listen. This is important. Does this place look familiar?"

Kendel walked closer to the pods and pointed. Covered in a thick layer of dust, each pod had a name and a number engraved above it in tarnished silver letters. A few pod doors lay open, one half off its hinges. Others were closed.

"No. I've never been here before."

Something tickled the back of my mind—an old memory or perhaps an infusion-stoked dream.

The space was extensive. On either side lay row upon row of numbered hatches. There were hundreds of them. Most hatches lay open and empty, but a few were closed. Above each hatch, a number was displayed in tarnished silver letters.

"C'mon, let's walk a little further," Kendel said.

"Kendel!" Noah said. "Did you hear her? She's upset."

"Brother, I know these passages better than you. It's quicker to pass through this way."

This space terrified me. Yet another part felt curious. There were so many mysteries demanding answers.

My legs gave out, and I stumbled. A flush of humiliation crawled up my neck as Noah steadied me.

"What are you doing? Don't touch me!" I cringed away from him.

"Sorry. I didn't want you to fall," he said.

A First Nurse would approach this challenge with grace and dignity. I forced myself to stand straighter, and a dull ache began in my lower back. A transparent window to one pod gave a vantage to whatever was inside.

"There's a light flashing on that one." Noah shone his flashlight at the pod's door. A red light blinked.

"Kendel thought you might know what these were for." Noah pointed to the number above the pod 11334.

Do the numbers mean anything to you?" Kendel asked

"No. Should they?"

Kendel sighed. "Well, you are from this crazy place, so I had hoped they would. Come on a bit further, and we'll show you the way out."

We passed row after row of the strange pods. The dread in my stomach grew. How could all of this lie beneath The Hive without us knowing? When I returned, I would convey a message to Dr. Whisper so he could investigate.

Noah pointed to one pod in a long row. His brow was furrowed in concentration, highlighting his powerful jaw and framing his gentle blue eyes. I couldn't help but notice he was very handsome—the most attractive male I'd ever seen.

"Well? What do you think?" He pointed above at the number. *4091 Persi Scion*. My number followed by two words. I scanned a few others, *4090 Myrrhis Scion and 3090 Ian Scion*. Dad? I walked closer and tugged at the edges. Anxiety fluttered inside my belly, but the pod prompted no other memories. The quality of the materials was like our infusion pods, but they didn't look comfortable. How long had they been waiting?

"What does this mean? Persi...Scion." The word sounded strange on my lips.

"Your family name?" Kendel asked.

I shook my head. "Our numbers are our family names."

"A number isn't a name. Family names have to be actual names."

Kendel's tone irked me. "Numbers are better than names. They're more precise."

"Persi Scion. Now that's a nice name," Noah said.

When he said those words, something vibrated deep inside my chest. It shook so hard it shot a wave of nausea through my body.

"Stop it."

"Persi Scion? Saying your name."

"My name is Persi 4091."

Noah shrugged. "Sorry, I see I'm upsetting you—"

"You're not upsetting me. But *Persi Scion,* what kind of name is that?" The instant I said the words, I regretted it. A blinding wave of pain sliced through my brain, and strange images flashed before my eyes. People dying, a haven that became, that became…."

When my vision cleared, I sat near my pod on the cold, damp concrete floor: correction, *the* pod. I stood, wanting to put as much distance between it and myself as possible.

"Are you okay?"

"I'll miss The Selection if you keep stalling! Plus, a virus is attacking my cells, and I need my infusion. If you don't help me find the way out, I'll do it alone!"

I hurried back toward the ladder we'd come up. With all these new points, selection as First Nurse was within reach, and I wouldn't let them mess it up for me.

"That's not the fastest way. Come on, we'll head out."

"Do you promise? No detours?"

Noah nodded. Having no choice but to trust them, I followed.

When we reached the last row, Kendel paused. "No one has ever mentioned these pods?"

I shook my head. As we stepped through the arched entryway, I took another look back. I couldn't stop thinking about what I'd seen. What were those strange, archaic pods for? Perhaps they were an old method of giving infusions? But if so, what happened? That poor person had appeared dead. Yet Dr. Whisper had conquered death from disease, death from microbes, and death from ill health. We were all guaranteed to live an extended life span and perhaps become immortal. Maybe these machines were no longer needed.

With this explanation working through my brain, the anxiety diminished. We stepped through another doorway similar to the one we entered and descended a long series of spiral stairs. Soon we returned to the dank, dark concrete of the underground space. A furry creature ran in front of us. "What the hell was that?"

Noah put his hand on my shoulder, and I felt my body pressed against his. He felt warm and strong but much too close. My heart beat fast, and I stepped away.

"It's just a rat," he said.

"Hominoids eat rats."

A rumble escaped from his throat. I thought he was choking for a moment, but he seemed fine.

Noah shrugged as we kept walking. "They bite if you hassle them. And they carry disease."

A shudder ran through my body. I needed to return to The Hive and report my symptoms. They would test me and perhaps give me a modified recipe. Then, with all the points I'd have gained, I'd upgrade and join Myrrhis in time for us to head to The Selection together. She'd be proud of me and wish she'd never doubted my plan.

I placed my hand against my waistband and touched—nothing. My brother's safety gun was gone. "My safety gun! Have you seen it?" I said, voice a strangled croak as I checked my waistband again.

Noah and Kendel looked at me blankly. Tears stung my eyes. "It held so many points. I'd have become a First Nurse!"

"We'll help you look," Noah said, eyes full of sympathy. "Do you want to retrace our steps?"

We'd just reached the base of the stairs I'd descended.

"No, thank you. It's too late." This had been a disastrous failure. Returning to the dismal surroundings was too much to bear, and I had no time left.

"Well…here we are, Persi. Thanks for trusting us." Noah pulled his lips back over his teeth. It was such an odd expression that I drew back. We never show our teeth when we smile. It's considered unsanitary. Noah blushed, and I turned to go up the stairs.

"Hey, wait!" Noah called.

I paused and gazed down at them.

"Meet us again in three days. Bring Myrrhis. Piper insisted you both come," Noah reminded. Kendel gave a brief wave. Too tired to think straight, I nodded.

As I continued up the stairs inside, I shook my head. The chances I'd leave The Hive were zero. And Myrrhis? Less than that. Somewhere down here, the safety gun lay, promising points and my redemption. Now I just needed to come back and find it.

CHAPTER TWELVE

WHEN I RETURNED to Zone One, the ward was alive with activity, people emerging from their pods, but I barely registered their presence.

At least I had a signal—my garland was no longer dark. However, I had lost another full stone for missing an infusion. How had I allowed this to happen? It hadn't been intentional. I thought of Noah, Kendel, but most of all, Noah and his kind, gray-blue eyes.

My motives had been good, but now I returned with nothing and—

Myrrhis's voice pierced my thoughts. "Where have you been? Angelica came looking for you. You missed an infusion *and* Selection Day! What happened to your face?"

I stumbled back, my hand flying to my cheek, feeling the burn of more blisters for the first time. "I missed Selection Day? No. How...I couldn't have been gone that long." I said, but Myrrhis was relentless.

She stepped closer. "Look at you. You'll end up like Piper....or Carum!" The warning bell for the first shift rang, adding to the weight of her words.

"Take that back!" I wrung my hands. "Please." I was dizzy, my head was swimming, and I felt I couldn't get enough air. "Nothing went as planned," I muttered, wishing I could undo my choices.

"Well, anyway, I have news." Myrrhis glanced down at the floor. "The doctor has selected me as a First Nurse." Her face flushed. "I won't be able to visit again."

For a moment, I thought I'd heard her wrong. "You? First Nurse....but you never...your feet...you always said—"

"True, I never minded much one way or the other. But Dr. Whisper selected me from all the others, and I must serve where needed. Also, my health got upgraded during the infusion. My feet are healing."

"You accepted?"

"Of course I accepted!"

"But you never *wanted* to be First Nurse. You told me it was out of reach all this time."

"Well, not out of reach. We both knew it was possible, just not that likely. But now it's happened, so--" She wouldn't look me in the eye.

"Piper wants us to leave The Hive. Both of us," I said. "He sent two people from out there to rescue us...they want to meet us in three days."

"Out where? The Desolation? To rescue us from what? Did you hear me? I will become a First Nurse. Why would I want to leave? Why would *anyone* want to leave? What is wrong with you, Persi 4091?"

"Piper must have had a reason. We need to learn why. I met some people—" I left out that they weren't people, but hominoids, a dangerous and sworn enemy. But Noah did not seem dangerous. He seemed kind, not to mention handsome. How could I convey that to Myrrhis? She would only understand if I convinced her to come with me. Right now, that felt imperative.

"Didn't we establish the other day that Piper lost his mind? You told me he was eating. And then I will never forget what I saw you did."

"Yes, I know." Tears stung my eyes. "I'm ashamed. What I did was unforgivable. But they've done far worse than me. Lister," I whispered, looking around. "He eats and drinks."

Myrrhis raised her eyebrows. "Lister is a jerk, that's for certain, but you expect me to believe he is an eater?"

"Yes, I scanned him for eating!"

"Well, if you did, you...you'll gain many points. You'll be able to upgrade." Her eyes brightened.

"But I lost the safety gun."

Myrrhis backed away from me. "You poisoned yourself with food,

Persi. I don't recognize you anymore. Now I can't be late for my First Nurse practice… goodbye."

She left but then turned back. Her eyes looked dull and glassy. "One more thing. If Dr. Whisper knocks, let him in, that's the key."

* * *

When I returned to my ward, I found Angelica and Lister waiting.

"You missed Selection Day *and* your infusion," Angelica said, shaking her head.

If Lister felt any shame over what I'd seen him doing, it did not show.

"I'm on time for my shift. I'm breaking no rules at this very moment," I said.

Angelica nodded. "No, no, not currently, you aren't. But you lost a stone when you missed your infusion. That means a demotion."

A sly, closed-mouth grin spread across Lister's face.

They led me past the regular area where I worked in bear assembly. Anxiety pooled in my gut as I thought of the safety gun lying far below. When we reached the toy bear assembly line, Angelica stopped.

Lister whistled tunelessly as he followed behind. He still had a slight wound on his head from where Noah had hit him. If not for that, someone outside would have noticed nothing amiss.

"Lister, you suggested a new position suiting Persi's status, correct?"

"Aye, I'll be taking you off stamping duty," he said as he led me into the noisy assembly area, which had poor lighting and a reputation for being the most dangerous. Several others waited in the room in front of a long conveyor belt. Most stood staring at the floor, waiting for the starting siren.

Aside from First Nurses, there are three chief occupations in The Hive: ward nurses (preservers of health), sanitary clerks (preservers of safety), and toy production (preservers of happiness). In The Hive, there is no such thing as a bad working area. Dr. Whisper wanted to ensure everyone would find joy in their duties. Most tasks involve manufacturing toys that get sent to sick children in other Free Cities. Our hard work in making handmade bears, dolls, and plush turtles spreads happiness where it's needed most.

But toy assembly was the most dangerous, especially for someone as clumsy as I was. It involved using machines with sharp needles and cutting tools. There had been mutual hatred from the start, but now I feared for my safety.

Now that I knew Lister's secret, hatred was nothing compared to the poison that poured from him. My resolve strengthened—I would return, find that safety gun, and give Lister what he deserved. Not just to rejoin Myrrhis, but also for the community. Lister was a criminal eater and a hypocrite who must be punished.

* * *

Lister was waiting outside my pod even after the warning siren had sounded. He stood with his greasy brown hair plastered to his forehead and hands clenched into balls. "I'm monitoring safety," he told the ward nurse when she entered.

"Please," I begged the nurse. "Couldn't you leave it open a bit?"

"All pods must be closed for the health of all," was her reply.

This time, I tried to lie still in the confined space and willed the infusion to kick in faster, but my fear was more potent, and The Fright was worse than ever. Just as the pod was about to close, I blocked it, and Lister crowed with glee.

"Violation! Interfering with public health." He pulled out his safety gun and took more points away from me. With tears in my eyes, I didn't dare look at my garland. Things had gone from bad to worse. Then, lying in the dark, my heart pounding, the knocking began again.

Answer it.

I had already lost my brother, sister, and most of my points. What else was there to lose?

Come in.

I opened a door in my mind, and Dr. Whisper stood there, as handsome as always. Unfortunately, his once benevolent smile had been replaced with a stern expression of anger.

"Hello, Persi 4091. I hoped you would answer, but it takes some longer than others. I've wanted to speak with you."

CHAPTER THIRTEEN

"Back again, I see," Carum greeted me with a hint of annoyance as she gazed into The Desolation, her pale eyes flickering like lightning in a stormy sky.

Several infusions had passed, and I'd lost more points. I stood, staring at her, unsure what to say, my heart pounding.

"I bet you wanna taste some of that soup we had last time, hmm?" Her thin pink lips made a smacking noise, and she chuckled.

I mustered the courage to speak. "No. Carum, I need to find Noah. I've decided to leave The Hive."

Carum raised an eyebrow, tapping her chin with a bony forefinger. "Interesting. I didn't see that one coming. But if you're sure that's what you want, I won't stop you."

With a sly smile tugging the corners of her thin pink lips, she beckoned me toward the dark, twisting passage that led to the hidden entrance. "C'mon, let's go. Your journey to freedom awaits. What changed your mind, girl? And what about your sister?" she asked over her shoulder.

"Myrrhis is a First Nurse now. She won't come, and they have banished me to Zone Zero. My sister wouldn't want to see me even if she could."

The thought of Myrrhis becoming a First Nurse instead of me filled me with a dull ache. The idea of facing her again shamed me.

"What happened to *your* dreams of becoming a First Nurse?" Carum asked as if reading my gloomy thoughts. Her torch barely pierced the dusty air.

"I was stupid to think it would ever happen."

Carum grumbled to herself as she lifted the door to the hidden entrance. We clattered down the long metal staircase.

"Myrrhis is gone," I said. "Piper abandoned us. There's nothing left. "

"What about the safety gun? You could gain enough points to become First Nurse, no?"

"I lost it. Nothing ever works out right for me."

Carum grinned as we reached the bottom. "Perhaps it was your destiny."

"What's a destiny?" My voice echoed in the space.

"Uncovering what you were born to do…and making it happen. So *what* is your destiny? That is the question, Persi. Hmm?" she deepened her voice at the end.

"To become a First Nurse," I said.

Carum gawked at me for a second and then burst into peels of laughter that echoed back, discordant. "Just two minutes ago, you said you'd given that up. And they call me crazy. Holy spaghetti. If you can't be First Nurse, what then? C'mon, have a seat. This is our meeting place."

We sat on a rusty metal barrel. Across from us lay the silver door I'd seen Carum exit from last time. Waiting in silence, I had no answer to her question. Leaving The Hive—was that my destiny? Finally, the silence got to me. "What's yours?"

Carum opened her mouth, closed it again, and grimaced. "Answering a question with a question. A bit of a cop-out, but understandable."

I waited for her to say more, but silence fell again, and I heard nothing but a distant dripping and the soft hiss of a pipe above us. "Are you certain this is the right place?"

The sound of footsteps perked my ears. Carum shushed me. "Someone's coming." Then she frowned. "Don't recognize the sound of those feet. We better hide."

She led me behind a wall into the shadow of a large, hulking piece of machinery across from the maglev track. The footsteps reverberated as they grew closer. Whoever this was did not disguise their steps. My heart rose…and then fell when I saw Kendel alone.

I stepped out from behind the equipment. "Where's Noah?"

"Back home in his kitchen," Kendel said with a sigh. "Feast days are coming, so I'll have to do. Where's Myrrhis?"

"Myrrhis refused to come. I told you she wouldn't. It's just me."

Kendel shrugged. "Well, c'mon then. Noah won't come back here for a while, and neither will I. This is your last chance."

"How will you get her there?" Carum asked.

Kendel stretched out her long limbs, first her legs and then her arms across her chest. "I take it you're not coming?"

Carum scowled. "Might do. It depends on how you plan to get there."

"A maglev."

Carum grimaced. "I figured that might be the case. Hopper 902?"

Kendel nodded. A metallic whirring sound filled the space. The ground beneath my feet trembled. With breathtaking speed, the maglev arrived across from us, pushing a blast of stale, foul-smelling air, light blinding me. Just as I thought it would plow into the other side of the chamber, a massive humming sound filled the air, and the enormous vehicle stopped almost instantly.

"Ride that thing? I don't know about that."

"Not ride on it. Ride in it. We need to be quick, though. Follow me."

Kendel walked the length of the train, looking for something. Crude numbers painted on the side of one read: *Hopper 902*. She pressed a button on a recessed receptacle. A door slid open. Inside, there was a compartment not much bigger than our infusion pods.

"Cosy, but it beats walking."

Carum shook her head. "Count me out. I don't trust these machines," she muttered. "Good luck to you, Persi 4091. I hope you find your destiny."

"You as well," I said and noticed her face redden.

Kendel folded herself into the tiny compartment and beckoned me to get into the one behind her. "C'mon. It's leaving soon."

"In there?" Panic flooded my body. The space was tiny, and my body froze at the thought.

"Persi!" Kendel shouted. "Move it!"

I was about to tell her I couldn't get in when Carum screamed.

"Watch out!" Suddenly, something hit my head from behind.

"Where is it?" Lister shouted.

With a *hiss* and a *click*, the door to Kendel's hopper slid shut. Perfect timing—if I had been inside.

Lister lunged at me and drove me to the ground. He placed me in a headlock, and my legs lay draped over the tracks. "Carum! Help!" I shouted.

The smell of his sweat sickened me, and my body went limp. Part of me wanted to struggle, but a larger part just gave up, like I always did. Then, with a squeal and a magnetic hum, the train lurched forward. Lister grunted and fell back. Carum yanked me to safety just before the maglev's rail sliced my legs in two.

"You, traitor." Lister stood, rubbing his head. "After everything I done for you?"

"Leave her be, Lister."

"Hand over the safety gun!" Lister shouted at me.

"She doesn't have it."

Lister's eyes narrowed, and his tongue darted to lick his cracked lips.

The maglev picked up speed, leaving with Kendel. Lister tried to get at me again, but Carum stopped him. "Lister! You want her, or you want this?" She held up the safety gun.

Carum had it all along?

Howling, Lister dove toward Carum, catching her off guard. Both of them nearly ended up pulverized by the maglev.

"Persi!" Carum shouted. Carum wrenched her arm back and tossed the safety gun in the air. Flashing silver in the gloomy light, it arced through the air. For a moment, I panicked, then I thought of the hours I'd spent moving my limbs in coordination…maybe it wasn't always perfect…but. These thoughts lasted milliseconds.

My left leg glided forward and to the right. It required superb technique. When my right arm crossed to the left at the same instant, I readjusted on my left leg, I'd fall without perfect timing. Like a fulcrum, I balanced. This was called Second Position in the dance of the First Nurses. I'd tried it before and always ended up falling on my face.

The safety gun hit the palm of my right hand — a *slap* much harder than I expected. My grip failed, and the smooth silver object tumbled and fell toward the tracks. It bumped up and over and exploded into a million pieces as the maglev's chassis hit it.

"Don't just stand there! Run!" Carum shouted as she pushed Lister hard, and he tumbled over a rusty barrel. "To the meeting place."

Although I wasn't sure which way to go in my state, instinct served me well. Moments later, I stood, sweat dripping from my forehead, in the area where we were supposed to meet Noah. I might have been wrong, but I felt that if it had been Noah here and not Kendel, things would have gone much more smoothly.

I waited, despondent, near the silver door. Where did it lead? After several hard yanks, it was clear the door would not budge. A few seconds later, Carum arrived, a grim look on her face.

"You had it all along."

Carum nodded. "Sorry. It may seem like I have nothing to lose...but it's all relative."

"Where's Lister?"

"He won't bother us if we keep moving. Lister fears this place. He got lost once, almost didn't make it out. C'mon, let's go. Now that I got on his bad side, there ain't nothing for me here."

"Go where?" My voice shook.

"Where else? The Desolation."

CHAPTER FOURTEEN

WE STOOD IN the heart of The Desolation, surrounded by nothing but barren dirt stretching to the edge of the world. The only sign of life was a gleaming set of metal tracks cutting through the emptiness, disappearing into a distant tunnel.

As I gazed at the desolate landscape, I expected to drop dead at any moment. My throat felt tight, and my skin crawled with the fear of toxic pathogens.

"We're alive!" I turned to Carum in wonder.

"At least for now." A grim smile spread across her lips as she coughed. "Let's move." Carum kept her eyes fixed on the silver tracks. "We've gotta make it to that tunnel before the sun rises and fries us to a crisp."

"The sun?" I asked, skeptical. "The sun's dead."

"Nah," Carum shook her head. "She ain't dead. You just never been awake to see her. Now get those legs moving!"

With that, she took off at a brisk pace, leaving a cloud of dust in her wake. I trailed behind, struggling to keep up as my throat burned and my lungs filled with grit. I wasn't so sure about our chances of survival anymore.

Health above all. Everything felt precarious.

Hurrying across the tundra, we choked in a self-made cloud of dirt and pathogens.

"How much time do we have? It seems too far."

"Not long. Hurry! We should be safe there...if we make it."

Although I wasn't a good estimator of distance, I didn't see how we'd ever walk that far. A rumbling, whining noise echoed across the playa. Just then, a maglev roared from The Hive and crossed the distance to the tunnel in seconds. The tunnel swallowed it whole, and silence returned.

Carum shook her head as we got closer. "The tunnel's narrower, a lot narrower than I realized. There won't be much space when the next maglev comes."

Soon we stood outside the opening. Cool, musty air wafted from inside, and a chill went up my spine. "It's awful dark in there."

Carum winked. "That it is. But I came prepared, kiddo. Maybe not everything is going to plan, but at least I have this." She took out a tiny cylindrical object that emitted a beam of light.

Noah had had one. It made me feel funny to think of him. Would we meet again? I was still alive, so at least there was that. But for how much longer? I kept waiting for "it" to happen. For my eyes to pop out of my head, to fall to the ground, and to begin projectile vomiting. These were all expected effects of pathogens without the infusion recipe.

"Do you think we're still protected with the infusion?"

Carum shrugged. "Not me. If you are, it won't last forever." She stepped into the tunnel. It was pretty tall but just wider than the tracks.

"Stand on that side." Carum pointed to the right side. "Press yourself against the wall."

I hopped across the tracks and did as I was told. It seemed there might be room for the maglev to pass.

Carum nodded. "Okay. That's not bad. Let's pick up the pace."

We continued. At first, being out of The Desolation was a relief, but the farther we walked, the more oppressive it became. Tons of rock, dirt, and stone must have laid above our heads. What if the tunnel collapsed? I felt a whisper of The Fright. Our footsteps fell into a syncopated rhythm. *Step, step, step,* hop over a joist and step some more.

I turned back. I could no longer see the entrance. "Where are we going?"

Carum shrugged. "Wherever these tracks lead. To Noah's people? To the eastern Free Cities? We've been delivering the toy bears and all that crap to someone. They might help us." She coughed and spat on the ground. Her saliva was bloody. She held her hand to her chest. "That hurt. Not good. How are you feeling?"

My heart pitter-pattered in my chest. "Okay, I think. My legs are shaking. My sores hurt. My wrists ache. It's hard for me to breathe... but."

Carum panicked when a wind began rushing behind us. "It's too narrow here! We need to go back the way we came. That one area before was wider. Hurry."

By then, I was numb, so tired I could barely walk. "How far back? I can't go much faster!"

"That's because you won't eat!" Carum had brought food with her —small bars of some disgusting thing wrapped in silver foil. Remnants stuck in her teeth like brown dirt, and a peculiar odor emanated from her mouth. I had to admit Carum seemed to have more energy than I did. Perhaps there was something to this eating thing... *But, no.* Eating stole my brother from me and caused everything to unravel.

Carum grabbed my hand. "Did you hear what I said? A maglev is coming. It's too narrow here. We'll be crushed. It wasn't supposed to be this long...this damn tunnel. Did we miss a turn?"

No, there had been no turns, just endless darkness punctuated by the shrill light of Carum's torch. Carum arced the narrow beam of light above her and passed it over the silver-gray surface of the tunnel. There were just a few inches between the tunnel walls and the maglev.

"We can lie down," I said.

"Lie down? Now you have lost your mind."

"There's space beneath the maglevs. I remember from when Lister attacked me. But we'd need to lie flat and right in the middle."

"You're thinner and smaller," Carum remarked. "It'll never work for me. I eat too much." She snorted with laughter at what must have been a look of disgust on my face.

The rush of wind grew stronger. "We have no choice." I knelt on the tracks and lay on my belly. The metal surrounding me hummed and warbled as the maglev drew closer. I glanced up to check on Carum. She stood on the tracks, trying to jump up and reach a metal joist several feet above. If she could jump that high (she could not) and had the strength to hang onto it (doubtful) then what she attempted might have worked. But in her case, this was suicide.

"You'll never be able to jump that high!" I shouted. Her eyes darted my way and then turned back toward the rush of wind, panic flooding her face in the blinding light. The tracks vibrated and hummed so loudly that they shook my entire body. Without looking, I knew that the maglev must be seconds away.

"Get down!" I screamed. Carum continued her mad leaping and jumping. After her third leap, she fell, and her ankle bent in a direction ankles were not supposed to turn. She slumped down half on the tracks, half against the wall.

"Carum!" Without thinking, I leaped up and ran toward her. Light blinded me as the maglev bore down in a shower of sparks. The wind tore at my body. Using my momentum and sheer desperation, I tackled her and pulled off the track. Then I forced her head down and pressed mine to the side.

Would this work? Was there enough space for the maglev to pass, or would we be scraped up and pulverized? Seconds later, we got our answer. The maglev hummed over us so fast it sucked the air from my lungs. I screamed as we got pulled along, but it was only the air pushing us forward. Miraculously, we were otherwise unscathed. The vehicle went so fast that it was gone before I could think.

I sat up, gathered myself for a few seconds, then rolled over to Carum. She pushed herself to her knees, ankle bent behind her.

"You saved my life," she panted.

"Now we're even."

A lopsided grin splayed across her face. "You were right, after all." She winced as she spun her leg around and massaged her leg. "Well, now we know. But you're going to need to go ahead. I'll be no good holding you back, walking with my ankle in this state."

"Just leave you here?"

"Find Noah, bring help."

"How will I find him without you?" Tears stung my eyes. Now I felt angry. "What were you doing? I told you to lie down."

"Well, I'm sorry! I didn't know what to do. Haven't you ever been scared half to death?"

I mulled that over and thought of The Fright. "Yes. Anyway, I'm not leaving you. I don't know how long it'll take to find Noah or if I'll even be able to find him."

We continued much more slowly. Finally, after a long while, the tunnel ended.

"It's dark out!" I said with a smile.

"Phew." Carum wiped her hand across her brow and pointed to a series of rocky formations. "That way. Keep following the tracks."

Carum continued to hobble.

"Here. Does it help to lean on me?"

Carum leaned on me as she walked, lungs rattling. As we approached the rocks, I noticed a mound of something. Dread pooled in my gut.

"Am I imagining things or...."

Carum let out a wheezy laugh. "Well, I was gonna ask you the same. I'm burning up. I thought I was hallucinating."

The closer we arrived, the more details popped out. Bodies lay amongst strange, rusted metal contraptions. Hundreds. Most were just skeletons, but three bodies had arrived recently. A man with sunken cheeks, eyes dark and hollow, and two women in a similar state. It was difficult to see the faces of the First Nurses with the blinding lights and sanitary shields. However, I had memorized the look of their feet. One woman had a mole on her left foot, and the man had prominent veins resembling blue snakes. These were two of the First Nurses who had disappeared.

My legs trembled. "What is this place?"

Carum jutted her chin toward a rusted hunk of metal. "Look at that pile of junk. It used to be a farm a lifetime ago. Now?" She hacked a wad of phlegm onto the dirt. "We made the right call leaving The Hive, that's for sure."

"Dr. Whisper needs to know about this," I said, desperation creeping into my voice.

She let out a sharp laugh. "You think he doesn't already know? The man has eyes everywhere."

"No," I said, shaking my head. "This is different. Something's not right in the Free City."

"Ha!" Carum chortled. "Free City? More like False City. We're all prisoners there, living in his delusion." She stumbled, and I reached out to steady her, but she fell to her knees, breathing hard.

My throat felt raw, and my eyes were teary, but I pushed the feelings down. "We have to keep going."

"Leave me," Carum said, closing her eyes and lying on the dirt. "I need to rest. You go on without me."

"No way," I said, fear and panic rising in my chest. "I'm not leaving you here."

"Go, damn it!" Carum yelled, but I just sat down next to her.

"Not without you," I said, tears rolling down my cheeks. "You need me to help you walk. Just rest a bit, okay? You'll feel better."

"Yeah," she said, her eyes closing. "I'll be fine. Don't give up, kid."

I closed my eyes and tried to ignore the harsh world, pretending I was back in The Hive, safe in my pod.

CHAPTER FIFTEEN

DUST FILLED MY mouth, and I choked. Rolling over onto my back, I gawked in terror at the orange sky. All my life, I'd woken to the somber light of my ward. Outside through the few windows in The Hive, I saw the stars and occasionally the moon, but most days were cloudy. The sky remained a tranquil velvet black. Now the sun tore everything apart.

"Carum?" She lay beside me, unmoving. "Carum!" I shook her. No response.

Red streaked across the bruised horizon like a bursting vein. My body shuddered and trembled, and a coughing fit struck. Soon I'd suffer the same fate as Carum; only my death would be beneath the giant blazing ball above. It would be over fast—at least, I hoped. Would it hurt?

I pushed myself up on my knees, squinted, and adjusted my eyes to the blinding light. If this strange, horrible sight was the last thing I'd ever see, I might as well make the most of it.

It was too bright to keep my eyes open for long as the harmful solar radiation pummeled me. But, for now, the warmth felt...good. My jaw dropped in wonder when I gathered the courage to open my eyes again. My surroundings were brighter and filled with colors I'd never seen.

The cliff in the distance was painted an iridescent orange. Details of the rock face stood out from each other — black, orange, and gray. Above them lay ominous green areas of vegetation that were no doubt toxic. All edible plants had perished during the great scourge. How tragic that such a vibrant green could do nothing but destroy. Meanwhile, the sun, that giant ball of fire, continued rising. It was miraculous that it didn't just tumble from where it hung and roll through the desert until it burned me and everything in its path.

But the sun did not fall from its perch. Instead, it climbed higher, and the sky became a dazzling blue, the same color as Noah's eyes. I'd never seen this much color all in one place. The color or some bacterial reaction flooded my stomach with nausea, and I knelt on the earth, dry heaved, the foul taste of dirt in my mouth.

Something about the sky made me keep looking at it, even though it made my head spin. It went on forever, unlike the black velvet void of night. That black could annihilate you if you thought about it too long.

The convulsions started again, and my legs grew weak. Now my heart fluttered in my chest—too rapid to be healthy. I was dying. When I drew my hand away from my mouth, it was red with blood, and breathing became difficult.

I lay down, gazed at the sky, and waited for death. "Thank you, Doctor. Thank you, Myrrhis and Piper. Carum, thank you. I'm sorry I failed you all."

* * *

When I woke, blackness surrounded me.

Dead?

I struggled to sit, but my muscles were too weak. My mouth tasted like desert dust and cobwebs. A soft mattress lay beneath me. The room was too dark to see much. To my right sat the shadowy bulk of a wooden chair. The air smelled strange. Wherever I lay, they did not use disinfectant. The odor reminded me of wet bandages and the dismal tunnels I'd explored with Carum. Poor Carum. Had she somehow survived, too?

A murmur of voices grew louder. Seconds later, two people entered the room; voices lowered to a whisper.

Kendel stood hallowed by the light in the doorway. She clapped her hands together, and I flinched at the loud sound. "See, told you. She's awake! I'll get Crane and Senior. Fetch her soup."

They both left. Not long after, the second girl returned—slender, with dark eyes hooded beneath long lashes. She placed something on the table beside the bed and turned on a light. It emitted a comforting amber glow. "Good morning—well, it's afternoon, but it must feel like morning to you!"

Her shrill voice pierced the silence. "I've brought you a healing soup." She handed me a metal object. It felt cool in my hand.

"No, no! You don't hold it from the round end. Haven't you ever seen a spoon before?" She spun it around my hand.

She motioned to the vessel on the table beside me and stood watching. Steam rose from it, and I saw shapes of things floating in a murky, mystery liquid. A rat bone stuck up from one side, flesh frayed at its end. My stomach roiled.

"Yum yum?" she lifted the bowl and breathed in the aroma with a groan of pleasure. She gestured that I should take it from her. If I'd had the energy, I would have moved as far away as possible, but I felt too tired.

She sighed. "Do you need me to feed you? Alright, I'll pull up a chair." Then, groaning louder than the chair squeaked, she pulled it over and sat beside me.

"Here." She grabbed the spoon from me, scooped up the liquid, and shoved it toward my lips.

"Please, no," I murmured, scared that if I opened my lips too wide, she might force it in.

"Silly cow, you need to eat food. You're dying!" A few seconds later, a gentle knock at the door, and then it opened. Noah stood in the frame. Taller and more handsome than I remembered, he walked toward the bed.

"The dumb girl won't eat!" she said. "She doesn't even know how to hold a spoon."

Noah raised his hand. "Patience, Mercy. Let me handle this."

"But, Crane said—"

"Mercy, it's okay. I've got this."

Mercy put the soup down and left.

Noah waited for the annoying girl to leave and sat in the chair. "How are you feeling?"

"Weak. Where am I?"

"In The Cliffs, my home. We found you starving, dehydrated, and half alive."

"How is Carum?"

Pain crossed Noah's face. "Dead when we arrived."

A swirl of emotions circled in my gut, and I blinked back tears. Noah was about to say more when two people entered—a woman with an older man.

"Oh good, you're awake!" A woman with cheekbones as sharp as a blade and silver blonde hair walked to my bed and adjusted my covers until they were straight and neat.

"There, that's better. Now, your name is Persi?"

I nodded.

"Good. My name is Crane. And you come from the place you call The Hive?"

I nodded again.

"Mother—" Noah started. Crane raised her hand.

"Is your memory intact? For example, do you remember who you lived with, what you did there, and so forth?"

I thought back to the infusions, my sister Myrrhis, my goal of becoming a First Nurse, and many more memories.

"Of course." My voice shook with weariness.

"Wonderful. I'll return to speak with you when you're stronger. You *must* eat, or you will die. Senior, see that she does. Now I have a Council matter to attend to." With a slight nod to Senior, she glided out of the room.

"Sorry about that," Noah said with a sheepish smile. Senior approached, a cheeky grin on his gray-whiskered face. "Mercy tells me you don't like our menu, hmm?"

"Menu?"

"This is a delicious soup." Senior sat down and dipped the silver tool they called a spoon in the evil liquid. "A spoonful? Just one?"

I looked at Noah, his eyebrows raised, hopeful. I shook my head.

Senior kept raising the spoonful, and I pressed my mouth together, ready to resist him with all my will...which unfortunately wasn't much.

Instead, Senior popped it into his mouth. Seconds later, they shared the same spoon spreading pathogens between them, not to mention whatever toxins lurked in the soup. My immediate concern was for Noah, since he had been kindest to me. However, they both seemed quite happy, and no noticeable harm occurred. The bowl soon lay empty.

Mercy returned and jumped up and down, clapping her hands when she saw the empty bowl. My ears rang with the noise. "Well, I'm glad you listened to someone. Now, wasn't Noah's soup amazing? He's a culinary genius." She batted her long lashes at him, but he did not appear to notice.

"Noah's soup?" I asked.

Senior nodded. "He made it just for you. Full of medicinal herbs and nutrients to help heal you."

Noah's face reddened. "Was it too salty? Too much cilantro or healer's plant...oh, you don't know what that is."

"I didn't try it," I whispered.

Mercy puffed air from her mouth in disdain and exchanged a glance with Senior.

"Oh!" Noah chuckled. "Well, then. No worries. We won't force you, although, with full disclosure, we gave you herbal teas while you were unconscious. You'd be dead otherwise. But Crane is right. You need to eat."

"When is the next infusion?"

Noah shifted on his feet and scratched his chin. "We don't do that here, you see...well, that's not a conversation for now. Senior, Mercy, do you mind if I speak to Persi alone?"

Senior smiled. "Your soup has whetted my appetite. Just don't be so long that you neglect dinner." He winked. As for Mercy, Senior had to pull her by the arm to get her to leave.

Noah gazed at me for a long moment before speaking. "I'll make something you like, Persi, don't worry. I love a challenge. What bothered you? Please, be honest."

"It was murky, and, and dark—"

"The color wasn't to your taste? Tell me. I won't be offended."

"It looked like...toxic sludge."

He clenched his jaw. "Toxic sludge. Duly noted."

"Horrible bones were floating in it."

"Mountain gopher bone broth is excellent for recovery from a long illness, but okay, vegetarian it is."

"It smelled like feet and rotting things. Also, there was—"

"Okay, enough honesty. You can stop now." He burst into laughter, sat down, and grabbed my hand, spreading pathogens. "I will make something you like, I promise."

"Noah," I said, my voice weak and my eyes closing against my will.

I wanted to tell him that I'd never eat again, that the cupcake had been a colossal mistake, and that this entire situation was a mistake. What I needed was Dr. Whisper's recipe, an infusion. But as my eyes shut, I was consumed by a terrifying dream.

I stood on a stage, alone, in a place where the First Nurses once danced. Dr. Whisper was there with me, but he appeared different. His once slender and muscular body was bloated, like a giant balloon. In my dream, I fed him a shriveled toe, and as I did, his face turned red, white, and black. At that moment, I realized that I had killed him.

CHAPTER SIXTEEN

MUCH LATER, I'M not sure how long I bolted awake, shirt soaked with sweat, heart pounding. My body was tight and coiled like a spring—I had to move.

I stumbled to the door, a strange wooden thing that wouldn't budge no matter how many times I yanked and pulled at it. But then, like magic, the round handle turned, and the door creaked open.

A dark hallway carved from rock appeared before me. Amber light flickered from stones set in the walls every few feet. To my right, the light disappeared down a bend in the hall, but to my left, the way was lit up by a brilliant sunbeam. I knew the safety of an infusion pod lay in the darkness, but today I followed the sun.

After several twists and turns through the winding stone passage, I emerged. The sun was a hammer, striking my eyes and forcing me to my knees, tears streaming down my face. I expected to be captured at any moment, but I was met with silence, and no one appeared.

I looked up and saw that the place I'd escaped from was carved into the face of a towering cliff. Ahead of me was a narrow wooden bridge stretching across a deep chasm. Suspended bridges crisscrossed overhead, connecting dwellings, with people moving back and forth across the swaying structures. None of them saw me yet, but I had to move fast. On the other side of the bridge was another tunnel leading to who knew where.

I moaned as I crawled across. What germs crawled on my skin? My arms trembled with revulsion. Below me, several similar bridges crisscrossed. What a strange place this was. A path I hadn't noticed led to a wooden ladder to my left. The ladder led to a series of steep steps carved into the rock above.

Mortified that my skin touched the dirt, I forced myself to continue. The feel of grime against my body made me feel faint. What was the point of escaping if I died?

As I ascended the ladder, rough wood poked and chafed my hands and feet. Finally, at the top, I stopped to look down. Rock towered above me. The wind whistled through my hair, and from above, shouts echoed off the cliff face. The ladder ended at a landing. Two stairways were carved into the rock. One went to the left, one to the right. I chose the one on the right.

Somehow, I gained the strength to continue up the stairs. The stairs led to a dark passage that let out into a grove of trees nestled beneath cliff walls on all sides. Giant boulders surrounded the area. I stopped and leaned against one to catch my breath. I'd seen images of trees but never touched one. Its brownish skin felt rough and foreign against my hands. I wondered if toxins were present, but I needed to rest.

Through a gap in some bushes, a cluster of hominoids sat cross-legged on the ground. A fire burned in the middle. Something steamed in a pot in the center. A strange odor wafted over me, and water rose in my mouth. They held silver tools and shoved brown and green material into their mouths—eaters.

A wave of nausea mixed with a strange desire washed over me. The idea of shoving that material in my mouth horrified me, yet part of me wanted it. This was part of the disease process—a will to self-destruction. The cupcake had started this. Tears streamed down my face, and my belly ached.

Sneaking closer for several minutes, I watched, hidden in the bushes. Kendel, two women, and a man ran past on my left, looking for me. They approached the eaters.

"The girl is gone. Have you seen her?" Kendel asked. She appeared to have some authority. The eaters put down their tools and stood, scanning the area. "No. We were about to return to the fields," one said.

"Okay. Help me find her." Kendel hurried away.

The people scattered, leaving their tools behind in a messy pile. For several seconds, I watched and waited. Kendel was gone. The eaters were gone. I crept forward. Smoke from the fire stung my eyes, but the warmth felt good on my skin. It reminded me of our infusions, and an ache gathered behind my eyes.

Lifting one of the silver plates to my nose, I sniffed the food remnants and promptly dropped the plate. Cramps racked my gut. A few seconds later, the pains subsided, but when I tried to stand again, they returned, and I remained doubled over. Gentle fingers touched my shoulder.

"Persi! Are you okay?"

Noah crouched beside me. Although I knew I should not trust him, it felt good to see a familiar face. He lifted me into his arms, took me back into the room I'd escaped, and put me into bed.

"Am I a prisoner?"

"Persi. We want to help you. We're friends of Piper. At least, most of us are. We don't want to harm you. I'm going to leave and get you something I made. I hope you will like it. Will you stay here? Please?"

"My brother? Where is he? Let me see him."

Noah scratched the back of his neck. "We've tried to contact him, but I'll be honest, we don't know where he is. He was supposed to be back by now. The fact that he isn't has caused a few problems."

A sour taste filled the back of my throat. That sounded like Piper. At least the way he had been of late.

"How do I know you're telling the truth?"

Noah blinked hard and hung his head. "You don't, I guess. But I promise you, I am."

Part of me wished I could take my question back. I slumped back into the soft fabric.

He returned a few minutes later with a steaming bowl of clear amber liquid. Floating in the fluid were brilliant green squares and several round yellow objects cut in the shape of moons.

"Those look like the moon," I pointed out.

"Yes! Thank you for naming it. I made it just for you. Moon soup. It has medicinal tinctures instead of raw herbs. I kept it nice and clear, but it still has many benefits. The flavors are delicate since everything will taste strong to you at first. No garlic. No onions."

"I don't know what those are."

"Here, drink." He put it in my hands.

I looked toward the door. "I don't want to get scanned."

"Scanned by what?"

"A safety gun. I can't afford to lose more points."

"Safety guns?" He laughed. "Ah yes, I remember now. The day we first met. We don't use those. I was curious about what they were for. Here." He took the soup from me, put it to his soft, red lips, and slurped and swallowed. I shuddered at the sight. At the same time, a thrill traveled through my body. It was intimate with me looking right at him. And yet he had no shame. He handed the warm bowl back to me. "It's delicious if you don't mind me saying."

"I don't mind, but I still won't drink it."

He cocked his head and smiled. "Are you making fun of me?"

"No."

A rumbling noise that I'd never heard my mid-section make set Noah snickering. "See? Your belly is waking up to the difference between right and wrong. It's called instinct. C'mon! Before it gets cold."

I went to hand it back to him, but he wouldn't take it. He sat, hand on my leg that lay beneath the covers. His arm was furry and much more muscular than the men back in the Free City.

There was no place to put the liquid, so I sat with it there. Stubborn, glaring at him. Meanwhile, the delicious steam kept rising, and soon tears streamed from my eyes.

"What have you done to me?" I said as I brought the bowl to my lips. I sipped and then gulped.

Noah stopped me. "Whoah, easy." He tried to remove the bowl, but I wouldn't let him. The hole that I hadn't realized existed partly filled itself.

Limbs that had always been cold for as long as I could remember filled with a slight warmth. My mind cleared, which was exciting because I'd never realized it was muddled. Gasping, I looked at Noah, and he gave me the signature open-mouthed smile of these people. The same expression came to my face without meaning to before I shut my lips.

"More?" I handed the cup to him.

"Plenty more. Later. Yes. Moon soup it is." He laughed, and his deep voice echoed off the room's rock walls. "How's your belly?" He placed his hand on my stomach, and even greater warmth filled me.

"It feels...wonderful." Tears ran down my cheeks. "I don't

understand what's happening. Am I dead?"

"You're not dead. We do our best here, but heaven, this ain't." He let out a shaky sigh.

"I don't understand."

"Baby steps, okay? You've lived your whole life somewhere where things are different. If you can, make space and be open to new ideas. Take it slow. Our first task is to get you healthy and back on your feet again."

"Health above all."

"Yes. That we can agree upon. If you need help, ring this bell." He lifted a tiny gold object with the most delightful sound I'd ever heard. "Someone will come and help you."

"Someone?"

"I'll come as often as I can. But it will be good to introduce you to others. I want people to know you."

Noah took the bowl, stretched, and revealed a slight tuft of hair around his midsection. He caught me staring, and his cheeks reddened. He hesitated a moment and then left. The cramps had disappeared, but a wave of sleepiness washed over me.

When I opened my eyes again, Crane sat by the side of the bed, staring.

"Hello there, it's okay," she said. She made that expression: smiling. It looked different on her than Noah. I liked Noah's smile better.

"Where's Noah?"

"Sleeping. He slaved in the kitchen for hours, making Miss Fuss Body a soup she'd eat," Crane said with a sour laugh, and I guess it was a joke, but I did not understand. "Well, you look a million times better. Are you ready to answer a few questions?"

CHAPTER SEVENTEEN

FROM THAT MORNING on, Crane drilled me with endless queries about life in The Hive. Where did we sleep? (The infusion pods) What did the infusions do? (Keep us alive, destroy pathogens) What are the First Nurses? (Dancing angels of healing and inspiration).

Sometimes, I made stuff up when I didn't know the answer. That may have been my undoing. Noah said they were escorting me for my safety until I regained strength. But, no, there was more to it than that. They were watching me. *Good.* I was watching them too. It was mostly just Noah, but when he was busy in the kitchen, it was someone else. Piper still hadn't shown up, and I wasn't sure what to make of it.

Noah forced—okay, okay, strongly encouraged—me to eat every day. Some days, it was easy, and I couldn't stop devouring everything in sight. On other days, the idea of food revolted me. I even threw up once, which broke Noah's heart. He felt responsible, and that made me sad. The problem was there were so many things to eat. So many choices. It made me anxious and overwhelmed. But one day, I tried to explain how I felt to Noah, and to my surprise, he understood.

"All feelings pass, so there's no point in running from them," Noah said with a wise nod. "Good feelings come and go, and it's the same with food. Eat it while it's there, enjoy it, and then let it go. Get it?" he chuckled, "Food passes too!"

"I'll try," was all I managed, unsure what he found so funny.

"Sorry, I guess it was a bad joke."

One day, Noah invited me to watch him make the food. It happened in an enormous, sweating room they called the kitchen. It fascinated me to watch him concoct his recipes. I'd seen nothing like it.

Bare hands massaged granular materials. Strange and often colorful growths from the dirt, called vegetables, were dropped into the liquid Noah called soup. Fruit—the pestilence of trees—was attacked and cut into tiny pieces with wicked sharp knives. Greasy liquids called oils were placed in giant pans that sizzled and spit. How primitive and strange to shove substances such as these into my mouth, mash them into a disgusting paste and let them slide down my throat. But how could I refuse after he put so much work into making these things? Especially since I came to crave the poison.

The first time "it" happened, I burst into violent sobs. Stomach cramps became severe, and a foul-smelling beast crawled from a hidden hatch in my body that I'd never noticed. The stench overwhelmed me, and I realized I was dying. I rang the bell, and Senior answered. He told me this was normal—part of being human— as if he knew anything about that.

"Nothing to be concerned about, my dear," he said. But he wouldn't look me in the eye, and went to get Kendel.

Kendel brought a rag with warm water to clean myself. But when she turned, I caught her suppressing a chuckle. She led me to a room where these horrible actions were done "in private." Well, at least there was that. But the idea that they dedicated an entire room—a decrepit temple—they called a water closet to this physical abomination horrified me. Everything Dr. Whisper told us about hominoids was true.

Was I becoming one?

It bewildered me—the differences. Being an eater was one of our worst offenses back in the Free Cities, and here I got in trouble if I *didn't* eat. Much to Noah's dismay, I tried to avoid food after the water closet incident. Noah patiently explained that without the infusions, I would get sick and die if I didn't eat.

Whether there was some trick or something I missed from the equation, he was correct. Each time I tried, a strange impulse rose inside, and I ate with abandon and unable to stop.

"Trust me, you don't want to starve to death," he'd said. I'd never heard the word starve but agreed it seemed painful.

The geography of this place never failed to amaze me. It was like a labyrinth of homes built into towering boulders that stretched hundreds of feet high, interconnected by wooden walkways. But what caught my eye the most were the hidden groves and valleys nestled between these mammoths of stone. The lush green vegetation that thrived here was a marvel, especially since I'd learned it wasn't poisonous like I'd thought. It was just one of the many enigmas of this place.

Today, I sat in one of the gardens enjoying the sun on my face. Oh, yes, how could I forget the sun? It took a while, but I came to appreciate its delightful warmth on my skin. Yet, it left me in turmoil. Did Dr. W realize that the sun wasn't a promise of death, or was I an anomaly?

Lost in thought, I didn't hear Kendel's approach. This girl I'd found intimidating had become a friend. Nevertheless, I didn't trust her the way I did Noah. A caution existed between us; I wasn't sure if it came from her or me.

"Just a warning. Crane is on her way to speak to you. She wants to put you to work."

"Really? Where?" The birds chirped, and the sky was blue with gray clouds on the horizon. Clouds meant rain, and Kendel complained when the skies went dark and gray. As for me, I found the dark gray skies comforting.

Kendel touched my arm, and I tried not to flinch. She had touched me before, and I'd acquired no disease. No reason to think this time would be different.

"Did you find Piper?"

Kendel shook her head. "No, I wish we had, but he hasn't returned yet. That's not what I came to tell you, unfortunately. You'll be working in the fields," she said.

Blood drained from my head, and I sat down hard on the bench.

"I know it probably wasn't your first choice, but we all take turns. Some people like it so much that it becomes their life's work. Perhaps you will too?"

"Doubtful—"

Crane arrived with Noah. Noah's face lit up when he saw me. My cheeks curled, and I allowed my lips to part. Smiling this way felt odd, but with Noah, I couldn't help it. It only happened with him.

Crane scanned me from head to toe. "Good morning, Persi. You're looking well."

"Thank you, Crane."

Butterflies roiled in my stomach. I hoped Kendel was wrong. It wasn't that I feared work. What they called work seemed similar to the tasks we completed back in The Hive. Perhaps it was less useful without the points and possibility to upgrade, but...still. I'd grown a bit bored whiling away my days while other people lived their lives.

"You've rested for long enough. You've gained weight, and you're looking much less pale. Now you need to build your immune system, get out and do some physical work. Plus, we need your help. We're about to have one of our best harvests, and we have a long dry season coming. I'd like you to start in the fields this afternoon. What do you say?"

Noah met my eyes and raised my eyebrows. "Sorry," he mouthed, sympathy wrinkling his handsome brow. He knew how I felt.

"Will I be working with the people who grow those...I'm not sure what they are called."

Noah had a bag of them when we met in the Free City.

"Noah, what was that tea—" His face stopped me. Noah gave a violent shake of his head and interrupted. "Cradleberries. You'll be harvesting cradleberries. They make a nutritious jam, and we need three jars for every ten people. But it's time-consuming, and your fingers will turn quite purple. I remember the first time I harvested cradleberries—" Noah continued.

Noah seldom spoke and never rambled; now, he was going on about cradleberries. What had I done to get him so nervous?

"Yes, Noah. It's my opinion that experience is the best teacher. Not everyone's fingers turn purple. At least not permanently. Kendel, will you take her there this afternoon?" Crane asked.

"Why don't I?" Noah suggested. "I've finished my lunch prep and have the time. I'd be happy to give Kendel a break."

Kendel shot Noah a sideways glance. Her expressions were hard to read, but it seemed she also detected the tension.

* * *

Noah and I descended a winding path, the lush greenery of cliffside vegetation surrounding us. "Do you mind if we take the scenic route, or would you rather get there quickly?" he asked.

"Take your time," I said. "Delaying this won't bother me one bit."

"Not too anxious to pick cradleberries, then?" he teased.

"No, not so much. Plus, I like walking with you," I said, the words slipping out before I could stop them. When I looked at Noah, I saw a hint of a blush on his cheeks.

"Me too." He took my hand. I cringed.

"Sorry."

"No, I'm sorry. It's just—" I still didn't understand why people held hands. It seemed…unsanitary. He let my hand go, and regret settled in my belly. We walked together in silence.

Noah cleared his throat. "I need to tell you something about that first day I found you in The Hive," he said. "I gave you a small dose of Spirit Root tea. No one else knows I had it with me, and it's best if it stays that way. It could get me in a heap of trouble."

"Of course," I said, nodding. "I'm used to keeping secrets. But, speaking of secrets, you never told me why you were visiting The Hive."

"It's a long story, but the short version is that I go there to cook for Dr. Whisper as part of an agreement," Noah said. "I'd prefer if someone else did it, but he insists on me being the one to cook for him as much as possible."

The idea of Dr. Whisper being an eater was so absurd I was speechless. "Why did you bring the Spirit Root to The Hive if it's a secret?" I asked.

Noah's back tensed, and he hesitated before answering. "It was one of the medicines I wanted to give you and your sister. Just a small dose," he said.

"Where does it grow?"

Noah was silent for a long moment before replying. "I'm not allowed to say," he said, his voice low and serious.

CHAPTER EIGHTEEN

WE WOUND THROUGH a labyrinth maze of walkways, strung high above a yawning chasm, its depths obscured by a veil of mist. As we navigated in and out of the rock face, I caught glimpses of Noah's clan, engaged in a patchwork of odd and varied tasks.

A slender man dangled from one walkway to complete a repair with a noisy tool. *Bang, bang, bang!* The sounds echoed off the rock face.

He's using a hammer.

How did I know that? Farther on, we stumbled into a clearing where two girls tossed a ball back and forth. Children! They had children here. I wasn't sure what this meant. We could not have children back at The Hive.

A boy and his mother led a small black animal with white horns over to a bucket and squeezed a white liquid from protrusions on its belly.

It's a goat. They are milking her.

The scenes felt like sensory overload, with each person sporting a different head of hair and outfit, creating a chaotic tapestry of life. This primitive mess was the ideal breeding ground for pathogens, a situation that would have made Dr. Whisper's head spin. But maybe not, as he had always warned us about the dangers of hominoids.

"What's wrong?" Noah asked as I panted and struggled to catch my breath. "You look scared."

"I do?" I tried to steady my racing heart.

Noah's eyes softened with tenderness and a hint of sadness. "You must miss The Hive."

"No," I lied. "Things seem so much…better here."

"Really?" Noah appeared surprised. "You adjusted faster than I thought. People from The Hive are so brainwashed. But you seem different."

"Brainwashed?" I didn't know the word.

"Well, yes. You all think you're on the verge of being infected by non-existent pathogens; you're scared to eat…."

"Pathogens do exist."

"Yes, but a healthy immune system is all you need—"

"That's not true. Our immune systems were destroyed during the great scourge."

"And yet…here you stand." Noah lifted his eyebrows. "Aside from being overwhelmed, you're okay, yeah?"

"Yes."

"That doctor poisoned you with fear and those chemicals he pumps into you every night."

"The infusions?" My hand flew to my chest. "The infusions are a life-giving recipe. We owe everything to their invention." I realized I'd said too much.

Noah frowned. "Hmm. C'mon, let's get down to the field. Keep those opinions to yourself. I hope you'll change your mind once you've adjusted."

As we entered a crowded walkway, several people shot me suspicious glances and kept their distance. They were as wary of me as I was of them.

"People don't like me much," I observed.

Noah shook his head. "No, they're just cautious. Dr. Whisper did substantial harm to us over the years. At one time, he stole children from the community. That ended when we agreed to cook for him. However, his drone patrols keep us confined to these protected areas. We aren't able to expand or grow."

"But homin—your people try to attack The Hive. That's why we need the drones."

Noah sighed. "Let's drop this for now. I'm just saying people have good reason to be wary. Some think you're a spy."

"Is that what you think?"

Noah laughed. "No, I'm the one who convinced people to trust you this time. You were lucky to escape The Desolation alive."

My escape with Calum seemed a distant memory. A sadness rose in my chest when I thought of her.

Noah stopped me, put his hand on my shoulder, and looked deep into my eyes. "Listen, if you think Dr. Whisper is great, why did you leave?"

"It started with a cupcake," I confessed the truth. "My brother had one. He wanted Myrrhis and me to leave with him. I still don't know why."

"He wanted to bring you here to protect you," Noah said.

"Yes. But from what?"

Noah raised his eyebrows as if I should know, so I quickly continued.

"After I tasted that cupcake, things changed. I had odd dreams. New thoughts. I realized I needed to leave."

We walked down a long series of worn steps, and when I saw where we were going, I froze. "I'm not hungry."

Noah grabbed my hand and pulled me toward the open door. "You may not be, but I want a snack, and you might be sorry if you don't grab one too."

The kitchen was Noah's domain. Despite my conflicted feelings, whenever I set foot in this hot, boisterous space, it lifted my heart to watch him work. Everyone loved him. Walking from counter to stove to bubbling pot, he joked with his fellow workers, who all toiled in the heat with one goal: to make food.

A tall, sweaty-faced woman emerged from the back, wiping her face onto a dirty blue apron. "There isn't near enough fresh goji berry for the dessert you suggested, Noah!" she said as if there were some dire consequence. Noah nodded, thoughtful. "Hmm, I have an idea." Noah turned to me. "Wait here just a sec, Persi. I'll be back."

He turned and left with the woman while I stood, self-conscious. Trying to avoid notice or attention, I snuck to the back, stood out of the way, and watched. Noah trusted me. I could run right now. I had no chaperone. Part of me itched to but now was not the time.

Crane's voice knocked me out of my reverie. "What are you doing here all by yourself? Shouldn't you be working in the fields?"

Crane made me nervous, and people had a way of standing much too close here. Her long, delicate neck bent to the right, and she peered at me from beneath an arced, pale-blonde eyebrow. I stepped away.

"I'm not that frightening, am I? Where's Noah?" She stepped closer to me again.

Turning back to the busy kitchen, I could not spot him. "He'll be back in just a second. We just—"

"Come," she took my arm, and I cringed.

"Noah said to wait."

"We aren't going far. Just outside where it's quieter, I'd like to have another little chat."

* * *

"You must find it difficult here." We sat beneath the shadows of the cliffside just outside the opening to the bustling kitchen. Two painted wooden chairs were positioned at a table. A cloth...

A tablecloth.

A tablecloth lay draped over the table. It had a blue and green pattern of some bird I didn't recognize.

"Difficult...I don't know about that," I said. Agreeing with this woman annoyed me. "But it is different."

"Tell me more about home. Tell me about the doctor." She placed her elbows on her table and cradled her chin between clasped hands.

Surprised again, I paused, unsure what to say or not say.

"I've already told you everything. He believes in the principle of health, health—"

"Health above all," Crane finished.

It sounded weird, those words we all muttered like a prayer coming from her perfect lips and unreadable blue-gray eyes....much like Noah's, except lacking the kindness.

"Yes. And I despise him for what he did. I was banished for no good reason."

I glanced back toward the kitchen, hoping Noah would rescue me soon.

Crane reached out and touched my hand. "Relax. Noah will be back soon." I froze, eyes directed to where her fingers met my wrist. Where was a sanitary clerk when you needed one? I'd give anything for a disinfecting spray or to hop into a sanitizing shower. Was this too much to ask? For people to keep their damn distance and stop touching me?

"Did you hear my question? Persi? Are you okay?"

She removed her fingers from my wrist, and my mind cleared, but my heart beat fast. "No, I'm sorry; what did you say?"

"Tell me about the First Nurses."

This caught my attention. "How do you know about them?"

Crane turned at a sudden crashing sound from the kitchen, then shrugged. "We need to know our...well, enemies might be impolite... but adversary is not too strong. Their dances are beautiful, I'm told."

"The most beautiful thing in the world," I said, thinking of Myrrhis. However, when I watched her dance on the stage once before I left, she had not even looked in my direction.

"Would you show me how they dance?"

I stood to leave. "No."

"Then, sit. We aren't finished."

Just then, Noah emerged from the kitchen with a dusting of flour on his forehead and eyelashes.

"Persi! I was looking for you in the kitchen. You had me worried."

Crane looked at Noah. "Weren't you supposed to take her to pick cradleberries?"

He flashed Crane a guilty smile. "Mother, I'm taking Persi to the fields right now. I just got distracted."

"Persi," Crane swooped toward me. "Would you be willing to part ways with your garland?"

My hand flew to my chest. The idea of no longer having my garland felt unthinkable. It was the only thing left that connected me to Myrrhis and my only chance of becoming First Nurse.

Noah raised his hand. "No, mother. We shouldn't rush her into anything!"

Crane glared at him. "Give Persi a chance to speak." Her shrewd eyes landed on me. "Well?"

"I'll think about it. Of course, yes."

Crane cut the air with her pointed chin and smiled. "Wonderful. Have a pleasant day in the fields, Persi. I'm certain you'll find it enjoyable. We'll speak again soon." Then, after a graceful nod, she glided away down the walkway with grace and poise that I envied.

CHAPTER NINETEEN

TWENTY PEOPLE TOILED in a garden nestled between two jagged cliffs of white rock that lay along the midday sun's axis. The clouds were gone, and several workers wore giant floppy hats of a beige material that shrouded them in shade.

Shielding my eyes from the blinding light reflected from the cliffs, I attempted to get a better look. "What are they doing?" No answer from Noah. I shrieked as something attacked me from above, landing on my head.

"Oh, hey, sorry!" Noah's fingers brushed against my cheek as he reached up and straightened the object. "It's just a hat."

"I-I've never worn one." My skin tingled from where he'd touched me, and my heart still raced from the shock.

"I didn't mean to scare you." He put a hat on his head. It had the same wide brim and floppy top as the ones people wore in the garden, but it looked humorous up close. A giggle escaped my lips.

"Are you laughing at my hat?" He jammed his hands on his hips, thrust his pelvis forward, and pouted. "You don't like the look?" Then he laughed and took my hand. His cheeks glowed in the sun, and his eyes danced with delightful mischief. He stepped closer, and for once, I didn't step away…until our hats bumped against each other, and the moment ended.

Noah tilted his hat far back onto his head. "C'mon, I'll introduce you to your coworkers."

A few of the workers nodded greetings as we arrived. Most watched with wary eyes. I'd noticed this over the last few days. Hostility replaced curiosity.

What had I done?

We approached annoying but pretty girl I'd met the first morning. She carried an enormous basket of brilliant purple berries so laden with fruit she could barely walk.

"Mercy, will you show Persi your technique? You have the gentlest fingers."

Mercy put the basket down and caught her breath. Then she laughed, reached out, and stroked the scruff on his cheek with fingers as purple as her berries. "Why, thank you, Noah!"

An impulse to take some berries and mash them in her face made my arms shake. She glanced at me, and her smile faded as she looked from me and back to Noah.

"First," Mercy pointed to my shoes. "No shoes allowed in the berry groves. See the delicate roots?" she pointed to the ground. Tendrils of brown that wove and interconnected patches of compressed dirt extended the entire length. "They are sensitive. Keep to the earthen pathways and only barefoot."

"Walk in the dirt with bare feet?"

"Noah, does she speak English? Isn't that what I just said?"

"Mercy, c'mon, be friendly—" Noah folded his arms.

"Don't be a bore. I'm teasing. I know she's new here, so I'll take things slow."

"Yes. Bare feet. She lifted her left foot and wiggled her toes. The tops were white and soft with even pink nails, but the bottoms were black with dirt.

"You can wash your feet after," Noah added.

"Of course." Mercy nodded. "Now your fingers…well…."

"You might have purple fingers for a while," Noah admitted.

"Yes," Mercy reached out and stroked Noah's muscular bicep as she watched for my reaction. "But see, it won't stain anything…or anyone. You seem to get stronger every day, Noah."

Irritated, I yanked off my shoes and stood in the dirt. I refused to let her intimidate me. The shock of the earth against my toes took my anger away.

The soil looked warm, but it felt cool. Perhaps it was my imagination, but I felt something crawling beneath the sole of my foot.

"Well, I need to get back to the kitchen," Noah said.

"You're not staying…." I said.

"No, you're in expert hands here. Isn't she Mercy?"

"Of course, albeit purple ones." She waggled her fingers and winked.

Anxious, I watched Noah leave and looked for a way to escape. Before I could react, Mercy took my shoes, walked over two rows, and handed them to a boy who went to stash them somewhere. Even if I dodged their watchful eyes, my bare feet wouldn't last on the jagged rocks and splintered walkways.

Mercy handed me an empty basket woven from a crude beige material. "Time to get to work. We only have five days left of harvest."

Five days? Making it through five minutes would be an achievement.

She demonstrated how to pick berries. Although it was not complicated, it took multiple tries not to crush the soft fruit between my fingers. Each berry had to be grabbed from its stems with a gentle but firm tug. If I pulled too fast, I yanked off the entire branch. Too slow, and they turned to mush between my fingers. Not a pleasant feeling.

Soon I settled into a steady rhythm. Mercy stood a few paces to my right, glancing over occasionally and picking at least ten times faster.

"What do you call that thing again?" Mercy motioned toward my neck.

The top of my shirt, which I kept buttoned, had come open, and my darkened garland glinted in the diffuse light.

"It's called a garland." Not feeling like speaking, I left it at that. The air felt sultry, yet the earth remained cool, and I kept glancing down to ensure nothing was crawling toward my bare feet. Meanwhile, a branch scratched me, and I worried I'd cut myself and get a horrible infection.

"Garland? Such a strange word."

"It keeps us healthy, and they are pretty—"

"Pretty?"

An odd defensiveness rose. I stopped picking. "Well, not right now. It has no signal here. Or maybe I broke it in The Desolation. Back in The Hive, it displayed colors depending on how many points I earned."

"Electronic items don't work here at all. Didn't you wonder why we don't use any of that stuff?"

"You have illumination."

"Biophosphoreence. They're alive, technically speaking. We grow them in a pond. My favorite necklace is silver and purple. Back home, what does it look like, your garland?" She continued picking, then glanced at me when I didn't answer. "I'm just making conversation. If it's too challenging for you to talk and pick at the same time, I understand."

"The stones turn a brilliant blue when you earn a point and darken when you lose one."

"Darker shade? Do you mean that hideous black? But what are the things for? I still don't understand."

"Yeah, your understanding of technology is a bit...primitive. Our garlands also tell us when we're due for our infusions and keep track of whether we are good citizens...."

There was another function I'd learned that I hadn't mentioned, and I certainly wouldn't tell her.

"Oh boo for you. You must be sad your silly toy doesn't work here."

Sweat stung my eyes, my head ached, and Mercy's questions and comments infuriated me. "Piper is your brother, isn't that right?" she asked.

Tired of talking, I nodded, trying to focus on the berries.

"The handsome drone pilot. I'd never guess you were related."

I ignored the insult. "You said electronic devices don't work here? How does his drone fly?"

Mercy gestured toward the tall cliffs surrounding us. "Above the cliffs, the magnetic force dissipates. So he lands up there."

"How do you get all the way up there?"

"Oh, not easily. Nothing grows, and the cliffs are dangerous. Why do you ask? "

"The view must be amazing."

"Oh yes, you can see clear to The Hive."

We continued to pick while I strategized how to get to that area undetected.

"Good for you, you poky thing. You finished your first small basket. Come now." Mercy picked up her much larger basket, filled to the brim with berries, and led me along the path.

With each step, I took care not to step on the roots that interwove the path and also watched I didn't step on anything hazardous. Picking the berries and speaking to Mercy, however awful she might be, had been a distraction. But now that I was walking, discomfort and unease crawled up my legs.

"How do you cope with standing in this disgusting dirt all day?" I blurted as we reached a shaded, covered area with wheeled contraptions holding hoppers that fit the baskets.

"Cope? I *enjoy* being barefoot." To my disappointment, she shoved an empty basket, larger than the other one, into my hands. "Water?" She grabbed a wooden mug from a nearby rack that looked filthy and poured water from an open container. I shook my head. She shrugged and took a swig. "You need to drink in this heat." She put it back down.

"Come, we've rested long enough." We trudged back into the sun. I pulled the brim of my hat down further, trying to shrink from the light.

"Is this all you do, all day, every day?"

"No, it depends on the season. Plus, we rotate depending on people's skills and interests. The cradleberry harvest will be done soon, and then I'll return to my favorite task." She rasped her hands together.

"What's that?" I asked.

"Helping in the kitchen. I *love* watching Noah work. He's a culinary genius. And the things he can do with his hands."

My head throbbed, and the headache went from bad to worse.

Mercy turned. "Persi, dear, are you okay? I insist you go back and have some water. I won't have you dying on my watch."

Stumbling back under cover of shade, I slumped down onto a stool, sweating and exhausted.

Mercy stood gabbing with a frizzy-haired girl. They glanced at me, and their shrill laughter rang across the fields.

CHAPTER TWENTY

THE SUN VANISHED behind the towering cliffs, cloaking us in the twilight. My fingertips were stained a deep, inky purple, my back felt like it was on fire, and my feet were caked in dirt. I'd swigged twice from those grimy mugs, desperate for hydration.

By the time Noah arrived, I'd tried to wash away the grime with Mercy and a few other girls. Unfortunately, they didn't use proper sanitizers, just murky, tepid water and a rough block they called soap.

My body was a stick compared to theirs, with their generous curves and bountiful breasts. Back at the Hive, men and women looked almost the same, with women having only broader hips and narrower shoulders. But with Noah, it was different. He had a scruff of facial hair that made him look rugged, while the men in the Hive remained smooth-skinned. No matter how hard I scrubbed, I felt filthy inside and out and ashamed to face him.

"You made it." Noah placed a comforting hand on my shoulder as he led me out. "Let's take a detour on the way." I felt Mercy's gaze bore a hole in my back as we left.

We followed a shaded walkway made from a woven tangle of tree branches. Suddenly, a turquoise bird burst from a dark nook, swooping past me with a startled flap of its wings. Noah grinned. "A whole flock of them live there," he said, pointing to a towering tree that seemed to grow right out of the rock face. "But they always catch me off guard, popping out when you least expect it."

We climbed a narrow set of stairs carved from the rock. It led to a wooden walkway that swayed in the breeze as we crossed a deep chasm. Then a winding ramp followed the cliff-side down. For a moment, there was darkness, as if we descended straight into the earth. We emerged onto a garden terrace on the other side of the cliffs, bathed in purple and orange light as the sun set.

"Grapes." Noah pointed at the maroon globes that hung from a sprawling terrace. "There's a secret place hidden behind those vines."

He led me up through a gap and two steep stairs. Hidden behind the grapevines, a small bench overlooked the rock face on the other side. From here, I saw people were still hard at work even as the light fell.

"They're all growing...food?"

"Food, medicine, materials we need."

I nodded. It was still taking time to process all this.

"So," Noah said. "I wanted to prepare you for what's coming. Senior and Crane spoke to me about you today."

"Crane doesn't want me here."

"Crane is complicated. She's protective of our community. What we've carved out despite...challenges is special. But she also has a black-and-white way of looking at the world. Others are uncomfortable for different reasons. Enough cliff-dwellers raised the issue to qualify for a vote."

"What will go to a vote?"

Noah glanced at the ground. "Whether you can stay. If you stay, you'd likely be pressured to remove your garland. It didn't do Piper any harm, but it hurt another visitor."

"You've had visitors other than Piper? Who?"

"That doesn't matter right now. I wanted you to know what was at stake."

"What did Senior think?" Of everyone I'd spoken with, he had seemed friendly but curious about me in a way that made me uncomfortable, as if I were a novel object that needed an inspection. "Or is it up to Crane?"

"It's not up to a single person. It's up to the community."

"Everyone?"

"Of course." He shot me a quizzical look as if what I'd asked puzzled him.

According to Noah, I'd only met or seen a fraction of those who lived and worked hidden in the terraces or within the cliff caves. The idea of all those people deciding seemed insane.

"It should just be one person. It must be chaos. How do you function?"

"We function well. At least, I think we do. Haven't you noticed?"

True. I couldn't argue. People seemed peaceful and happy here—but deluded.

"When over fifty percent of people call for a vote on a specific issue, we hold a Council meeting. Everyone votes, and you can stay if more people vote for you to stay than to leave. If more people vote for you to leave, you must leave."

"Where would I go?"

"I'd take you back to The Hive. You could see your sister again."

"Yes, maybe I could...."

"But anyway, I'm confident people will vote yes. That's why I wanted us to speak." Noah stood, walked to a long vine, and popped a giant purple grape in his mouth. He offered me one. I shook my head.

"Delicious, but they'll make better wine. This will be hard to explain, but some people see you as different from us."

"Well, I am different. You are all eaters."

"Yes, although you are now, too."

My face flushed.

"The thing is...they don't see you as human."

That set me laughing. "Me?" All this time, I'd been afraid to tell Noah my secret fears about *him*, and they had the same worries about me.

"I'm not a hominoid."

"What's a hominoid again?" Noah asked, perplexed.

"Android humanoids left over from the war," I spoke before I thought. For one thing, maybe I shouldn't be telling Noah. For another, Noah's people did not seem dangerous. Indeed, much less hazardous than my fellow Free Citizen, Lister.

Noah stepped closer. "We aren't androids. We're flesh and blood, like you. But that's where it gets complicated. I'm born from a mother and father."

"I have a mother and a father. But they're both dead."

"You're part of an experiment. Your doctor, well, he's changed you in ways that make some people uncomfortable."

I curled my toes beneath my feet. "Yes. We wouldn't be alive if not for Dr. Whisper's recipes. Plus, the result of his work will be immortality. Or would have been if I'd stayed."

Noah nodded but appeared unconvinced. "I'm glad you know. I wasn't sure if you did. Just so you understand, I wasn't sure at one point, but now I am. You're human, just like me. You have a soul, a spirit."

"What's that?"

"Too complicated to get into right now. The point is that other people need to get to know you so they also see that you aren't different from them. Not at your core, anyway. Otherwise, they'll see you as the doctor's experiment—a non-person we can exile without care for your safety."

"But that's how we think of hominoids," I said, speaking without thinking. "Which one is true?" Down below, people finished their duties, chatted, and stowed equipment away. The sweet scent of grapes wafted through the vines as the air cooled.

Noah scratched his chin and gave a rueful smile. "It appears, neither. Anyway, I want you to meet more people. And I'd like you to have dinner at our full moon celebration tomorrow."

"Eat? With all of you? I don't think I could."

Noah had convinced me I needed to eat from a practical standpoint. Admittedly, I enjoyed some things he made. Or perhaps I just enjoyed being with him?

Now I understood that Dr. Whisper's infusions removed the need for the strange habit. Without the infusion, I *had to* eat, or I became weak and confused. Food was a drug that fostered addiction. It pained me that Noah took so much pleasure in its creation.

"It'll help people connect with you. Otherwise, they might vote you out because they don't know you. Persi, are you listening? This is important."

"When will all this happen?"

Noah sighed. "The Council meets in a few days. Please show them the Persi that I know. Don't take this the wrong way, but you come across as a bit...sour to people. You seldom smile or make eye contact."

"I'm trying to be polite. And I don't understand the need to smile."

"But you often smile with me."

I felt a slight pull at the corners of my cheeks.

"See." Noah grinned and pointed, and I couldn't help it. My mouth opened like some strange toothy flower. My cheeks ached, and my heart beat too fast.

"Yes, but I don't know how to—"

Noah stepped closer. Heat radiated from his muscular body, which was much larger than mine. He stroked my hand. "It's okay. Your customs are different. I get that. It wouldn't be a simple task for you to return to The Hive, and I'll protect you as best I can. The more you can do to help, the better, understand?"

I nodded, confused as to the warmth that spread throughout my body.

"Well, we have little time to lose. Let's go."

CHAPTER TWENTY-ONE

WE LEFT THE grape terrace and headed back the way we came. The wooden walkways swayed beneath our feet, and the creaking became hypnotic as if each board told a secret story.

Noah paused. "The Commons will be quiet now. That's where people come and barter food and other items. There's a woman I'd like you to meet. Be curious. Ask questions...and smile. Okay?"

I spread my lips open. "Good?" I asked through clenched teeth. My cheeks felt stretched and uncomfortable, jaw sore and tight.

Noah's brow furrowed. "Hmm. Okay, don't smile unless you feel it."

"I only feel it with you."

Noah blushed. "Just do your best." As we continued walking, the pathways became busier. People stopped and stared and sometimes pointed. Again, a few appeared friendly, but most were not. Soon we reached The Commons. It was an enormous vaulted chamber carved inside the rock. Luminescent stone shone above, almost as bright as the sun.

Motion took my breath away. People hurried in every which

direction, following no order or correct traffic flow. "I thought you said it was winding down?" It was all so inefficient, and if anything this disorderly happened for just a few quick seconds back in The Hive, scanning them would give me copious points. My finger twitched at my side.

Noah led me into a quieter area. A woman stood in front of a table filled with colorful fabrics.

"Dasha wove these from our cotton," Noah explained.

Dasha cocked her head and looked me in the eye.

"Ah, this is…."

"Persi," Noah said. "This is Persi."

"Our new visitor." The woman nodded. "How are you enjoying your time here?" Dasha smiled at me. It did not light up my heart like Noah's smile did. My cheeks trembled as I tried to reciprocate, but Noah tapped my foot with his shoe.

"The fabrics are pretty. What are they?" I stammered.

"Dry season hats. It's warm for them today., but chilly night air isn't far off."

The woman put a green hat on her head. "Would you like to barter for one?"

Noah smiled. "I'll barter on her behalf. Choose one that you like, Persi."

"Really?" I missed my clothes from The Hive, but the only item that had survived was the white pantsuit bottoms. The sterile fabric Dr. W used was durable, and further, it was impregnated with antibacterial substances that killed pathogens. With its rough weave, this hat was likely a nest for nasty beasts that might make me sick.

"Has it been sanitized?" I asked, eyes narrowed.

Dasha looked at Noah and then back at me, face blank.

"They're brand new hats, Persi. They are clean."

"Of course they're clean!" Dasha frowned.

Perfect. I was supposed to be winning people over, and already I was saying the wrong thing. Maybe it would help me fit in if I looked more like everyone else.

"The yellow one with the blue diamonds."

Noah nodded. "I like that one too. It'll look good on you." He handed it to me. Noah and the woman began discussing the price, but I found the conversation confusing and challenging to follow. I was more intrigued by how the fabric felt between my fingers: more delicate than our uniforms but with so many nests for pathogens to hide. Bracing myself, I put it on my head and held my breath.

Noah clapped. "You look beautiful. I love it!"

He introduced me to a few more people on our way out of The Commons. The hat felt itchy, and I wondered if it was harming me. But no one had ever called me beautiful before. Each time we met someone new, my stomach tightened in a knot, and my mouth grew pasty. I tried various techniques, such as imagining the person was Noah or putting Noah's face in place of the person's body.

In one case, when we met Effie, a tall woman with the most enormous breasts I'd ever seen. The image of Noah with giant breasts sparked laughter that I disguised as choking. That didn't help. Effie gave me an odd look and left. Perhaps she thought I harbored pathogens.

By the time we returned to the narrow bridges that strung together the homes hidden in between the rocky outcroppings, I felt exhausted.

"A good start, Persi. I know that wasn't easy."

"It was that obvious?"

Sending a snort of air through his nose, he shrugged. "I'm not known as a social butterfly, either."

"I've never heard that before."

"Oh, I prefer keeping to myself."

"Can I take the hat off now?"

Noah grabbed it off my head and sighed. "I'll give it to Kendel. But we need to find you new clothes.."

The walkways grew more and more narrow. It required more skill to walk in the dim light without tripping. We could no longer walk side-by-side and continued single file. This seemed like the best moment to ask. I stopped and turned.

"Noah, Mercy said you have people helping you in the kitchen?"

"Yes, true."

"Can I help you there instead of in the field? You said you want people to see me in my best light, and I don't think the fields will help."

"You still have a little dirt on your forehead."

"What?" I scratched at the side of my head.

Noah stepped closer and brushed my forehead with warm fingers. "There, gone. Just a few specks of dirt."

"Why didn't you tell me?" Horror filled my gut. "Pathogens, germs —"

"Oh, c'mon, stop that. A little dirt is good for you. I found it

101

endearing…, and I thought other people might as well."

We continued, but I found it difficult to calm down. I'd been walking around with disgusting dirt on my head and hadn't noticed. What was happening to me?

"Senior wanted you to finish the harvest with them. Cradle berries are key to several delicacies popular during feast time. I'm seeing Crane in a few minutes. I'll ask her."

My heart sank. "Crane hates me."

"No! She doesn't. I told you, she's complicated."

Our conversation filled me with a sudden burst of anxious energy. I continued along the wooden walkway ahead of Noah. Below us, the drop descended past several other rope bridges. A dizzying fall to the bottom, which I'd become accustomed to.

"Hold the ropes on either side," Noah warned. "I don't want you to fall."

Ignoring him, I continued, aware of his eyes on me. Then, bringing all my attention to my feet, I did the third opening of the second movement of the dance of the First Nurses. It doesn't require much space. It is a forward motion—three quick steps followed by a pause to balance on one foot, then a slight step to the left with a bowing of the head and slinging of the arms back, and then forward again to repeat on the other side. The bridge cooperated and danced with me, swaying and bouncing in rhythm with my stride.

"Wow! Don't get cocky!" Noah said, clapping as I finished with a long hold of position nine. "You're very graceful. I'll be curious to see what you think of our dancing."

"You dance?" I asked.

"At the festivals, yes. You'll see." Noah pointed. "Up ahead, take the next walkway to your right." This one became even more narrow. Just a single plank, just wide enough to walk with a single footstep on each side. I loved it. I stepped onto a platform leading to a door set in the rock. Noah arrived behind me, took the metal objects they called keys out of his back pocket, and opened the door.

"These will be your new quarters."

"Unless I'm banished."

Noah didn't respond to that. He opened the shutters. I followed, noting that it was a sheer drop from each window.

"I'll let you know what Crane says. Goodnight, Persi."

His mood had darkened, perhaps because of my comment. I wanted to lighten things, but nothing came to mind. When he walked to the door, I followed him.

"Are you going to lock me in again?"

He paused for a moment. "Yes."

"Please, don't."

"I don't want you dancing around these walkways at night, Persi." he waggled a finger at me in mock warning. But his demeanor felt forced.

"What if I promise I won't go on the walkway?"

"Well, if you won't go out anyway, what difference does it make if I lock the door?"

"Are *you* locked in at night? It just doesn't seem—"

He put his hand on my shoulder. "I get it. It's not up to me, though. I'm sorry."

Perhaps he had a point. Besides, it felt wrong to mislead him. With one last glance at me, Noah left and closed the door. The lock turned. From the window, I watched him walk onto the walkway. He gave a self-conscious wave and continued winding his way down. I watched until he disappeared into the maze.

After he left, I stood, lost in my thoughts and plans. In the distance, I heard the boards creak and groan as someone passed. A few minutes later, a woman walked past, giant burlap bags slung over her shoulders. People worked hard here but appeared to have something missing in The Hive. What was it? What was it that was different about these people? We had so much more back in The Hive. We did not need to go to all this work to gather, process food…and yet, and yet…

I was deep in thought when the creaking walkway boards snapped me back to reality. A man was passing by, his footsteps distinct from the woman's. He hesitated for a moment and then continued on his way. I might not have had a clear view of his face if he hadn't stopped at that moment. But he stood on the walkway just below my dwelling, looking around as if he was lost or on the run from someone.

He was dressed like many people in this strange place: a simple fabric shirt and pants made from a patchwork of distinct patterns. As he looked up, the moonlight illuminated his jawline. Our eyes met, and at first, they were blank, but then they widened with recognition. A snarl spread across his face.

I was paralyzed, gripping the window's edge so tightly that I lost feeling in my hands. It was Lister.

CHAPTER TWENTY-TWO

ALL NIGHT, THE sounds of creaks rustles and sighs from the interconnected wooden structures echoed through the air, each one sending shivers down my spine. Lister? Was this an elaborate trick, or had he somehow followed me? My mind raced with fear.

As I paced back and forth, my reflection caught my eye, and I gasped. My sores, every one of them, were gone. This small change brought hope to my darkened world, but my fear remained intact.

In an attempt to find comfort, I lit a candle. The flickering orange flame danced and wavered, casting shadows across the ceiling. If I squinted my eyes, I could imagine I saw the First Nurses dancing and swaying in a private show just for me. Unfortunately, candles were not a luxury we had in The Hive, and when it flickered out, my eyes filled with tears as if part of me got extinguished with it.

Come morning, when Noah arrived, I felt such a wave of relief that I couldn't stop shaking. But I also felt frustrated. "Did you know he was here all along?" I asked, referring to Lister.

Noah looked confused. I reminded him of the man who had tried to strangle me, the man he had saved me from. "No. It must just be someone who looks like him," he replied.

"I know what I saw, Noah. Right there." I pointed to the spot where Lister had stood, staring at me from the wooden walkway below.

Noah frowned, deep in thought. "Hmm...," he murmured.

"You don't believe me?" I asked, feeling hurt.

"I believe you saw someone, but I don't see how it could be this guy from The Hive. Let's get you something to eat and a hot drink. You're shaking," he said, trying to comfort me.

This morning the sway of the walkways made me nauseous. Noah led, and I kept checking over my shoulder. No dancing. Several times I stumbled.

"Did Crane agree to me helping in the kitchen?" I asked as we arrived at the bustling area where much of the food got made.

Noah chewed his lip. "No, she thought it would be best if you continued the harvest." He turned to me. "But I won't let you out into the hot fields in this state. You look like you barely slept." He led me to a quiet nook with a small table and a padded bench off a side passage. "Have a seat."

I sat on the bench. He turned to leave. "You're safe. Even if he is here—"

"He is."

"Okay. If you see him, shout. There are plenty of people around to help. I'll mention it to Senior." Noah gestured to the people bustling about. Not long after, Senior arrived.

"Good morning, Persi." His kind smile set me at ease, yet a strength emanated from him that intimidated me. "Noah tells me you had a fright last night?"

"Not just a fright. I know what I saw...." I mumbled.

"No one says you didn't, but that's not what I'm here to talk to you about."

He took my hands and pressed my palms, closing his eyes. Then he asked to see my tongue. "I'll give you a calming tea—Noah's right. It would be best if you rested today. No cradleberries. We'll find a quiet task for you to help with."

Being in the kitchen wiped away all thoughts of Lister. For one, I got to watch Noah work firsthand. Today he prepared a strange food meant to be eaten as a delicacy after the main meal. Meanwhile, a bushy-eyebrowed boy named Petrof came and assigned me my task.

"These are for the Culmination Sweets," he pointed to a rack growing full of one-inch by one-inch circles of a dark substance with a cradleberry on top. We need one cradleberry for each dessert, but they must be washed and dried first, or it melts the sugar.

"Deserts? Like The Desolation?" An image of its blank dryness promising death flitted across my mind. Thinking of The Desolation made me think of Lister and the sickness that had disappeared returned.

I was too wrapped up in emotional turmoil to notice my comment had provoked Petrof into a fit of laughter so hard he stood doubled over, wiping tears from his large brown eyes. "I'm sorry," he said. "It's just—these are such exquisite delicacies and so difficult to make. We are only allowed one each. To compare them to The Desolation…well, it's so opposite it's hilarious." He burst into laughter again.

He stopped when I didn't join him. "Hmm, you're not the sort that finds contradictions amusing, I see. Unfortunate. Life is full of them. I'll be back."

Petrof returned with a basket of cradleberries. "These will turn your fingers purple—" he noticed my fingers. "But I see you're ahead of the game, so this task will be perfect." He led me to a stone cistern where a bubbling pool of cool water flowed.

"Dip each cradleberry into the water. Shake it gently…not too hard. If it loses its shape, it gets used for pie, and you can put it in this bowl. If it keeps its shape, put it here, and I'll take them to Grayson, who will dry and prep them for the next stages. At that moment, Noah exited from the thick of things. He rolled a ball of something white and sticky in his hands, and his face was flushed with excitement.

"Cradleberries, after all, huh?"

I smiled. "I don't mind if it helps. I'm happy not to be in the fields."

"Every hand helps. So many delicacies, so little time. My goal for this full moon feast is to create at least two flavors that no one in history has ever tasted. Tastes so unique they do not even have names!"

"How many flavors are there?"

Noah's face lit up. "Oh gosh, that's complicated—"

From behind him, there was a shout. "Noah, it's burning!"

"Hold that thought!" And he was off again.

I continued to wash berries and put them in the small bowl. Once ripe, they became even more purple and gave off a pleasant aroma. To my surprise, I wondered what it would be like to pop one into my mouth. Instead, I focused more fully on the task. Five gentle swirls to the right, five gentle swirls to the left, a gentle bob up and down, and then remove. Now here is where I often made my mistake. After this treatment, the berries were tired. If I shook too hard, this is where several times, they squished between my fingers. But if I allowed them to drip and carefully placed them in the bowl, they tended to be okay.

"Someone weaseled a promotion pretty fast." When I looked up from the cradleberry I'd just placed in its bowl, Mercy stood sweaty, fingers even more purple than they had been the day before. "How did you finagle that, I wonder?"

I didn't know how to respond, so I picked up another berry and washed it. Then she pushed beside me and sat on the bench. She smelled tangy and sour, a combination of sweat and cradleberry. The berry plopped from my fingers into the water.

"I'm onto you," she leaned so close I could feel her breath on my ear. I cringed. "You might have fooled Noah, but you haven't fooled me. When everyone votes against you, watching you get sent away will feel so good."

She stood and left. Not knowing what else to do, I kept washing berries. Only there was no use. My hands were shaking, and I kept crushing them. I blinked tears away.

Around then, Petrof returned. He'd complimented me on my work a few berries earlier, but not this time. "Oh..." was all he said. "Why don't we stop what we're doing? I'll finish up. You rest a bit." He pointed to a stool by the doorway...a dark corner befitting my mood.

Petrof continued where I'd left off. He could wash the berries at three times my speed, even at my fastest. He was so immersed in his work that he no longer noticed me. When I stood, he said nothing. I stepped out of the kitchen and followed the hallway to the entrance. I heard Noah's voice deeper in the kitchen but didn't see him.

Stepping outside onto the walkway, the light blinded me. The fear of Lister being nearby was palpable, but I had to take the risk. I didn't have many options and felt pulled to go up. I set off toward a small path leading to a steep staircase, unsure of what I'd find at the top.

CHAPTER TWENTY-THREE

THE PATH MEANDERED past several homes carved into the rock formations that loomed like giants. A wooden stairway snuck through a narrow gap and let out into a clearing. From nearby, I heard the distinctive sound of Crane's voice. I froze. She stood below in a hidden garden. It was filled with strange plants with colorful fruit: pink, blue, purple, and green of all different shapes and textures.

Flowers.

Crane spoke with an older woman who appeared to be giving her some sort of lesson. They couldn't see me from where I stood, but I stepped into the shadows just in case. I was about to continue upward when Crane bent to point at a flower, and that's when I saw it. At first, I thought I was hallucinating. Hidden beneath the bright color of her purple blouse lay a series of dark patches—a garland. Crane had a garland, the same as me!

Backing away, I hurried up the steps. Did Crane come from The Hive? The thought filled me with confusion. Why hadn't she told me? She didn't look familiar. When had she lived there?

Still reeling from what I'd seen, I wasn't paying attention to where I walked and who might be around. At the next landing, I had the choice to turn left or go straight ahead, and ignoring my instinct, I continued straight. Seconds later, Senior approached me from the other direction. At first, his face remained friendly, but a frown appeared when he noticed I walked alone. He raised his hand and stopped me.

"Where are you going, Persi?"

"My legs were stiff, so I went for a walk. Walks are healthy. Health above all."

"Yes, indeed." He rubbed the gray stubble on his chin. "However, aren't you concerned you might run into the intruder you mentioned…what was his name?"

"Lister."

"Yes, Lister."

"You told me to shout if I ran into trouble," I said, thinking fast.

"In the kitchen. But there aren't many people around here. It just happened you're headed toward my apothecary. Does Noah know you went for a walk?"

I shook my head, remembering I'd promised to tell him if I went anywhere.

"Please follow me."

Senior led me back the way I'd come and took a shortcut I hadn't noticed—a set of wooden stairs so steep they were almost vertical. "Be careful going down the ladder," Senior called from several feet below. "Take your time."

Moments later, we approached the kitchen, and I expected that's where he'd take me, but he led me toward my room.

"But Noah—"

"I'll have a chat with Noah. Rest in your room. You'll be safer."

With no way of refusing, I entered, and Senior left, locking the door behind him.

* * *

By the standards of The Hive, my room was comfortable, except that it did not have a sanitizing shower. Frustrated, I went and lay on my bed. Although I missed the infusions, beds had no hatches to close, thank goodness. There was plenty of space above, and I hadn't had The Fright here even once.

However, back home, I sanitized twice per day. At The Cliffs, it seemed to occur once, if that, and with plain water and the white soap blocks. I missed the pungent chemical sanitizers that left my skin blistering red. My motto was that if it didn't burn when I washed, I must not be truly clean.

A soft rapping came at the door. Leaning out the window, I tried to see who it was but couldn't from my vantage.

"Who is it?" I called out, unnerved. The door rattled again, this time harder. "Who is it?" I said again, louder. Again, the door shook and vibrated.

"Go away!" I screamed. "Help!" I shouted out the window. The door shuddered, and then everything went silent. My heart beat so loud in my ears that I heard nothing else for a moment. Taking deep breaths, I forced myself to calm down. I crept over to the door and put my ear to it.

Bang, bang, bang. With my ear so close to the door, it deafened me. I stumbled back and fell to the floor, hitting my head against my wooden bed. The door flew open. I screamed.

"Hey! It's me." Noah stepped inside and shut the door behind him. "Are you okay?"

"Lister! He tried to get in." Legs shaking, I stood and walked to the door. "He banged the door so hard I thought the whole thing would break."

"The door got stuck. Maybe it was Senior?"

"No! When will you believe me?"

"I believe you." Noah wrapped his arms around me, and I froze. What was he doing? He pressed our bodies together until I could feel his heartbeat against my body.

"Hugging you, is that okay?" he leaned back to look me in the eye. I wasn't sure it was okay, but I didn't want him to stop. I gave a short, jerky nod and yielded. It felt like falling. My body grew warmer and began to shake.

"Hey, it's okay. You were terrified." Noah stroked the back of my head. He had showered recently. Whatever he'd used to disinfect himself had a pleasant woody odor that I lacked words to describe…or maybe it was him. After a few moments, my heart rate calmed. Maybe there was something to this hugging.

"Senior said he found you wandering around alone."

"I know, I—"

"Persi, I want to win people over in your favor. If you wander around like that or don't follow our rules, it'll make that difficult."

"Maybe I don't understand the rules or what they're for."

"You're our guest…."

"Guest or prisoner?" I tried to say it jokingly, emulating Noah, but failed.

"You are a guest, but you must follow our rules. I'll tell Senior what happened. Someone will remain outside your room all night. Me if necessary."

"No, you don't know, Lister. Now that he realizes I'm here, he'll find a way… I won't be able to sleep. Or what if he tries to hurt you?"

Noah flexed his biceps. They bulged from beneath his shirt. "I don't think so."

"You don't understand. Lister is mean and sneaky. He might bring a weapon! Maybe I could stay with you?"

Noah hesitated. "Hmm. I could get in a lot of trouble,"

"What if I left in the morning? You won't be breaking a rule. Not really. You're supposed to be my chaperone…doesn't it make sense?"

Noah smiled, and I smiled back. "You can be annoyingly persuasive. Did you know that?"

"I don't mean to be annoying. I just—"

He laughed. "Okay, come on. Just tonight. Tomorrow, we'll figure something else out."

Every step higher filled me with new feelings of excitement. We passed no one along the way, to Noah's relief. "If anyone asks, we're out for a walk before bed."

Noah's dwelling lay off a spiral staircase carved in thick, gray stone. A charming wooden door made of wood the same color as his skin. "This is home," he said as we entered.

I had seen nowhere like it. In the Hive, we built our rooms for cleanliness, with all surfaces being shiny and capable of being sprayed and wiped down. The most important part is the pod, where we receive our healing infusion. Aside from a small receptacle beneath each pod to keep items such as a safety gun, everything we need is provided. Here, people had beds which were rather rudimentary replacements since they allowed for nothing but sleep. They also had many more objects, most of which I had never encountered.

In Noah's room, every inch of the walls gave me something new to look at. Tiny shelves held small sculptural objects—I recognized some of them from old stories—animals from before the Great War, figures of people.

"Are you okay?" Noah touched my arm.

"I-I'm just not sure where to look. It makes me dizzy."

Noah blushed. "Okay, so I like to collect stuff. Kendel thinks I go overboard, but everything I have here has a story."

"Everything? How is that possible?"

Noah frowned. "Possible? It's how things are. We can never run out of stories and experiences. Not until we die."

Yes, that explained it. I'd forgotten they lived much shorter lives than we did in The Hive. That must be why they needed to clutch to their stories.

He showed me a piece of wood carved in the shape of a bird and told me the story behind it. His best friend, Sedrick, carved it during their first sleep-out. Then he picked up another object from a shelf. "My father gave this to me." With bent brown ears and covered in a tattered fuzzy material, it appeared to be a toy animal. "It's a toy bear from before the scourge. Look, it still works."

He turned a knob on the right-hand side. The bear made an odd clicking noise, and when Noah put it down, it gave a few jerky steps before it fell over on its side, legs twitching.

Something about it filled me with something between sadness and disgust.

"You don't like it?" Noah said. "It's just a kid's toy." He put it away. "But my dad gave it to me...."

"What happened to your father?"

Noah adjusted its position on the shelf and turned to me. "Dr. Whisper killed him," he said, voice breaking.

My breathing quickened. I didn't know what to say. Should I ask questions? *How? Why?* Of course, I didn't say what I thought out loud: his father must have deserved it, but I felt terrible for Noah. A deep sadness collected in my heart.

"I'm sorry."

He shook his head as if to clear his mind. "I didn't mean to bring that up now."

"But you cook for Dr. Whisper."

Noah's eyes hardened. "Yes. What he did and has done isn't your fault. And there's a good chance you can help make things right."

"What do you mean?"

He stood close to me. "It's been a long day for us both." He brushed my hair back from my face, and my skin tingled where his fingers touched me. "I'll make up your bed."

It took quite a while before I could be certain Noah had fallen asleep. For me, sleep still felt odd and was often elusive. There were no warning sirens, ward nurses, or healing infusions to stop my brain from thinking.

Night after night, I struggled. Sometimes I fantasized that a ward nurse came and pierced my vein to deliver the healing recipe. That relaxed me a bit. Tonight, my insomnia—that's what Noah called it—served me well.

After he had been snoring for a good, long time, I crept to the door. Would he have locked it? I turned it and pulled, but nothing happened. Leaning closer, I inspected the mechanism. I'd seen him move something after he shut the door. Yes, this door locked from the inside. I moved a lever and tried the knob again.

Finally, it opened. Outside, heart pounding, I shut the door behind me. Lister lurked somewhere, which made my foray much riskier than I liked, but I had no choice. I had to reach the clifftops. My mission was far from over, and destiny called my name. Carum would be proud.

CHAPTER TWENTY-FOUR

I TIPTOED ALONG the platform, my senses on high alert for any sign of Lister's presence.

Up, find your way up.

To my left, a wooden walkway stretched out beyond Noah's dwelling. To my right, a series of wooden steps spiraled downward to a lower walkway branching off in four different directions.

I headed left, quick but cautious, glancing behind me in fear of encountering a dweller or, even worse, Lister. When I arrived at Senior's dwelling, it surprised me to see his light still on. I crept by, making sure not to make a sound and praying that he wouldn't look out the window at that moment.

From there, I faced a series of steps carved into the mountain. They grew steeper and more treacherous with each step. I had to use my hands to maintain balance, and I dared not glance downward for fear of a potential fall. Eventually, the steps transformed into a ladder that seemed to reach for the stars.

Climbing the wooden ladder was difficult and dangerous. The entire structure trembled. Noah would be worried if he knew what I was attempting. I could almost hear his husky voice talking me out of my insane venture.

A flush of shame at my dishonesty flooded my body, but I pushed the feeling away. I rolled onto my back, chest heaving when I reached the top. A moonlit series of circular rock shapes stretched from one side of the protected valley to the other side of the cliffs—within these dome-like structures lay Noah's people. Beyond it, although I couldn't see it from here, lay The Hive.

I walked to the highest point, steadying myself on a rock, and tapped my garland three times. The remaining stones glimmered like brilliant white pearls, and I closed my eyes, waiting for Dr. Whisper to connect. Moments later, I heard the knocking sound and let him in. I was transported to The Hive, seeing the world through his eyes.

"Hello, Persi," he said. A chill traveled up my spine as it had the first time we met like this. "You're late for our meeting."

"Greetings, Doctor. There were complications. I've done my best. Did you tell Myrrhis why I left The Hive? I don't want her to feel abandoned. How is she?"

"Myrrhis is fine."

"When will I see her again? Before I left The Hive, you promised that—"

"Do you have any news on the spirit root? Or Crane?"

"It's been impossible to follow Crane without being noticed. People are protective of the spirit root. I haven't been able to find out where it is. But, there is one thing…."

I paused, not sure how to tell him.

"Crane wants me to remove my garland. Soon they will vote on whether I can stay. I told her I would think about it."

For a moment, there was silence. Then my view shifted as Dr. Whisper looked out through a massive circular window. It was odd to see The Cliffs in the distance and know that I looked at myself, or at least in the same direction as the point where I stood.

"You told her you'd consider it?"

"I-I didn't know what else to do."

"And the spirit root? I'm disappointed with how little progress you've made. I told you how important it is that I obtain it—for the health of us all. I will reward you. You will dance with your sister as First Nurse in the front row and receive all available upgrades."

"That's extremely generous of you! Yes, I've tried, but where it grows is a secret. Not even Noah knows."

"He's lying."

"Noah wouldn't lie to me."

Dr. Whisper laughed. "You are perplexing, Persi 4091. It would be best if you were the same as the others, yet you are not. You appear to be..." he paused and spat the rest out with obvious distaste, "Quite an *individual*." An uneasy feeling crawled through my body.

"Please understand that the hominoids hold a different worldview from you and me. Simple. Barbaric. Eaters."

"Yes. But now I am an eater too." I felt the need to remind him. Or maybe it was out of loyalty to Noah. Part of me wanted to tell him how much I enjoyed Noah's cooking, but I suppressed the urge.

"Noah's cooking?" Dr. Whisper asked. "Who is Noah?"

"Pardon me?"

"You were thinking something about cooking."

"Yes, they cook food here. Noah has helped me. He knows where to find the spirit root. I need a little more time."

"Good. Eating is a temporary sacrifice while you complete your most important mission. Upon your return, I will provide a customized infusion recipe to decontaminate your body. After that, your system will cleanse and adjust."

"What should I do about the garland?"

"If you let them take away the garland, we will be unable to communicate, and it will kill you. It is integral to your health."

"Health above all," I whispered out loud, wondering how Piper was still alive. For a moment, it knocked me out of my connection. I sat atop the cliff, the wind rustling my hair and drying my tears.

Dr. Whisper wrenched me back. "We aren't finished yet."

"I miss Myrrhis. I'm not strong enough to do this. Maybe I should come home?"

"No. You do not have permission to return. I would not have sent you if you weren't strong enough. Are you questioning my judgment?"

"Of course not. I'm sorry."

"Here. As a gesture of my faith in you."

The area around my neck tingled. When I looked down, my entire garland was lit up. I'd regained every stone I had ever lost and then some!

"If you do well, there will be more, and of course, I will arrange for you to see your sister and dance with her. This is what you tell them."

As Dr. Whisper outlined his plan, my heart raced with the weight of the task at hand. "Remember, Persi, that wisdom is the foundation of true health. Superior minds shepherd the weak. Without this, people make unhealthy choices, not knowing how to live. Unfortunately, these hominoids lack guidance and pose a danger to themselves and others. Discover where they cultivate the Spirit Root and force Noah to serve you. Bend him to your will."

"Yes, Doctor. I will not disappoint."

"Good girl. Go now."

Dr. Whisper released the connection, and I slumped back on the cliffside, exhausted from the meeting. The coolness of the rock seeped into my skin as I gazed at the starless sky above. Doubts about Noah filled my mind.

Would Noah deceive me?

Why not? You are lying to him, after all.

My stomach churned at the thought. I had to tell Noah the truth. It was the right thing to do. Dr. Whisper's motives were pure, and once Noah realized he'd understand. But Dr. W. forbade me to mention this to any of the hominoids, unfortunately, that included Noah.

As I mulled this over, a startling realization came over me—I trusted Noah more than the doctor.

CHAPTER TWENTY-FIVE

As I LAY in the cramped pod, I felt a sharp pain in my left arm where the needle had punctured my vein. Despite the infusion not being complete, I awakened, feeling suffocated by the oppressive enclosure. My heart pounded with fear—The Fright—and I thought it would burst from my chest.

"Persi? Persi? Are you okay?" a gentle voice whispered, and I felt fingers touch my hand. "Please, leave the pod open—just a bit."

"Hey, there's no pod here. It's time to wake up," the voice spoke again, and my eyes fluttered open to gaze upon a familiar yet unfamiliar face—it was Noah. He stood shirtless before me, his muscles rippling in the dusty swatch of sunlight that illuminated his stubbled chin. A lock of hair hung over his brow, and his smile was warm.

"You had me scared. I thought you weren't going to wake up," Noah said, taking my hand in his.

"Of course, I'd wake up," I replied, feeling exhausted and burdened by a sense of guilt that draped over me like a heavy cloak, making me irritable. "What did you think I was dead?"

Noah's face turned red, and he stammered, "No, I saw that you were breathing, but when the other...I don't know. I guess I was just being crazy."

He took my hand again. "You have a splinter."

I gasped. A piece of wood lay stuck in my finger. It must have been from the ladder the night before.

"You relax and wait right here."

The events of the previous night kept replaying in my mind. Did Noah suspect? No, of course, he didn't. What time did I return? I'm lucky I made it back before he woke. The walkways were confusing.

He returned with a small green bottle and a box with various silver tools. "These are tweezers. I'll disinfect your finger and remove the splinter."

At the word *disinfect*, my heart swelled. "Thank you, Noah." Tears welled up in my eyes. I wanted to tell him everything but didn't know how to begin. How could I make him understand?

When he removed the tiny piece of wood, his fingers were so gentle it did not hurt. After he finished, he bound a white cloth around my finger. "To keep the dirt out." His focus on sanitation reminded me so much of The Hive and Myhhris that I almost burst into tears.

"When I was a kid, I smelled like this stuff constantly." He told me stories of various adventures and mishaps. They transported me away from my worries, at least for the moment.

"Are you hungry?" he asked, concerned.

"Not right now."

He caressed my face. "You sure you're okay? You look tired."

"I didn't sleep well."

Noah settled closer to me. I curled my knees beneath my chin and gazed through the portal carved into the rock. From this high vantage, I could see the crisscross of walkways that connected the various dwellings carved in the immense boulders and massive cliff-side. Far in the distance, the formations ended, but I could see nothing—just a blank, blue sky.

"What lies beyond this place?"

"The cliffs descend, and these rock formations end. Beyond that, there is the last depot before the maglevs leave the island."

"Island?"

"Yeah, didn't you know that? This entire area is on an island—The Hive included. A massive chasm separates the island from the mainland."

"What's over on the mainland?"

"The maglevs stop and unload cargo. A tube connects this side to the other, but no one has ever made it across. I tried or thought about trying. My best friend, Sedrick, died trying. We were thirteen. Sedrick was the more adventurous one, but I suggested going that day. I still remember the sky that morning…a pinkish light that lasted well past dawn. We snuck some—"

A knock at the door stopped him in the middle of his story. Frowning, he turned. He wore a light pair of sleeping shorts but was naked otherwise. I'd never seen a man with so few clothes, and his body fascinated me. My eyes traveled from his large, bare feet to his muscular buttocks and broad back…and then he stepped out of sight.

I should have felt pleased with what I'd accomplished the night prior, but I felt hollow. I stood closer than ever to my goal, yet a profound sadness gathered. What was wrong with me? *You are only a temporary eater.* I reminded myself. Dr. Whisper would fix me when I returned.

Outside, I heard voices raised, and an argument ensued. Sitting up, I slid out of bed and moved closer to the door.

"How many got damaged?" Noah asked.

"At least half!" Mercy's voice.

"Less than half." A man's voice I didn't recognize.

"I'm telling you, Bernard, no one else could have done this. Persi is —" then Mercy lowered her voice, and I could no longer make out the words.

"But no one saw anything?" Bernard said.

"I know her. Persi wouldn't do anything like that." Noah said.

"She's not in her dwelling!" Mercy shouted. "Who else could it be?" There was a long pause. Then Noah called my name. "Persi? Will you come here?"

First, I wrapped a blanket around myself. Although the temperature was pleasant, having bare skin exposed to the air still felt odd.

Mercy stood with Bernard, a man I'd seen but never met—tall with bulging arms and hair tied tight in a ponytail. When Mercy saw me emerge from Noah's chambers, her face went pale; her mouth dropped open in shock.

"You let *her* stay with you? Haven't you learned anything, Noah?"

"Was she here with you all night?" Bernard asked.

I waited for the question I dreaded, but it never came. Noah neither looked at me nor questioned me. "Yes, she was here the whole time. It couldn't have been Persi."

"Who else would do something like that?" Mercy crossed her arms.

Noah turned to me, his expression grave. "Last night, we had an issue. Someone went into the kitchen and stole a bunch of food. Two rows of Culmination Sweets were knocked over. A lot of stuff got damaged."

I couldn't help but think of the culprit immediately: "Lister."

Noah nodded in agreement. "She's right. We need to search the area. Who knows, he might be hiding nearby."

"Do you really believe it's one of the Hive people slipping in undetected every day?" Mercy asked, skeptical.

Noah shook his head. "What if it's Kallum?"

The man shook his head. "Kallum must be dead by now."

Noah turned to me. "Persi, tell me again what Lister looks like?"

I described Lister's stringy hair, nervous twitching mouth, and noticeable gap in his teeth.

Noah nodded, a look of recognition on his face. "That sounds like Kallum."

Mercy and Bernard exchanged uneasy glances. "Crane wants to see both of you. Meet her in the kitchen now," Mercy said, her gaze locked on Noah's eyes. She was about to leave but then stopped. "Why do this, Noah?"

"Because this time, things are different," he replied, his jaw tight with determination.

"Come on," Mercy said, pulling Bernard's massive arm as they left.

My situation was growing perilous. I couldn't shake the feeling that something dreadful lurked just around the corner.

CHAPTER TWENTY-SIX

NOAH AND I proceeded along the wooden walkways, both lost in thought. I kept grappling with the urge to confide in him about my secret meetings, but every time I worked up the nerve, I lost it.

When we reached the kitchen, it was bustling with more activity than the previous day. Upon our arrival, voices hushed, and every eye turned to me.

Crane stood at the kitchen entrance with Mercy by her side. Crane stepped forward, her voice unwavering. "Noah, Mercy will take over your supervision of Persi, and Persi will return to working the cradleberry fields."

Mercy watched me with folded arms and a cold gaze. Noah, however, was not having it. He raised his hand, jaw clenched with determination. "I started this and will see it through to the end. Unless we put it to a vote."

Crane appeared shocked by his words. She opened and closed her mouth several times before speaking. "Fine. As you wish. We will expedite the proceedings, but be warned, Noah, you may not like the outcome. Reconsider and let Mercy take over."

Noah pushed back the hair from his forehead, his eyes flashing with anger. He held my hand, and I could feel the heat radiating from his grip. "No," he said.

"Noah!" Crane's tone sent a shiver down my spine. "If not Mercy, then let Kendel do it. Can't you see you're making the same mistake?"

Noah ignored her, pulling me along with him toward the fields. As we walked, I couldn't help but ask, "What did she mean by 'making the same mistake'?"

"Never mind. I'll explain later." I'd never seen Noah this upset.

"Won't you lose points?" I asked.

Noah scowled and let out a bitter laugh. "Points? Maybe." And with that, he led me further away from the kitchen.

* * *

We were the first to arrive at the fields.

Noah rubbed his hands together. "Well, we might as well start. I need to keep myself occupied."

"You're going to pick with me? Don't you need to be in the kitchen?"

"For a change, I'm happy to be as far away from the kitchen as possible. And if I leave you unsupervised..." he rolled his eyes. "Well, then I will lose points, at least in a manner of speaking." Noah handed me a basket. "I'm sure you remember these."

Barefoot, we stepped through a row of bushes with bright purple berries lit in the morning sun. Surrounding the berries and my feet... was the now familiar dirt. Row upon row of soil. Dirt everywhere! By now, I should have become accustomed, but I was not. How could I be?

Noah began picking. "These are good and ripe."

A buzzing creature flew and landed on my arm. I waved it off. "What the hell are those things?"

Noah stopped and cocked an eyebrow. "You're joking, right?"

I returned to picking.

"A fly. An insect. They don't have those in The Hive?"

"No."

"How do you keep them out?"

I shrugged. "Dr. Whisper says that science, properly executed, is indistinguishable from magic for those uneducated in its mechanics. I don't know how ninety percent of things work in The Hive, only that they do."

"Careful. Noah put his hand on mine. You're making cradleberry juice." He pointed to the crushed berries in my basket.

"Gosh, I'm sorry."

"Have you tasted one yet?"

My stomach rumbled, but I declined. "No. I'm not hungry."

One, two, three, four, berries. Counting helped take my mind off my troubles.

Noah popped one in his mouth. "You've got to try a cradleberry at least once. Tell me you couldn't resist their delicious smell last time?"

I shook my head. They smelled pleasant, but taking something off one of these dirty bushes and putting it in my mouth made me cringe.

He popped another in his mouth, chewed, and spit the seed like a tiny projectile. It hit a large stone on the ground. "The way I see it, it's important to know what you're picking tastes like. It helps develop a connection to the food. A sense of presence. Do you get what I'm saying?"

"Noah, eating food is one of those things that I will never understand. I'm eating because I need to, that's all."

"Really? Oh. You said you liked my cooking."

"Noah, I do, but—"

The anger left his face as quickly as it came. He popped a berry in his mouth, chewed it, and spit the seed at my forehead. To my shock, it stuck there, and I brushed it off.

"Noah!"

He grabbed another berry and spat out another seed. It hit my cheek. "Sometimes you piss me off."

"Stop that!" I put down my basket.

"Make me."

Another seed, and then another hit me. One stuck in my hair and then right on the tip of my nose. Now we were both laughing. I grabbed a berry and popped it into my mouth. Flavor flooded my cheeks, making my lips spread in a wide grin. Sweet, but tart and juicy. It revitalized my entire body. Giggling, I puckered my lips and spat a seed at him. The first one missed. The second hit him right on the chin.

Noah wiped it off, laughing. "That's some aim you've got!"

We played like that with the cradleberry seeds for another while. Soon though, Mercy arrived, and both of us felt her icy stare as she stood on the rise, looking down at our antics.

For all the good things about The Hive, I now noticed something missing. Here I felt alive. And yet, their lives were so short. It filled me with sadness. They needed Dr. Whisper's help but didn't see it...and maybe—and this was a new thought—Dr. Whisper needed theirs too?

"Noah, what is the oldest anyone has lived until here?"

"One hundred and twenty-four."

That confirmed my suspicion. Many of us lived to ages well beyond, and Dr. Whisper was at least twice that age.

"Perhaps it's because you live and work in unsanitary conditions. Or maybe it's because you lack the infusions."

"Huh?"

"The reason you don't live as long as we do in The Hive."

He gave me a long, hard look, chewed his lip, and then returned to the berries. "Watch out, or you'll get another cradleberry pit on your nose." This time he said it with little humor. "How old are you, anyway?" he snapped.

"Sixty-four," I responded. "How old are you?" Something fell behind me. When I turned, Noah's basket lay on the ground. Several berries had rolled out and laid in the dirt. I was torn between fascination with the strange look on Noah's face and the cluster of dirt on the bright purple berries.

"What did you say?" he snorted as he bent to pick up the berries.

"Sixty-four," I repeated, confused. "What's so funny?"

"Seriously?" he stood with his basket, a strange lopsided grin on his face.

"How old are you?" I asked. "And what's so funny?"

"Uh, sixteen."

"Sixteen? No way. You look *much* older than sixteen."

"There is no way you are sixty-four. Another one of Dr. Whisper's lies."

"He does not lie!"

A pained look crossed Noah's face. "Persi, believe me. You are *not* sixty-four."

"No, you are *not* sixteen."

"Okay, what does a sixteen-year-old look like then? What did you look like when you were sixteen?"

"I was..." I tried to remember how I looked, or Myrrhis, or maybe Piper. But the thought just spun in my brain. No memory came to mind. A headache gathered behind my eyes. "I don't remember, but that's not the point. You're in your forties, at least. You, Noah, are the one who is being lied to."

Noah put down his basket and looked over his shoulder. Mercy stood with a few of the other workers. Most of them had their heads down, busy picking cradleberries.

"Do you have the energy to climb up that ridge with me? I'll prove that you're wrong." He pointed to a spot close to where I'd stood when I connected to Dr. Whisper.

"I'd rather do that than pick berries."

"Fine, let's go then. We started picking early. We can afford a break, but we'll have to work double-time when we return." He put his basket down. "I can see that you're gonna keep on getting me in more trouble every day that passes."

"What's that supposed to mean?"

"Just c'mon. Sixty-four." He turned back, looked me up and down, and laughed. "Crane isn't even sixty-four."

At the end of the last row, we arrived at a gate. Noah opened it for me and pointed to a series of jagged steps carved into the rock.

"I'm warning you. It's steeper than it looks. Maybe this isn't a good idea."

"Uh uh," I continued, thinking of the climb I had managed the night before. "I'm not letting you get out of this. You say I'm not sixty-four. You expect me to believe that you're sixteen? Well, you better prove it."

Several minutes later, I regretted my hastiness. Noah ascended at a much faster pace than me. Soon, my breath burned in my lungs, and we weren't even one-quarter of the way. My legs still ached from the previous night's exertions. On the other hand, Noah seemed tireless, which only increased my stubbornness.

"Stop and rest!" Noah shouted from ahead.

We stood shoulder-to-shoulder overlooking the fields below. Each quadrant was distinguished by its own color, but some areas were a mismatch of different plants and crops.

I shook my head. "If it were up to me, I'd make them all the same. All the purple should be with the purple. It's so chaotic."

Noah cocked his head and looked at me. "Hmm, I get what you're saying, but we need diversity in each field. It keeps the plants strong and helps keep the pests away. The plants are much weaker if you grow one thing with no variety."

"Well, I know nothing about that, so...."

"You'll let things slide on that one?" he turned, grinning. Now we stood face to face.

"Yes, I'll let that one slide." My lips curled into a smile. The taste of cradleberry lingered in my mouth, and I put my hand in front of my lips, careful not to touch my face.

Noah put his hand on mine and guided it down. "Don't hide your smile."

He leaned closer, and I noticed the musky odor that surrounded him. Although he didn't smell sanitary, I enjoyed the scent.

Before I knew it, Noah pressed his lips to mine. His action surprised me. What was he doing? I froze, unsure of what was happening. Noah pulled away. "Was that okay?"

"What was that?" I asked, confused.

"A kiss."

"It sounds familiar, but I don't remember that word."

"I won't do it again if you don't want me to," Noah said.

"But, I... maybe I want to try it again," I said, feeling an unfamiliar craving. "I've felt nothing like it."

Noah leaned in, and we kissed again. His lips felt warm and moist, and I felt we were doing something forbidden, perhaps even worse than eating. Yet I yielded to him, allowing him to taste me as I tasted him—the taste of Noah.

I pulled away, gasping. "I'm not sure what we're doing."

"Kissing. I told you, it's—"

Suddenly, a whining noise echoed through the sky above. We looked up to see a drone flying overhead in a wide arc, heading towards a distant area beyond the fields.

"That's from The Hive!" I pointed. A wave of fear coursed through me. Perhaps Dr. W had seen me up here tasting Noah. Now he sent a drone to punish me.

Noah's face froze. "A drone? My god, you're right. Wait, yes. It's okay. It's your brother's drone, Piper. He must have got our message."

The original mission forgotten, we scrambled down the steps.

CHAPTER TWENTY-SEVEN

NOAH DASHED DOWN the last series of steps and paused at the bottom, waiting. My thighs trembled. I bent over, struggling for oxygen, lungs burning. He pointed to the sky.

"Look—there are *two* drones. This is bad." The second drone circled the first as they maneuvered in the boundless blue, one chasing the other. Their whining noises filled the entire area. The first drone banked up and just missed hitting a jagged outcropping of rock on the cliff's face. "If they get closer to the boundary, they'll crash!"

The second drone arced and tried to follow, but it did not have enough time—it careened lower, and its blades hit the rock. It plummeted toward the cliff slide and erupted into a ball of sparks and massive flame that engulfed the second drone. The second drone spun in a lazy spiral and crashed in the distance.

"Oh gosh, Piper. What was he thinking?"

"Wait, no! Piper's not flying *in* the drone. They use remote control, unless—" I stopped the thought.

"Yeah, of course. That's how he got here." Noah stopped and grabbed my shoulders. "Do you want to wait while I go ahead?"

"No! If my brother's hurt, I should be there for him."

It felt like hours before we reached the site. Bits and pieces of metal lay strewn across an orchard of nut trees. Above, the other half of the drone lay embedded in the rock, smoke billowing from its center. Down below lay a mix of charred wood, electronics, and metal pieces. No one could survive that.

"He must have flown in the other drone!" Noah shouted.

My hand flew to my mouth, and my legs shook so hard that Noah held me to stop me from falling. "Gosh, I hope so."

We continued, and I tried to run, but my legs would not cooperate. The physical and mental exertion was too great. Noah stopped me. "You're pushing yourself too hard. Wait here. Right here. I'll find your brother and bring him to you." His eyes bore into mine, and there was another meaning he didn't want me to see. If he did not find Piper or found him dead or macerated in a mound of smoking metal, he did not want me to see that. Maybe I didn't, either? It did not matter. I was too exhausted to continue.

"Okay." I slumped down on a wooden bench set into the stone wall behind me. I recognized the spot. It was just a few feet from the door I stumbled from in my escape attempt when I'd first arrived here.

Noah spun on his left foot, and his calves flexed as he took off, a blur, down the walkway. Before I had a chance to call after him to be careful, he was gone. It was better this way. He'd been holding himself back because of me. If Piper was hurt best that Noah got there fast.

I put my face in my hand, trying not to think the worst. I'd seen no possibility of survival in the first drone. What about the second? At least the second one appeared to have missed the cliffside. But there were many rock formations throughout this strange area.

I knew little about drones, but drone pilots did not fly *with* their drones. They piloted them from a distance. How had my brother managed it? I settled back to wait. The cool stones of my garland comforted me as I stroked them one after the other. Each one lay cold and inactive.

"Interesting conversation?" Kendel stood not far away, a bemused expression on her face.

My hand flew to my mouth. "Was I talking out loud?"

"More like mumbling. I guess you heard two drones crashed. Noah sent me to find you. Aren't you worried about...the man who is after you?"

I looked over my shoulder. The drones distracted me so much that I forgot Lister could be anywhere. "If Piper needs help, I want to be near. Plus, it calms me to be outside." A surprised sigh escaped my throat. I never thought I'd rather be outside, but here I was.

Kendel's eyes glistened, and she gasped. "What? Noah didn't mention that. I hope Piper's not hurt!"

I clutched my stomach. Waiting felt more excruciating than running. "Do you know where the second drone crashed?"

Kendel pointed in the general direction. "Over that way."

"Yeah, but do you think you could find it?"

"Probably, but—"

"Persi!" Piper's voice rang out behind me. Noah, a grin more expansive than I'd ever seen spread across his handsome face, led my brother toward me. Piper didn't have a scratch. To my surprise, Kendel ran to him, wrapped her arms around him, and pressed her lips to his.

Kendel and my brother?

Relief flooded my body. The rush of exhaustion that followed was so intense the sight of my brother and Kendel in each other's arms did not phase me. Even more surprising, my hands were dirty, and for a change, I did not care.

* * *

Sitting at a low table and watching my brother shove food into his mouth had me gawking. I forced myself to eat soup, but my stomach churned from the day's excitement.

After dinner, I usually went to my room, but today, they built a fire and invited me to stay. Noah, Kendel, Piper, and others I recognized but didn't know by name drank a foul-smelling liquid together.

"Pass the cradleberry mead!" My brother's words sounded slurred. Watching him eat, drink, laugh, and smile, Kendel nestled under his right arm; he appeared so at home here it jarred me. A burning began in my stomach. How could he be laughing and talking about nothing? It made me feel out of place. Here I thought I had adjusted so well, and Piper had done it better. No matter how hard I tried, I never seemed to measure up. Would Piper get all the points again?

Finally, I'd had enough.

"Stop it!" I shouted and banged my cup so hard against the table it shattered. Its broken pieces reminded me of the drone I'd seen crushed against the cliff wall. The drone I'd thought my brother had perished inside.

Tears filled my eyes. "You owe me an explanation, don't you? How dare you abandon Myrrhis and me! Why did you leave?"

The table went silent. Drinks sat frozen in hands, and even the constant chewing ceased—at least for a moment. Piper's eyes cleared, and his cheeks reddened, but he forced a smile. "Long story, sister. But you're here now. Safe."

People ate and drank again, but I'd spoiled the mood. My brother's smile faded. "I'm sorry. You're right. I was relieving some stress, but you've been through a lot too. Let's talk tomorrow when we're rested."

* * *

The following day, my brother arrived alone at my room, munching a long yellow fruit I'd never seen. It seemed he could wander as he pleased.

"Do you want to taste it?"

I shook my head. "Did eating come easy to you, or did it take a while?"

Piper laughed. "Pretty easy. I noticed you slurping down Noah's soup last night."

"I only eat if Noah made it."

"Yeah, he's awesome. Come on. I'll show you how I got here. It wasn't easy."

We plodded along the creaking walkways, which were now becoming familiar. Every day I'd had a chaperone, mainly Noah, but sometimes Kendel or the first day out in the field, Mercy. Today, it was just Piper and me. They trusted him a lot more than they did me.

"How long have you been coming here? Kendel seemed to know you pretty well."

He nodded. "It started on one of my missions. We were supposed to shoot hominoids if we saw 'em. It's hard to fly in these canyons, and the doctor doesn't have many drones left. I flew mine to the area nearby—The Desolation. There were three...hominoids. I'd never seen one before. I zoomed in to get a better look. With the electricity shortage and the drones taking so much power, they trained us to kill in one shot...I was the best during target practice. But something held me back."

He blinked away tears. "They killed many people from here throughout various missions. On that day, there were three of them, and one helped the other. The one in the middle couldn't walk. Hominoids were supposed to be savage, dangerous android subhumans. That's what Dr. Whisper told us. But that's not what I saw with my own eyes."

"Who were they?"

"People from here, and if I had followed orders, they'd be dead. Soon after, I met Noah and Kendel down in Zone Zero."

We reached a clearing. Ahead, his silver drone sat intact on a flat section of rock. "Come and see."

Piper led me toward the drone. Using a crate to stand on, he helped me inside. There was a warren of wires and electronics. It smelled of sweat and fried circuit board.

"Thanks to them, I learned some other stuff—more about Dr. W's experiments. I knew I needed to get us out of there. I hacked a drone and managed to control it from the *inside*. That's how I escaped. I wanted to mod the drone to take you and Myrrhis with me, but I got caught and barely escaped. Noah agreed to help. He was already going to The Hive because of his agreement with Dr. Whisper."

Stooped over in the drone, even inactive, it felt warm. Buttons and lights flashed everywhere.

"Don't touch anything."

"I'm not." A blinking button read *Home*.

"What does that one do?"

"It returns to base. To The Hive. But it's no home of mine anymore. Nor of yours. Is it?" Piper's eyes narrowed. "Why do you still have your garland?" A row of red scars lay where his had once been.

"It reminds me of Myrrhis. And it's pretty!" I said as I clutched the stones.

Piper raised his eyebrows. Pretty might have described my garland just a short time ago when I'd stood on the cliff tops, but no longer. Without a signal, it lay black as night. It had all the beauty of a dead snake.

He lowered his shirt. "Are you afraid of the scars? Kendel likes mine." He stroked his fingers along his collarbone.

"I'm just not sure I want to remove it."

"Persi, get something straight. We were all brainwashed by that man. The only person Dr. W is looking out for is himself. He conned us, we were just part of his experiment."

"That's nonsense. You mean his experiment to grant us eternal life?"

Piper snorted as if I'd told a joke.

"Wait, no one told you?" He helped me out of the drone. It felt good to stand in the fresh air.

"Told me what?"

"I guess Crane doesn't feel that you're ready."

Piper was about to say more when Noah arrived carrying a package. Piper shut the drone's hatch and strode away. "C'mon, tonight's the Full Moon celebration, and no one's gonna stop me from getting smashed." He shot me a dirty look as he walked away, leaving me with more questions than answers.

CHAPTER TWENTY-EIGHT

NOAH ENTERED THE clearing and presented me with a package. The broad smile on his handsome face made me forget Piper's warning— well, almost. The drone loomed nearby, silver and gleaming in the sun, a constant reminder of my roots.

"For you." Noah placed the item in my hands. I unwrapped it to find a shimmering blue and gold fabric.

"What is this?" The incredible, soft texture of the fabric was unlike anything I had ever felt before.

"A dress," Noah said. "I had it made for you for tonight's celebration. I know how you love to dance."

"Noah, I don't—" I started to say that I couldn't go, but the look of disappointment in his eyes stopped me. "Thank you," I said instead.

"Are you okay?" Noah asked.

I told him about my brother's words about me not being ready, and he chewed on his lip. "Piper exaggerates sometimes," he said. I knew this all too well, but combined with Dr. W's warning, I had reason to be worried. I thought about telling Noah. Would he still want to dance with me if he knew the truth?

"Well? Are you going to try it on?" Noah led me past a tall, scraggly tree to a ramshackle storage hut.

I nodded, feeling both nervous and excited. Putting on the dress was easy as if I had done it before. The way it hugged my curves and brought out the green in my eyes left me in awe. A healthy glow had replaced my pale and sallow complexion from when I first arrived, and I felt beautiful in the dress.

"What do you think?" I asked as I emerged, feeling a sudden rush of insecurity.

Noah's jaw dropped. "Delicious." He came and took my hands. I looked into his eyes. He leaned in and kissed me. Something inside me became untethered, just a little more, but still not all the way.

"Me?"

"Yes."

Noah kept telling me that *life* was delicious. True, I had had tastes of that here and there. But why did something get in the way just as things smoothed out?

"We should go." He grabbed my hand.

There was no way I could say no—not after his incredible gift.

* * *

Never had I seen so many people gathered in one place. Since my arrival at The Cliffs, I had seldom ventured out of my quarters at night. But tonight, the big moon reminded me of the lights back in The Hive. I had grown to love the sun, but the moon's peaceful glow made me feel serene.

The tables were overflowing with food, more than I had ever seen before. Silver platters brimming with hot bread and meats sat next to hot and cold soup bowls. Beads of sweat formed on my forehead as the sight overwhelmed me. People were milling about, snacking on the various "finger foods," as Noah referred, placed on tall circular tables throughout the celebration.

Strings of lights crisscrossed the ample space like shimmering necklaces. Noah led me through the crowd, but I felt hostile eyes turning toward me. They had gathered in an area Noah called The Commons, at the base of the network of trees and walkways. Noah described it as the nestled womb, the belly of the place. This description made me feel uneasy.

A few seconds after we arrived, music played. In The Hive, the only music we ever heard was the same song played each morning to wake us from our nightly infusions. Here the music was made live by men and women wrestling with peculiar instruments. A cacophony of sounds, sometimes discordant but most often melodic and with a beat that made my body want to move.

"They're dancing!" I grabbed Noah's arm and pointed. Noah looked down at where my hand rested on his solid bicep.

"Sorry," I said, not knowing why I apologized.

Noah drew me close to him, and I didn't push away. "Don't apologize," he said. "Did you know it's the first time you've touched me on your own?"

He was about to say more, but the music grew louder as we drew closer and more people entered the dance floor. Effie danced so close to Petrof, who was so much shorter than her, that his head almost disappeared into her breasts. Dasha wore one of her colorful hats as she danced with a younger woman, hands clasped and spinning with tremendous speed. Piper danced, too, but nothing like the First Nurses. He moved fast but with little grace. I stood, gawking so enamored by the whole thing that I forgot my troubles, forgot all my worries of Lister and Dr. Whisper. There was just the dance.

The music changed, and more pairs appeared, whirling around each other so close I thought they might collide. Amazingly, it seldom happened, and when it did, it seemed to result in raucous laughter and good humor. Back in The Hive, any such behavior would have resulted in a massive demotion of points.

"How stupid."

"What's that?" Noah shouted over the noise.

"Nothing." I smiled at him.

Noah gestured to the floor. "Would you like to?"

I shrank back. Part of me yearned to be part of this…to move, to dance. But I didn't know how. These were not my people, and this was not my dance.

I shook my head. Noah shrugged. "We can watch for a while."

Noah clapped his hands along to the beat. I'd seen no one clap like this before.

Or perhaps you've seen it and just forgotten?

Right now, this was new to me, and I loved it. Noah was right. Life could be delicious. Mercy caught my eye, dancing with a handsome man dressed in beige. They parted ways, and she glided across the floor.

"Noah," she gave a slight bow to him and then, without a word, grabbed his hand. Before I could react—I'm not sure how I'd have responded, although I know what I would have liked to have done—Mercy pulled him out onto the dance floor. My stomach burned as I watched them dance, chest to breast. As I continued to watch, I noticed a pattern and protocol to their wild antics.

People exchanged partners, often switching with fellow dancers or scooping up participants at the side. I drew back, fearful of being approached, as unlikely as that may have been. Meanwhile, I continued to watch their movements, and it reminded me of all those days, those snatched moments when I mimicked the dance of the First Nurse.

Had Noah forgotten me altogether? Kendel passed and offered me the drink Piper loved. I grabbed it and drank it in one gulp. Fire burned my throat, but my limbs flooded with delightful warmth.

The next song began, and Noah and Mercy swirled across the floor. I had had enough—something snapped. I moved onto the dance floor. Raising my arms as I'd seen others do and making the three and then two steps forward and then back, I revolved across the floor and caught up to Noah.

Bowing to Mercy, I placed my right hand on his left shoulder and spun him to me. A flash of anger crossed her face, but she did nothing to stop me.

"I knew you would love this!" His eyes shone. "You're so graceful."

Heat rose to my face, and my heart swelled with...something.

You are in love.

A flutter of emotion swelled. As we danced, I noticed a happiness and freedom I had never felt before. The controlled and rigid movements of the First Nurse faded as I lost myself in the rhythm, the misty air caressing my face and the feeling of being alive surging through my body.

I hadn't realized how dead the infusions made me. Of course, my sores were gone, but that was just the start. My mind was clear for the first time, and I felt happy. I hadn't even known it to be possible.

Despite feeling as if I were betraying Dr. Whisper and Myrrhis, I couldn't help but bask in the joy of this moment. This dance with Noah was a true celebration of life, and I did not want it to end.

CHAPTER TWENTY-NINE

BACK IN NOAH'S room, giddy and wide awake after an evening of dancing and two more fiery drinks, I watched him roll a ball of ji between his fingers. From my spot on the low cushion close to the warm, earthen floor, the fragrant aroma of herbs reached my nose. He dipped the ji in the green sauce and put it in his mouth. My fascination with watching him chew still had not left me.

"You're making me self-conscious." He placed a hand over his mouth, shy. "You act as if you've never seen anyone eat before."

Still, I didn't take my eyes off him. "Until you, I never had. I don't enjoy watching other people eat. Just you."

"Why me?"

I decided not to tell him that watching his comrades eat disgusted me. Noah was an exception. Something about the way his mouth moved, the tensing and releasing of his powerful jaw muscles, the subtle expressions of pleasure that flitted across his handsome brow. Then there was the brief pause as if he savored the moment, followed by the swallow. I envisioned the food, moistened by his saliva, traveling down his throat and landing in his belly.

"Are you going to eat, or are you having issues again?"

"I'm not having issues." I rolled the dough between my fingers.

"What you're doing is playing with your food, and it's considered impolite," he said, teasing.

My face reddened.

"What are you thinking about?" he asked.

"How incredible it is that you can take these objects...."

"Around here, we call it food—"

"Yes, food, and you place it in your mouth and destroy it...."

"Chewing."

"Yes, I know it's called chewing. Stop being so difficult. I'm trying to explain how I feel!"

Noah rested his hand on my bare knee. His skin against mine caused a tingle to travel through my thighs. "Yes, I apologize. So you were talking about this...destruction."

"And then creation. It lands in your stomach, and somehow, it becomes something new, energy, life. Everything you need to live... with no outside help. No infusion recipe."

"Food is medicine. At least it should be."

"Food is medicine?"

The idea disappointed me. I liked the idea of food being separate from the infusions they gave us back in the Free Cities.

"Yeah. That's why we're so passionate about our food. We live in a bit of a precarious situation, as you know. Living close together could allow diseases to develop, but we stay healthy because we care for our inner terrains and keep our bodies balanced and strong."

Noah put his fingers on mine and removed the ball of ji.

"I will eat it, I promise. I'm not playing with it. Or I don't mean to."

Noah leaned closer, dipped the ball in the bright green sauce, and held it toward my mouth. Now it was messy with the sauce. How was I supposed to eat it? Perhaps he noticed my hesitation. When I tried to take it from him, he stopped me.

"Let me feed you."

My heart fluttered in my chest. "What? Why?"

"At least I won't have to watch you play with your food. Open up."

An irrational fear filled my gut. I'd barely grown accustomed to eating—becoming an eater—alone. The idea of being fed pushed me too far.

"C'mon." A smile played at the corners of his eyes.

Something inside me released, and I opened my mouth. "Fine."

M.S. Kaminsky

"Wider and close your eyes. If you trust me."

Taking a deep breath, I closed my eyes and opened wide. He put the ji in my mouth, fingers grazing my lips. "Now bite. I don't want you choking."

I bit down and cut the delicate ball in half with my teeth. Just in time, he moved his fingers out of the way. He watched while I chewed, and I lowered my eyes as shame washed over me. Finally, he took my chin and tipped my head back up. "Let me see your face."

He took the other half of the ji and put it in his mouth. We watched each other, chewing and eating, and I forgot my discomfort. We swallowed together, and his face broke into a smile that I returned.

The idea of the food traveling to our stomachs simultaneously—that shared ball of ji felt like the most intimate thing I'd ever done. However, little did I know that the next experience would eclipse it.

Noah leaned in and placed his mouth on mine—kissing. I detected the delicate wine they drank in his mouth as we tasted each other more deeply than last time. A surge of passion rose in my breast, and I forgot everything else as I allowed myself to experience him.

His hands rested on my shoulders and then traveled down, undoing my blouse. "Is this okay?"

"Yes."

He stroked my body with warm fingers and left a warm tingle everywhere he touched. He caressed places that even I would not have dared to venture. But his tender fingers lingered, causing shivers of delight to travel in waves up and down my spine and into my belly.

We moved to the bed. My entire body trembled, but it wasn't with fear. My legs felt weak, but it wasn't with sickness. Even that day beneath the Free City, when I missed my infusion, did not compare to my desire for him.

We snuggled beneath the covers, and his lips left a trail of kisses along my body. I touched the spots where his lips grazed my body and felt tiny traces of moisture he had left behind. I ran my fingers over those places. He grabbed my fingers and put them in his mouth. I gasped as he sucked on them, looking me deep in the eye.

"What's happening?"

"Are you scared?"

"Yes, no, I don't know."

"We can stop if you like."

"Don't you dare. I didn't know I could feel like this."

We continued. Deeper waves of pleasure thrummed through my

140

body, and I became bold. I ran my finger down his muscular chest, stomach, and farther down. My mouth ran along his body, tasting nipples, the crook of his arm, nibbling at his hair. He let out a sharp cry of pleasure when I touched him. I leaned back, and he lay on the bed. This was the first time I'd seen a man unclothed.

"What do I do?"

Noah laughed and trailed his thumb along my thigh. "Whatever comes naturally."

"No one taught me."

Some things don't need to be taught.

So I let my mind go. My body knew what it wanted to do, just like eating. We continued to eat each other, and I found him delicious.

Now on top of him, our eyes met. We shuddered at the same time. A flash of white light blinded me for a moment. Waves of sensation burst through my body as instinct overtook me. A flash of uncertainty crossed his face. I was leading him onward.

"No," he gasped. "This is too fast."

I slowed. How could I be teaching him something even I didn't know? All my life, I thought science was a mystery and that technology held every secret, but I didn't realize the biggest secrets sat locked inside me, waiting to reveal themselves. Noah moaned, a deep rumble in his chest.

Over and over again, I brought us to the top of a giant cliff. It overlooked the universe. Then I took us down, and the view from below awed us. Up again until we screamed and shouted like animals. A small part of me felt a distant embarrassment, but it crashed beneath the next wave, leaving exhilaration and an aliveness so intense I thought I might cry.

When the last wave tumbled, I leaned forward and kissed him again. A strange sense overcame me—we were not just eating. I fed him, and he fed me. The joy that rose in my chest threatened to overwhelm me.

"I love you, Noah. I love you. I love you."

I slumped on top of him, and he stroked my hair. We lay stuck together with sweat.

He whispered, "I love you too, Persi."

We fell asleep in each other's arms, and it's fair to say that I didn't know what sleep was. I woke up ravenous. We ate food again and then ate each other again; this time, I savored the experience even more.

That morning, when we walked out into the garden, hand-in-hand.

Crane stood, watering her collection of flowers. She glanced up at us when we walked past, and her eyes traveled to our hands. Her gaze locked on Noah, face an impenetrable mask. Noah grasped my hand tighter.

I smiled at her. It just bubbled up. She was the first person I'd smiled at except Noah. But she did not return my smile. Instead, she glared, eyes cold. The flower that had opened in my heart withered, but it did not die.

CHAPTER THIRTY

LATER THAT AFTERNOON, head throbbing, I stood with Noah and Piper beside the drone—correction, Piper's drone. Piper slapped the metallic surface. "Did you see the other drone crash and burn? Man, what I'd give to know who piloted that back in the Free Cities." Piper spat on the ground. "Guaranteed, they won't send another patrol for a long while." He clapped his hands together.

"Can you keep it down a bit?" My headache and Crane's reaction that morning made me irritable. Piper's loud behavior made it worse. A hangover, Noah called it. My brother's arrogance provoked me to challenge him. "How do you know they won't come back?"

"Yeah, how can you be so sure?" Noah asked.

Piper's face lit up. "The drone that crashed the other day was the last one. I've taken them all down except for mine."

Without drones, how would the Free City defend itself against hominoid attacks? I worried about Myrrhis. Then I remembered that there were no hominoids. Just this community I'd befriended.

We stood on a large, flat rock that offered a breathtaking view of the surrounding rocky terrain. The farmlands were nowhere to be seen, which was peculiar since we should have been able to spot the path we had taken. I bent over and tried to change my angle of view, searching for the direction we had taken to reach this spot.

"You won't see anything down there," Noah said, pointing to a distant cliff face. "We use electromagnetic oscillators to refract light and hide the community from above."

I raised an eyebrow. "I thought you were anti-technology."

"Not at all," Noah replied, shaking his head. "Technology is a useful tool, but it should be used wisely."

"Is that what you wanted to show me over there?" I asked, pointing to the ridge we had walked the day before.

Noah and Piper exchanged a look that I couldn't interpret. They were keeping something from me.

"What's going on? Why did you bring me here so early?"

"Look over there," Noah said, pointing. "That's where we walked the other day before Piper's drone crash-landed."

"Have you told her yet?" Piper asked.

"I thought it might be better to show her."

"Guys, I'm standing right here. Show me what?"

"The truth," Noah said. "Starting with your age."

"You mean like the idea that Noah is only sixteen years old and I'm not sixty-four?" I said, glaring at Noah. "That's how this all started, right?"

"Persi, he's right—" Piper started to say.

"C'mon! Don't tell me you're going to join him with this insanity. You were there on my sixtieth name day, remember?"

Piper took a step closer. "What about the birthdays when you were young? Like a kid or teenager. Do you remember those?"

I tried to recall those days. "No, but that's just because...I don't know why. It was a long time ago."

"Why do you think there are no teenagers in The Free Cities, no children?"

Piper was as ignorant as Noah.

"The toxins. Everyone knows that. We're lucky to be alive. Thanks to the infusion we—"

"You don't have the infusion now, but you seem fine," Noah said, interrupting.

"That's true." I had no explanation.

Between my headache and Piper's irrationality, I snapped. "Fine! Why wait? Please show me what's over there. Show me right now!"

Noah laughed. "It's a half-day walk from here, plus the climb. I thought you said you had a hangover."

True. A half-day walk did not appeal to me.

Piper rubbed his hands together. "Well, that was the idea I had, Noah. Three minutes tops, and I can get us over there. It'll be fun." He smacked the side of his drone.

Noah shook his head. "Piper, no way. It's dangerous."

"Not really, Noah. What could be dangerous about it? There are no drones left to shoot us down, and there's no pilot better than me."

"Well, it involves flying in that…contraption. At high speeds."

Piper smiled. "You're scared, ain't you?"

I massaged my temples. "If it saves us walking half a day, it works for me. Maybe Piper and I can go on our own?"

Noah sniffed and flashed a hurt look my way. "It might be challenging to find the right spot without me. I'm not scared…it's just —"

Piper clapped Noah on the shoulder. "Then it's settled. Let's go for a ride!"

* * *

The three of us climbed into the drone. Because the machine was not designed to be flown by a pilot, my brother had created an area to lie down while he operated the controls. It included a sizeable piece of padding—the same material we used for our infusion beds.

"Comfy?" Noah and I sat between a circuit board and two vibrating silver cylinders—perhaps motors. Tight spaces freaked me out, but this didn't feel too bad. Of course, it didn't hurt that all the flashing lights lit the space and to have Noah next to me.

"You can lie back." Noah guided me down until my head rested on his chest, his face close to mine. Now I felt as if I could lie there forever.

The drone had not budged, but already the ride had begun. A mix of feelings and impressions flooded my body: fear and excitement. Beneath my ear, Noah's heartbeat sounded steady and strong. His chest felt warm against my head, like a small furnace. His powerful muscles moved beneath me when he shifted positions. It reminded me of the night before. When he spoke, it sounded like thunder. It tickled my ears.

My next thought got obliterated by the drone's engines. The metal objects surrounding us vibrated, and a hideous, squealing, whining noise deafened me.

"I forgot to mention the noise!" Piper shouted. Maybe that's why he talked so loud all the time. Next, my stomach lurched. There were no windows, but I could see Piper's controller screen from where I lay.

Noah wrapped his arms around me, and I felt him tremble. I put my hands over him, and we held each other.

"Are you okay?" I asked.

Noah grimaced and nodded. "This is about as bad as I thought. Keep well away from the cliff-side, Piper!"

Piper didn't even look up, eyes locked on his screen, hands twitching the controllers back and forth. "I know what I'm doing." An alarm blared, and we landed back on the ground with a jolt.

"Damn, I thought I'd fixed that. Too heavy," Piper sighed. "One of us needs to get out."

"Well, I guess that'll be you, Piper. I'm quite comfortable here." Noah grinned, but I could see the relief on his face. "You're sure you want to do this?" he asked me.

"I'm still not sure what we're doing—"

Before I could say more, Piper helped Noah out. "We'll be fine! Don't be such a worrywart. We'll be back tomorrow morning."

Why would we be gone that long?

"Tomorrow morning?" Noah shouted. "What do I tell Crane?"

"Tell her we're introducing Persi to the truth."

With Noah's rather hefty, muscular body gone, the drone lifted fast. Rock and stone blurred past on the monitor as we sped toward the distant cliffs.

"The winds are powerful. I'll land just past the ridge."

Seconds later, there was a gentle bump, and the drone went silent save for a *tick, tick, tick,* of a component cooling. The smell of electronics filled the air.

We tumbled out of the machine and into the desert. I remembered this terrain well. It was like the area that me and Carum walked through what seemed like ages ago. I missed her sassy attitude and wished she could have experienced this community. She would have liked it.

"So what was it Noah wanted to show me?"

Piper pointed to the point of the ridge we stood on. "Up there."

"All this drone flying, and we still have to walk?"

"Yeah, but not far."

It felt good to stretch my legs, and we arrived at the top in just a few minutes. The view was expansive, and…my mouth fell open.

"The Free City!" I could see it there gleaming in the distance. "Is this what you wanted to show me?"

"Partly." He licked his finger and stuck it in the air. "When Kendel brought me here, the wind came from a different direction. Not ideal; we'll make do. Have a seat." He gazed up at the setting sun. The first one should arrive soon. We sat down.

"You know, you could just tell me."

"I could. Then again, Noah told you already, and you didn't believe him, so…let's just wait." We sat on the rock, and I gazed at the horizon and the endless blue. Mainly I couldn't take my eyes off the city. What was Myrrhis doing? Was she dancing with the First Nurses? No, they would avoid the sun. Everyone would be in their pods, infusing. Soon, the sun had set.

"Now listen close," Piper said. My ears perked up when the noise came. The distant siren signified the start of a new day. It made me feel homesick.

"Okay, I heard it. Morning. I get it—we avoid the sun at The Hive. We do everything at night."

Piper shrugged. "That's part of it. Now have a nap." We both lay back, comfortable enough with each other to lean against each other for support. The moon rose, first orange, then white, an enormous shining jewel of a moon when the sound came again. A few hours later, a distant siren signified the end of the workday. So their day was over in The Free Cities? That seemed odd. How could it have come so fast?

My legs were cramped. Piper poured us a hot drink, and we ate ji.

"Noah packed it for you. He said it was your favorite."

My heart warmed. Still, it felt odd to sit and eat with my brother, but I was hungry. And Noah made them for me. Then, a few hours later, the morning bell sounded again.

"Wait, that can't be. A new day hasn't begun yet!"

We sat through one more wake, sleep cycle, and by then, I shivered, but not with cold. I shivered at what it meant.

"They divide every day into four days in The Hive, so…."

"Divide your age by four. You're not sixty-four. You're sixteen years old! We thought we were living longer, thanks to that garbage he injected into our veins. But it's all a shadow play."

Numb, I nodded. Piper was right. I would not have believed it without watching it myself.

"Are you okay?"

Bending over, I stretched my legs. "Yeah, I need to wrap my head around this."

Four days were equal to one. Anger and confusion surged through me. I knew one person who might know the truth about The Hive. The questions I had for her were long overdue: Crane.

CHAPTER THIRTY-ONE

BERNARD, THE TALL, muscular man who seemed omnipresent in front of Crane's dwelling, stiffened as I marched toward him the following day. He held up his hand and stopped me.

"Is Crane expecting you?"

"No, but I need to speak with her."

"She's not available. Whom should I say called?"

I glared at him. "You know who I am. Persi. But it's important."

"I'm sorry. She can't be disturbed. I'll tell her you called."

Not to be deterred, I headed up the stairs around her dwelling, following the path where I'd seen her from the garden. Perhaps I could get her attention from there. When I arrived at the landing, loud noise and the smell of food greeted my nostrils. My finger twitched at my side. How many points for scanning each of them? The thought made me smile.

A young girl heard looked up and pointed me out to her companion. In a panic to step back, my hair got tangled in a scraggly branch hanging above. Humiliated, I endured their laughter while I extricated myself.

"Persi." Crane arrived and helped me untangle myself. "If you wanted an invitation to our breakfast, you could have asked. You don't need to hide…and spy on me, do you?"

"I wasn't spying. I need to talk to you. Bernard wouldn't let me."

Crane led me down the stairs and past Bernard, who watched, face as impassive as the cliff above. Then, before I could protest, she sat me at the table with eight others—six women and two men. Of the guests, I only recognized Kendel and Mercy. None of the others looked familiar, but that was no surprise. People here changed clothes daily, and I couldn't keep track of the faces and names. They became a blur.

Crane sat me next to Mercy, and her cheeks turned the same color as the fuzzy fruit on the table.

Peaches.

Cheeks the color of peaches, with eyes as wicked as the daggers Noah used to slice meat. She grumbled and made space for me, and I felt just about as enthusiastic. Kendel passed a woven basket of steaming bread which I declined. I'd eaten nothing but the food Noah had prepared for me. It felt wrong and dirty to share such intimacy with these people.

Crane raised her glass. "A toast. To unexpected pleasures." A few titters rose around the table as glasses clinked, sounding like tiny bells. Perhaps it was my imagination, but I felt they all mocked me.

"Her sort don't realize how rude it is to be invited to eat and not accept what we offer. Surely you will eat with us, break fast, Persi?" Mercy said with a fake smile.

"They don't know how to eat at all, perhaps?" a waifish girl I'd never seen before said.

"Untrue," Mercy continued. "Anything Noah makes, she gobbles like a mountain hog." Mercy snorted through her nose, and two of the other girls snickered.

Crane raised her hand, and they stopped. "You won't make me regret my invitation, Persi, will you?"

With some hesitation, I took a piece of bread. It felt rough and warm, like one of the cleaning sponges I used to wash my body. I wondered who had touched the bread. Who put it in the basket? But I forced myself to take a nibble.

"Well, you said you came to ask me something?" Crane peered down her nose at me as she popped a round, brown object into her mouth. When she chewed, it made a most unpleasant sound, like bones breaking. Did she eat a roasted finger? An animal bone? Nothing would surprise me. Noah's people ate anything.

"It might be better if I asked you later." I pushed food around my plate with the bread while the others shoveled items into their face holes. My stomach churned.

"I have no secrets from my guests." Crane opened her arms and shot me a generous smile. "Well?"

My chest tightened, and I could barely breathe. I didn't want to ask her in front of the others. The hostility directed toward me was palpable. Crane leaned forward, hands on one chin as was her habit while nibbling a carrot. As was also her habit, she wore a high-collared blouse of brilliant blue. The color reminded me of The Hive, although only First Nurses and those above Zone Three could wear blue uniforms.

"I know why you always wear those collared blouses," I said without thinking. The serene smile faded from Crane's face. Her face went pale, and she put the half-finished carrot on her plate. The others murmured among themselves, watching Crane with curiosity.

Crane cleared her throat. "Well, that's interesting." She finished the food on her plate while the others began an awkward conversation. The moment she stopped chewing, she motioned to me.

"Finish your vegetables, Persi, and then you are correct. After that, we shall converse in private." Using water to wash it down, I was teary-eyed by the time I'd forced the last mouthful down my throat.

Crane led me into her home and shut the door. Her chambers were dark and smelled of perfume. It was not unpleasant. She motioned to a bench covered in a soft, pink fabric and sat across from me in a hard wooden chair, back as straight as a pole.

"Well?" Crane said. "What did you mean?"

"My brother showed me something about The Hive. Dr. Whisper is distorting time to make us seem older than we are—"

"Not about that!" Her pale blue eyes looked almost white in the dim light. "About my high collars. What significance is that to you?"

A silence fell.

"You're from there too. The Hive," I said.

"What makes you say that?"

"One day, you were out in the garden. You bent over, and your collar fell. You have a garland. Same as I do."

Crane's eyes flashed with anger. "No. I do not." She pulled down the collar from her blouse and bared her throat. What I had thought was a garland were scars where the stones once lay embedded.

"Unlike you, I am no longer his pawn."

"I'm not—"

"You may have fooled the others, Noah, and all the rest. But you have not fooled me."

I glared at her. "When did you leave The Hive?"

"Years ago. Escaped, not left. And for the record, I'm *not* like you. I'm one of the stolen. Or maybe Noah didn't tell you about that part?"

I remembered him mentioning it early on, although I hadn't believed him.

"For years, they stole young children from The Cliffs. A hidden passage to The Hive lies not far from here. Dr. Whisper sent his followers to take our young. Then, once he perfected his cloning operation, we were no longer needed for his experiments.

Afterward, he tried to destroy us, but we fought back. However, his culinary skills still lag. He has systematized most things in his world, but true art has always eluded him. This is clear in his twisted interpretation of the First Nurses' dance. Though you may not comprehend, Persi, cooking is a long-lost art form, and it's something that we have perfected. Luckily, Dr. W is a greedy bastard, a real gastronome, if you understand what I'm saying."

"No, I don't understand. We have his infusion recipes. The doctor does not need to eat."

Crane erupted in laughter. "The doctor is using all of you as guinea pigs. It's not just his lies about time. He's searching for immortality."

"That's no secret. He's trying to make us all immortal," I said.

"You're just a means to an end. He lacks one crucial ingredient for his so-called recipes. Once he obtains it, he won't need anyone in The Hive anymore. I was a First Nurse before I left, and—"

"You? Impossible." I shot back.

"Believe me or not," Crane shrugged.

"My sister is a First Nurse," I said.

"You sound proud."

"I am proud."

"Yet you profess hatred for Dr. Whisper. The facts do not add up." Crane said, rising. To my amazement, she assumed the First Position. "Your sister is in great peril if she is a First Nurse."

With fluid grace that I had only seen hints of, she danced towards me, arms flowing at her sides as she transitioned to Second Position, mere inches from my face.

"It won't be long before he takes control of your sister's mind, completely and utterly," she whispered. Sweeping her arms over her head, she continued her dance, gliding across the room. "I barely escaped with my sanity. It took me months to learn how to dance on my own, in secret, during those precious moments we had to ourselves. By the time the doctor realized I had regained my independence, I had fled with some help. Your sister is unlikely to be as fortunate."

CHAPTER THIRTY-TWO

NOAH SERVED A dinner of all my favorite things, including moon soup, but I was not interested.

"I understand you're worried about your sister, but you still gotta eat," Noah said.

I nodded. "Okay, I'll try."

Noah ladled the steaming soup into a bowl. "Today is your three-month anniversary since you arrived here. That's why I made moon soup, and it's not an easy recipe."

"Back in The Hive, four of our months is equivalent to one of your years," I said.

Noah nodded solemnly as he served me food from an enormous silver platter.

"That would mean my sixty-seventh birthday is coming soon."

Noah chuckled as he speared a piece of okra and added it to my plate.

"Oh, no, okra, please."

"I thought you liked roasted okra?"

"Well, I may have pretended to like it a little," I admitted.

"There's no need to pretend."

"I didn't want to offend you. Plus, sometimes I want to eat, and sometimes I don't.

Noah chuckled. "That's called appetite, and it's normal."

"But I never had this appetite before. Hunger seems...dangerous. Life was simpler before I ate."

Noah held my hand. "Please, let me know what you like and dislike. Everyone's tastes are different, and I want to know yours, Persi. It's what makes you unique."

"Being unique is not healthy or community-minded," I said as I stirred my soup. "The only true health is collective health."

"But collective health starts with individual autonomy. The weakest link, remember? Pretending to like something you don't is unhealthy." He speared the okra off my plate and popped it into his mouth.

I hesitated as I thought of my last meeting with Dr. Whisper, Crane's warning about my sister. We sat close enough that I could smell the earthy scent of sweat from Noah's body. Tears stung my eyes.

"Noah, I—" I couldn't keep the secret from him any longer. But before I could continue, he leaned in, and his lips met mine.

For a moment, I got lost in the sensation of his moist lips against mine. It reminded me of the infusion in a way—a brief escape from my anxiety. But then I pulled away. "Wait—"

Noah leaned back, his eyes shining. "I couldn't help it. I have to leave for a few days."

Fear clutched at me like an icy wind. "Why? Where are you going?"

Noah cleared his throat. "The Hive."

My heart lifted. "To rescue Myrrhis?"

"Not exactly," Noah said. "But I'll do my best to find out how she's doing. We've had to make compromises with your doctor. Kendel has been going in my place, but Dr. Whisper insisted that I go this time. He wants me to cook for him."

"You don't enjoy going there?"

"No, I don't," Noah admitted. "The last time I went, I had nightmares for weeks. Kendel isn't affected as much."

A flash of inspiration struck. "Let me come with you."

Noah paused, and I thought he might agree, but then he shook his head. "No, I can't. If Dr. Whisper thought I betrayed him, he would retaliate. Crane and others think you're manipulating me."

"Is that what you think?"

"I trust my heart, and I'm ninety-nine percent sure I can trust you,"

Noah said, looking down. "But I've been wrong before."

Shame filled me. If I told the truth now, I doubted Noah would take me to The Hive. And yet, this might be my only chance to rescue Myrrhis. "What can I do to prove you can trust me, Noah? Couldn't I come with you without Dr. Whisper knowing?" My chest tightened with fear.

"I do trust you, Persi," Noah said. "But in The Hive, the doctor can manipulate people's minds. Crane told me about your meeting."

"Yes," I said, blushing. I should have told him. Why did I always need to keep parts of my experience locked away?

Perhaps because it's safer that way.

Noah stopped eating, for once losing his appetite. He cleared the table and put the dishes on a trolley for later cleaning. "Let's go for a walk."

* * *

Noah guided me through unfamiliar paths, spiraling deeper into the base of the cliff dwellings. Away from the hustle and bustle of the hidden groves and craggy nooks, we descended into the depths of the towering stone cliffs. The air grew thicker, and the light faded until it felt like being enveloped by a dark pod.

"Will you let me cover your eyes for the last bit?" Noah asked, halting our descent. I agreed, and when I opened my eyes again, towering trees surrounded us. Their trunks were as thick as forty men standing shoulder to shoulder, blocking the sky and leaving us in an eerie darkness.

"How do they grow here?" I asked, incredulous. Trees needed sunlight to thrive, or so I thought.

"We harness sunlight from The Desolation. It is bright here for a short time during the day, but these trees need little light to survive."

"Does anyone come here?" I asked, taking in the deserted and abandoned atmosphere.

"Few and rarely. It's always damp and mostly dark," he replied.

We reached a gap between two trees, and Noah led me inside. A narrow staircase descended further into the earth. A rich, earthy scent filled my nostrils, and I couldn't help but laugh in delight. "What is that wonderful smell?"

Moments later, we arrived in a cavernous space. The dim twinkles of light on the ground emitted soft illumination. I bent down to examine the source of the light and found amazing glowing roots of all shapes and sizes plump in the dark, fertile soil. Each root twinkled and shone with its inner light, creating a mesmerizing display.

"Spirit root?"

Noah nodded.

"This is where they grow?"

Now the most critical piece of my mission was complete. Why did I feel so empty?

"You could get in a lot of trouble for bringing me here, couldn't you?"

A sheepish smile spread across his face, and his Adam's apple bobbed. "Yeah. Especially since no one but me knows about this entrance."

There were hundreds of them. I knelt and examined the tangle of glowing, sparkling roots.

"What does spirit root do?"

"We are still learning. In small amounts, it provides primal health and well-being. Longevity."

"Immortality?"

Noah shook his head. "No, not immortality. There's no such thing."

"Dr. W is nearly immortal. I will be too, one day…I mean, I would have been if I'd stayed."

Noah gave me an odd look. "Why would anyone want to be immortal?"

His response stunned me. "Well, who does *not* want to live forever? Isn't that the whole point of growing these roots, so that one day— anyway, why does Dr. Whisper want it so bad if it can't grant immortality?"

"We're not sure. Spirit roots connect earth to spirit and reveal the soul's truth. He wants to break it down to its components so he can learn its secrets—assuming that's possible."

The weight of what Noah was showing me sank in. When he learned how I'd deceived him, what then? A knife hung from the side of his belt. I'd never seen him carry one before. Had he brought it in case we confronted Lister or—? I didn't continue the thought.

Noah looked down at the clusters of glowing roots, affection in his eyes. "These roots help us have a meaningful life while we're here—a long life, but not a forever life. The idea of immortality is corrupt. Life without limits is no life at all because our souls aren't meant to stay attached to a body forever. They need other sustenance and would die while the body kept living."

"But people here think I don't have a soul, anyway, so...."

Noah smiled. "You have a soul, Persi. Of that, I am certain. Anyway, we'll find out soon. Are you willing to experiment? If you have no soul, the spirit work won't work."

I hesitated. "You weren't supposed to tell anyone but brought me here. Why?"

"This is one of my favorite places, and I wanted to share it. Plus, it's the only way I'll know if I can trust you one hundred percent. With my life. Then we can figure out a way for you to return to The Hive with me."

Noah crouched and collected a glowing root from the ground. "A ceremony needs to be done first if you're willing." When the root left the earth, it stopped glowing and looked ordinary—unwashed and disgusting, ingrained with dirt.

He looked me in the eye, and I realized I stood on a fulcrum. If I said no, I'd lose his trust. If I said yes, I had no clue what it meant. Did I have a soul?

"Yes, I'm willing."

We sat in the ethereal light while Noah murmured words, root cupped in his hands.

"That's not English."

Noah continued without acknowledging me. Then he closed his eyes for a long while and broke it in half. He grimaced as he chewed and swallowed half. That caused me great anxiety. I'd *never* seen Noah express any displeasure over anything he'd eaten.

I waited for him to give it to me, but he stayed silent, eyes flickering behind his eyelids. Then he handed it to me. His pupils became so black the blue was barely visible.

"Eat. It's time."

My hand shook as I reached out and took it from him. Tears welled up in my eyes.

"Noah, I—"

"Eat, Persi. Everything else is just words. I'm no longer interested in those."

Intense bitterness flooded my mouth the moment I put it in my mouth. Noah sat, hands raised toward me in an odd gesture. He looked solemn and peaceful, and I feared I might throw up my dinner right in his muscular lap. Then something strange happened. Tendrils of sensation traveled from my mouth into my sinuses, and then it felt like it entered my brain.

"Chew," Noah commanded.

I bit down, and the flavor exploded. Bitter no longer described it. Every part of my body felt on fire with the odd taste of this root. And the sensations burst into my brain. A bizarre sound rose. It reminded me of the whisper of the First Nurse's feet hissing across the floor.

Shhhh.

Everything turned white, and then I saw Noah. He sat across from me in this white space but didn't have a body. Nevertheless, I recognized it was Noah and realized I saw his essence, his pure spirit.

As I looked at him looking at me, I realized he knew everything about me. He was aware of my appointments with Dr. Whisper and my ambition to become a First Nurse despite everything I'd learned. But I also discovered that Noah had not been truthful with me. I returned to my physical form, sobbing in his embrace.

"Noah, I've lied to you. And you've lied to me. But what does it mean? Who is she?"

"I'll bring you to her when I can."

"I'm sorry I betrayed you. I didn't know what else to do. If I reject Dr. Whisper, he'll destroy my sister," I explained, referring to the ultimatum Dr. Whisper gave me before I left The Hive. "If I bring him the spirit root, he promised to reward me with enough points to become a First Nurse. If I fail, my sister will suffer a grave punishment meant for me and think I deserted her."

Noah listened, his face expressionless. The only signs of his internal turmoil were in his eyes, which sometimes filled with tears or hardened with anger.

"You haven't seen your sister since you left?"

I shook my head. "No. I've asked about her, but he won't let me see her."

Noah remained silent for a long time, then let out a sigh. "I believe you, but there may be things you are unaware of," he said.

"Yes," I agreed. His words resonated with me, and I realized there were gaps in my understanding. But, perhaps with his help, I could fill in these missing pieces and understand what was happening.

"There may be a way you could go back and save your sister," Noah said as he helped me stand. "But we'll have our work cut out for us."

As we left, I felt like I had transformed. The weight of my troubles had been lifted, and I felt a glimmer of hope for the future.

CHAPTER THIRTY-THREE

NOAH HELD A meeting in the kitchen the next day. He instructed me to wait until he called me forward. Despite my lack of cooking experience, I felt a thrill of excitement as he went over the menu and assigned various tasks, each with its own set of instructions and precautions. When he got to my part, he announced, "As you all know, I'll be going to The Hive for a three-day tour of duty, and, as always, I'll need an assistant." He gestured toward me, and the group looked at me in confusion.

"My assistant will be Persi," Noah declared, causing a moment of silence before Mercy broke it.

"You have got to be joking. Kendel went with you the last three times." Mercy turned to Kendel, who stood across the room with a confused look. "Why the sudden change? And why pick a Hive person with no experience?"

"Persi, grab an apron. Your training starts today," Noah said, ignoring Mercy.

"What? Right now?" When he said he'd teach me, I pictured us sitting somewhere looking through the scribbles and scrawls that made up his "Bible," as he called it: *The World of Food According to Noah*.

"Noah—" Kendel started. But Noah was master of his domain. He clapped his hands once. "Well, that's settled. Let the magic begin!" People snapped out of it, perhaps eager to focus on the less stressful tasks of prepping a complex and intricate gourmet meal.

Kendel and Noah approached me at the same time. Kendel got to me first. "You're in over your head, Persi."

To my right, a girl slapped a giant slab of butter on a burning hot grill. The air filled with smoke and fire. Noah took Kendel and me aside.

"Kendel, I already have this planned. I will cook for the Doctor for the minimum of two days plus one day to travel—"

"We did three last time."

"Only because we owed him a day. That debt was paid."

"You'll never teach her in time. He'll recognize her."

"She's even more beautiful than when she arrived. Her face is healthy, and her body is strong. Plus, she'll wear a sanitary shield. That will help disguise her."

Noah found me beautiful? A warm glow rose in my chest, like a tiny sun. If there weren't so many people around, I would have wrapped my arms around him in a giant hug.

Kendel frowned. "What if something goes wrong? She'll be seen on the cameras."

Noah gave an impatient sigh. "Piper rigged the cameras in the stairwell, remember? There are none to speak of below Zone One."

"You have an answer for everything, perfect. But why? We just rescued her from that place!"

"Well, my sister—" I was about to mention my sister's plight, but Noah stopped me.

Kendel's eyes widened. "Her sister? That adds a huge element of risk."

"Not if we're careful. I will train her well, Kendel."

"Does Crane know of your plan? She won't be pleased."

Noah turned to one of his workers. "Dil cut back on the peppercorn. I can smell you're using too much from here!" Then he continued in a lower voice. "Crane won't be happy, you're right. But you're going to tell her you agree with my decision."

Kendel folded her arms. "Why would I do that?"

Noah leaned in and whispered something I couldn't hear. Kendel's face paled, and she looked like she might burst into tears. "You're making a mistake." She turned to leave.

"Kendel, wait. Persi will be my first chef today. We'll make a saffron souffle and savory donuts with an herbed cradleberry reduction. This is one of the recipes I'll make for the doctor. Then, we'll serve it to Crane and Senior for dinner, and they're gonna love it."

Laughter escaped Kendel's lips. "Brother, if you can achieve that in a day, you will have my full blessing. Crane will know something is wrong, though. The only person who might be pickier is the doctor himself."

"Wait and see." Noah turned, triumph lighting up his handsome face as if I'd already achieved the goal. Meanwhile, I was a girl who had never eaten until a short while ago. I didn't know my way around a kitchen sink, let alone this complex maze of a room filled with thousands of different utensils, ingredients of all colors, shapes, and sizes, and many ways to prepare it.

Noah must have noticed my panic. "We'll focus on this one recipe." He walked me through it and set me on my first task, making a cradleberry reduction. If Carum were still alive, she would tell me that cradleberries were my destiny.

"What's a reduction again?"

"Evaporate the liquid to tease out the sweetness, the flavor. But careful not to burn it. Persi, I'll be with you every step. I don't expect you to learn everything at once. But your skills will need to look convincing at The Hive, so I can't do everything for you, got it?"

Noah tried to oversee the most intricate procedures but was often called away. Plus, I started to have fun. Several times I noticed other helpers sneak tastes of their work. At first, I found this disturbing, but then I realized I had no other way of knowing if I was getting things right. And so I followed their lead.

Sweat dappled my forehead, and I became more appreciative of Noah's skill. A few days ago, a man referred to him as an artist when we walked through the square. I knew what an artist was—a person who painted paintings or made sculptures. Something as crude and awful as food could not be art. Now I realized I was wrong.

"Persi," the girl I knew as the butter girl called me over. "Watch this, will you? Petrof needs my help. Make sure it is crisped, not burnt."

She handed me a spatula, which I dropped. It fell beneath the stove. Then when I picked it up, I didn't know where to wash it. When I returned, the rolled doughs were perhaps a bit too dark. Ashamed, I removed them. Then I smothered them with sauce, hoping the strong flavor would hide the bitterness. Noah told me this is how a chef worked—adapting to any situation.

At some point, after I tasted the spice for the reduction and perhaps didn't follow Noah's instruction to the letter, I wondered if I was getting things right, but before I knew it, there was another task, and then another, and I had no time to ask. Meanwhile, Noah had to contend with a disaster when I contaminated their savory deep fryer with sweet.

Kendel came and insisted that she join Crane and Senior for their meal. "I want to taste it for myself," she said. "It smells fantastic."

I wondered and hoped that I wouldn't be forced to sit and watch whether I had passed or failed, and luckily I would not.

Noah placed a reassuring hand on my shoulder. "Persi, I want you to walk into The Hive's kitchen with confidence. Cooking is as much about attitude as it is about ingredients and recipes. Of course, intuition also plays a big role, but that comes with time. If the doctor visits, I need to present you as a seasoned pro."

Remembering the many dropped utensils, a burn on my thumb, a singed side of my apron, and a nasty cut on my pointer finger. The experience had not filled me with tremendous confidence.

Noah led me behind a decorative screen made from an opaque material surrounded by towering, lush green plants. The table was lit by flickering candles, and Noah attended to every detail. Dinner arrived on multiple small plates, each bite followed by a sip of lemon water to "cleanse the palate." I was still unsure what that meant, but I got the general idea.

"Don't worry. You won't need to stay here for the entire meal. Once you've seen how much they enjoy it, you can sneak out that way." He pointed to a stairway that led down toward the main walkway.

Nervously, I watched as Crane and Senior conversed while sampling various delicacies from silver bowls. I had worked on two dishes and assisted with a third, yet they hadn't touched those. And then it happened. Crane took a bite from one of the savory donuts, and her expression changed. I held my breath, hoping that her pause showed the incredible flavors she was experiencing. But seconds later, her mouth expelled the food into a napkin. "You plan to serve burnt food to the doctor?" she exclaimed. "Really?"

Senior scowled as he tasted my cradleberry reduction. "These spices are strange. All I can taste is cumin."

Noah rushed to me. "Persi, I think you better go. We'll sort this out tomorrow."

I blinked back tears. "How? Is it true the doctor is even more demanding? I won't put you at risk."

"Tomorrow. We'll work it out tomorrow. Just go now before it gets worse!" He made his way over to them.

CHAPTER THIRTY-FOUR

THE NEXT DAY, Noah informed me that they had accelerated the vote on my stay. "Today?" I exclaimed, my jaw dropping in disbelief. "Why?"

"It was my idea. Otherwise, they plan to hold the vote when I'm gone. If that happens, everything falls apart. You won't be able to come with me."

"But if I lose the vote then I'll be sent back to The Hive anyway?"

"Yes, but we won't be able to go together. Crane wants to deliver you straight to the doctor to avoid any retribution on his part."

I was at a loss for words, feeling like life was spiraling out of control. I hugged Noah and buried my face in his chest.

"It'll be alright. Come on. I want you to be as prepared as possible." He led me to a room I had never seen, deep within the rock formation. It was a chamber with arched ceilings that glowed with warm pale light and multiple rows of benches carved from rock, each with a long cushion.

"These are the Council Chambers. Every resident will fill these seats in a few hours, and you...." He led me up a series of steps, "will stand here to face them."

My knees grew weak.

"Alone?"

"You'll be alone when you answer the Council's questions, yes."

The thought of standing on that stage above my soon-to-be judges filled me with fear, but, I felt a moment of joy. It reminded me of the stage where the First Nurses danced. What if, instead of speaking, I danced to answer their questions? How better to communicate my answers than with dignity and grace?

"What are you smiling about?" Noah asked, a frown creasing his forehead. "This is serious."

"I'm sorry, I was daydreaming. It's a habit I have when I get scared. Now tell me—what do I need to do?"

"The Council has collected questions from each resident and will ask the ones mentioned most often. I don't know what they will ask but answer honestly. That's all you can do."

* * *

Hours pass rapidly when your fate hangs in the balance. Piper insisted I drink even though I could not eat. As much as I enjoyed some of the food he'd given me, an infusion seemed a more convenient way of gaining nourishment in this situation.

"Isn't there something you could stick in my arm? Must everything go through the mouth?"

Noah gave me a sideways glance. "Please keep those opinions to yourself."

"Sorry. I thought you said to answer honestly?"

Noah sighed. "Yes, but—" he didn't have time to finish his thought. As seats filled, a trickle of people filing into the room became a sudden torrent. Crane arrived and ushered me away from Noah onto the stage, where she sat me on one of the three stone chairs. "We'll call you forward when we're ready."

Soon, the room was packed. Looking out at the room of faces filled me with dread and wonder. With all its hidden nooks and crannies in the rock, I hadn't realized how many people lived here—several hundred at least, maybe a thousand.

"Persi?" Crane's voice echoed in the chamber. "Please stand." She motioned me to the center of the stage. Legs trembling, I did as she asked, and the questions began.

"Why did you come to our community?"

"I was trying to help my sister. I escaped with Carum. We ended up in The Desolation, lost." It still hurt to think about her. "And when I woke up, I was here."

"But you wish to stay?"

"Yes," I said without pause. Noah gazed at me from his seat and smiled. I hoped that meant I was doing okay.

"Do you consider the doctor at The Hive your leader?"

"Dr. Whisper was my leader once, but he's not anymore. I despise the man."

"Why?"

"Because they brainwashed us into believing things that weren't true. For example, about eating and how old we are. Now that I'm here, I've learned the truth."

The questions continued, and I got tired. Still, I continued to answer. After some time, the barrage ended. A woman brought me a glass of water and snacks on a tray. I noticed several people watching me. It was ji, and Noah must have made it. Of all the food I'd eaten, they were my favorite, and without hesitation, I popped one into my mouth and enjoyed it, feeling grateful for him.

Ultimately, it came down to this: I could stay under the condition that they remove my garland. Otherwise, I needed to leave.

"All those in favor of Persi staying with the conditions mentioned?" Multitudes of hands raised, but not Noah.

"All in favor of exiling Persi from our community and helping her find safe passage back to the doctor." Just as many, if not more, hands raised, but Noah again did not raise his.

He tried to catch my eye, but I looked away, too surprised and hurt to react.

"Persi stays by two votes contingent on having Senior remove her garland tomorrow."

Mercy's face soured, but Crane kept the same neutral mask she almost always had. However, both of them had voted for my exile.

Noah leaped up, and I'd never seen him angrier. "You're no better than the doctor. Removing it should be her decision!" He crossed to Crane and began a furious discussion.

Senior returned to the stage. I hadn't seen his vote, but he always greeted me with a kind smile.

"Come with me, Persi. Please." He led me off the stage through a back passage—a shortcut onto one of the narrow side walkways that swung and bounced as we walked.

"Congratulations," he said. "That was closer than expected."

I stammered a response. The experience overwhelmed me as if someone had just slapped me upside down—all the eyes on me, those questions, and Noah's reaction.

He led me into his quarters. It felt like I was stepping into the hollow of a giant tree, with walls covered in carved bark and orange light filtering from crystals in the ceiling. Everything back at The Hive was sterile and felt more advanced, yet they used technology here I had never seen before. Dr. W had told us that the hominoids lived like dirt creatures, wallowing in mud and filth.

Senior reached out and touched my garland. I drew back, protecting it. "Are you going to remove it right now?" My heart was pounding.

"I'm sorry," he said, tilting his head in a manner that reminded me of Noah. "Does it hurt when it's touched?"

I shook my head. "No, but it's not...sanitary, and I'm scared."

"Ah, yes. My apologies. Different customs. No, I won't be removing it right now. May I examine it a little further?" He blew on his hands as if that provided sanitation.

He touched my garland again, tapping it in several places. "Have you decided? I will only remove it with your permission."

I nodded.

Senior smiled. "Good. Noah doesn't want us to move too quickly, but I..."

"But please, not just yet." I put my hand over my garland and thought of Myrrhis, of how much I missed her. Tears came to her eyes. "It's all that remains of my time in The Hive, and it reminds me of my sister, Myrrhis." Everything I said was true, yet my gut clenched when I spoke.

Senior cleared his throat and looked at me for a long time. "A community is only as strong as its weakest individual." He paused, and I wasn't sure if he was waiting for me to respond. Did he consider me part of their community? Was I now the weakest link?

"When people stop thinking critically, society becomes fragile and susceptible to corruption and totalitarianism. Ultimately the soul of the community will be consumed, eaten," he said.

"Eaten?" I swallowed.

"A figure of speech," he explained. "But if you aren't willing to remove the necklace, you must leave our community, as that was the Council's decision. We have given you a short time to consider your decision and don't believe you pose an immediate threat. Your arrival has been a great gift in many ways."

"It has?" I asked, surprised.

"Yes. Noah was a broken boy before you arrived, but you have healed him. Not only do I love him like a son, but his cooking has reached new heights, and you are to thank for that," he said with a smile.

A chime rang in the room, sounding like tiny metallic birds and sending shivers up my spine. Senior bowed his head. "It's time to end our meeting. Think over what I've said and let me know tomorrow morning. Noah cares for you a great deal and is wise," he said, leading me to the door. "You're blushing. Do you have anything to say?" he asked.

"No, thank you. If I decide not to remove the garland, I will leave, of course," I said.

Senior nodded. "We take our decisions seriously and—" The door burst open, interrupting him. Noah stood in the threshold, fists clenched by his sides.

"Senior, we need to talk. Alone," Noah said.

CHAPTER THIRTY-FIVE

NOAH MET ME back in his room. His cheeks were pale and mottled with red, and he paced back and forth in front of me.

"You understand why I didn't vote, don't you?" he asked.

"I...I was surprised. I thought you wanted me to stay," I replied.

Noah slammed his hand down on a table, and objects on top of it wobbled. "Of course I do! Can't you see what they've done? They didn't give you a proper choice at all."

"If I remove the garland, the doctor will harm Myhhris," I said.

"Yes, and removing it could also hurt you! They're forcing you into this," Noah responded.

"I'm not worried about being hurt anymore, Noah," I said. "I just want to make sure no harm comes to Myhhris or you—that's all."

Noah resumed his pacing, unable to stay still. "They've shown no respect for you as an individual. We'd never treat one of our own this way. It's because they don't see you as human. They don't believe you have a soul. But I know you have a soul, Persi. And I won't let them bully you. You should be able to stay without conditions that could harm or even kill you."

"But what about my sister? I need to help her before it's too late," I said.

"Of course. You have the right to leave. But if we don't plan ahead, the whole thing will fail. Tomorrow there's someone you need to meet," Noah replied.

* * *

Later that night, as Noah fell into a restless sleep, I dressed and went to the door. The piece of spirit root I'd taken lay curled and dry in my pocket. Taken? *Stolen.* I hesitated, wondering if the Council was watching the door or Lister was waiting. So, I went through the window instead.

I climbed onto the dark ledge and made my way to the clifftops, careful to stay under cover of darkness. Once there, I stood in the light mist, shivering from the cold. That's when Dr. Whisper connected with me.

"We have no scheduled meeting. Do you have news?" he asked.

"I want to speak to my sister. I need to know she's okay," I replied.

Dr. Whisper grew silent for a moment. "You don't trust me? Your sister is happy and doing well. However, she has expressed concerns about your loyalty to The Hive. Before you left on your mission, you pledged to do anything to redeem yourself. You promised to one day look your sister in the eye as a healthy community member, knowing that you had contributed to the same extent as she."

"Yes, I do, but can't I just—"

"No! Don't you see what they have done to you? They brainwashed you. Poisoned you with their food and decrepit customs."

"Yes, of course. You're right."

"You will see your sister when you return with the root. Do you have it?"

Cramming my hand in my pocket, I pulled the root out and held it in front of my face. My skin crawled as I felt him lean forward and look through my eyes.

"Wonderful. What are you waiting for? Leave! Bring it to me!"

His voice blasted my head so hard I felt my brain shrink, and my resolve wavered.

"Y-yes, I will, of course. I didn't want suspicion to arise. How will I return?"

"I will tell Lister to find you. He will help you."

"Lister? No, but I—"

Noises and voices on the cliffside caught my attention. "Someone's coming."

"Your sister's punishment will be severe if you get caught," Dr. Whisper warned. He then cut the connection, leaving me crumpled on the rocks below.

As I lay there, I heard familiar voices. It was Crane's guard, Bernard, and Noah with him. "Why would she go up here?" Bernard asked. Noah responded, "I woke up, and she was gone. I'm worried someone has hurt her."

I lay there, hidden in the dirt and mud, as they searched the area. "How did she get the spirit root in the first place?" Bernard asked. Noah defended me. "You don't know that she stole it. What about Kallum? You should have believed her in the beginning. No one else could have gotten into the kitchen."

My eyes burned with tears. The best thing I could do for Noah was to follow Dr. Whisper's advice and leave The Cliffs as soon as possible.

Not wanting to risk the main path, I went a different way. It wound among giant spires of rock and ended at a sheer cliff. Fifty feet down lay a narrow ledge and the walkway below it. The voices grew nearer. Without thinking things through, I scooted over the edge.

My legs dangled in the air for a moment, looking for something to touch. Then, grabbing a large outcropping, I swung my legs down and wedged them in a deep crevasse. Lowering myself farther, I shuffled along the groove, making progress across and downward. Soon, the big groove in the rock ended.

Above me, the cliff face protruded outward. Below, I hunted for an outcropping to brace my feet, but the nearest one was too far to reach. My hands trembled, and my grip weakened.

Reaching up, disaster struck. With a loud *crack*, the brittle rock broke off in my hand, and I slammed myself against the rock face to avoid being hit. I flailed and grabbed another smaller outcropping lower down just in time.

Several other pieces followed, and for a moment, it seemed a massive rockslide would take me with it. But the barrage of rock stopped, and all I could hear was my breath racing in my lungs. Fear paralyzed me as the wind whistled through the chasm, and the air chilled. The weather was changing, and rain might come soon.

"Help!" I shouted. My voice got drowned out by the wind. Besides, I wasn't sure what kind of help I could count on unless Noah found me here, which seemed unlikely. Somehow, I needed to figure this out myself, or this was the end. But if I died, what would Dr. Whisper do to Myhhris?

This gave me the strength to continue. Realizing I could not move up or down where I stood, I moved along the crevasse. Again, I tried to drop my right leg and connect with the outcropping below, but my arms shook so hard I had to stop. I jammed first one toe and then the other as hard as possible and leaned against a slight indent in the rock.

For the first time since I had descended, I rested. My mind wouldn't let me get comfortable for too long. It was figure this puzzle out or die. Now that my arms had rested, inspiration struck. The outcropping was too far to reach with one leg...but if I stretched down and used my body length, I would reach it. This would require keeping my grip on the crevasse with my hands and not tumbling backward when I readjusted.

I turned my knees hard to the right and shifted my feet. Not too far, or I'd fall, but too little, and the bed of my knee might push me off the side to my death.

After I'd bent as far as I could, I lowered my hands and jammed them into the crevasse. I released my left leg halfway and used my knees to stabilize myself against the rock—they must be bleeding by now—while I lowered myself. I tried to look down, but couldn't see how far the outcropping lay below.

Finally, the toe of my left foot touched. From there, it became easy. I reached a larger incline wide enough to scoot down on my butt for thirty feet. I fell to my knees and kissed the earth when I touched the ground.

"That's disgusting. You've reached a new low," I said.

Well, at least you didn't die reaching that low.

The thought shook me with a nervous fit of laughter. I stumbled to my feet and continued. Seconds later, the shadowy figure of Bernard appeared on a walkway below, and I realized that my escape was far from over. I crouched down and waited for him to pass.

CHAPTER THIRTY-SIX

THE MOMENT BERNARD went in the opposite direction, I moved. My legs were shaking so violently that the entire structure vibrated. I held onto the ropes on either side to steady myself and walked forward.

The climb down the cliff had depleted all my strength, and I needed to rest. As I passed one dwelling, I noticed the back door was ajar. I had seen Senior and Noah enter the building before and thought it might be a storage room for food. Noah had taught me well, and I realized I needed to eat and rest if I wanted to continue. I approached the building with caution, unsure if it was occupied.

The walkway swayed behind me, and I heard Bernard's voice. I had no other option but to slip into the darkness of the dwelling. I hid behind the door and held my breath, waiting for the voices to pass. The room was dimly lit and had a faint scent that reminded me of the herbs that Noah gave me on the day I woke up here. Back then, I had tried to escape, and now, I was trying to run again, but for different reasons.

The voices outside grew louder. My eyes adjusted to the dark, and I saw that the room had rows of wooden shelves lined with colorful glass jars. In the center of the room was a large table with smaller bottles and tools, which looked familiar from Noah's kitchen. Then, just as I was about to search for food, I heard a noise that stopped me. Someone was in the room with me. Slow and regular breathing came from a door on the other side of the room, which was ajar, leading into darkness. I tiptoed over.

Open it.

I'd learned to listen to my impulses even though I did not know where they came from. The door squealed on its hinges. I froze and waited. No other sounds arose except for the breathing—slow and somewhat labored.

Despite the squeaky door, the room looked clean and taken care of. Now I made out features in the dim light—the crook of a nose... something familiar about that. Hair splayed on a white pillow. Where was the light? I fumbled around, looking for the control to illuminate the space.

I found it on the stone wall next to the bed. A faint orange glow rose, and I blinked, unsure if what I saw was my imagination. Lying in bed, pale, dark circles under her eyes—was me.

Stepping closer, my mouth hung open, and the room lurched beneath my feet. I fell against the bed, jostling the girl's leg. So this was the girl I'd seen in Noah's mind when we ate the spirit root together. At the time, I hadn't understood.

She remained motionless. Either unconscious or in a deep sleep, her breath kept its steady rhythm. My pulse throbbed in my ears. Leaning closer, I saw scars on her neck where her garland had once been. My hand flew to my neck, and I felt relieved to find that mine was still there.

"Who are you?" I whispered. The girl did not answer. Noah's words came back to me—another visitor had been harmed when Senior tried to remove the garland. Was this her? If so, I could see why he hadn't brought me earlier. Even now, this was too much.

I touched her arm. "Hey," I whispered. "I need to talk to you." A desperate urge to communicate with this twin flooded me. "Open your eyes!"

Her eyes opened, and I gasped. "Can you hear me?" No response. Her eyes remained open, unblinking. I grabbed her shoulder and shook, but she showed no reaction. Her blank eyes staring up at the ceiling, set my spine crawling. "Close your eyes, please," I whispered, not expecting her to do it. But she did.

"She's in a coma," Senior's voice came from behind.

I spun to face him. He stood alone, hands behind his back, a small, sad smile on his face.

"Who is she?"

Senior shrugged. "You?"

"No."

"Well, your clone then, Persi. You must have put the pieces together by now. Ninety percent of the so-called Free Citizens of The Hive are clones. The rest, naturally born humans, were stolen from The Cliffs at a young age.

Noah's words came back to me. "Is this what will happen to me if you try to remove The Garland?"

Senior walked closer to me and sat on a chair beside the bed. "I'm continuing to study the matter. I feel we can do safely it this time."

"What was her name?"

"Persi. Just like you."

A sick sensation crawled through my stomach.

"Noah holds himself responsible. He convinced her to have her garland removed. There was no vote that time."

"Was she the same as me?"

"She sounded the same, looked the same... But her path has differed from yours, so only God can say if you are identical."

"This is why your people think I don't have a spirit, a soul."

Senior nodded, stepped closer, and touched the other Persi's forehead. "I fear she will die soon."

"When did she come here?"

"About a year ago."

I tried to wrap my head around this new information. What made it challenging was that I couldn't remember what I was doing one year ago....or even could conceptualize what a year was. We had no calendars in The Hive. I'd confirmed with Noah that what I thought was a day in The Hive was not a day. Everything related to time's passage had come from Dr. Whisper.

"That explains why Noah doesn't want me to remove the garland."

Senior nodded. "While I disagree with him, I understand the concern."

A sudden flood of emotion coursed through me. "You removed Piper's, didn't you?"

Senior sighed. "Unlike your brother, the Garland is embedded deep into your limbic system."

He cleared his throat and leaned against a table."Well, anyway. Now you know. The vote has brought a great deal of turmoil to Noah. But he is sensitive and intuitive. Food isn't just a meal for us...in some ways, Noah has become our priest."

"What do you mean?"

"I'm sure you've seen that he gets away with more than others. Perhaps too much. Maybe we should not have allowed him to escort you day after day. On the one hand, it has healed him. On the other, he fell in love with you again, didn't he?"

"I love him, too."

Senior blinked several times, and a pained look crossed his weathered face.

"I have a soul," I said, recalling that the spirit root had proven it. "At least, I think."

"Do you even know what a soul is?" he asked, eyebrow arched.

My mind went blank. Had I misunderstood Noah's words all this time? "It's...like a candlelight inside you that can never be put out," I stammered.

Senior nodded. "Hmm. Who am I to judge? But the vote has been made, and I can do nothing. If you have the spirit root with you, now would be the time to surrender it. Noah need never know you took it."

"I don't," I lied.

We stood facing each other in silence. Then, without warning, Senior slid out the door and locked it behind him. "No wait!" But he was already gone. I was a prisoner again.

The wind howled through the lone window. I leaned out and looked down at the dizzying drop. On closer inspection, I saw that the opening was natural, but someone had smoothed and rounded the edges to make it more like a window. I took a deep breath, trying to steady my nerves.

I turned and walked back to the girl who looked just like me. She lay there, breathing steadily. Then, an idea hit me. "Open your eyes," I said.

Her eyes opened, but she showed no response to my movements. "Sit up," I commanded. After a moment, she did as I asked, her hair longer and more disheveled than mine. And with this, I knew how I would escape.

CHAPTER THIRTY-SEVEN

TREMBLING, I COMBED the hair of the other Persi. A pungent stench of sweat and medicinal herbs filled the air. I couldn't bear the thought of my hair becoming so unkempt. It took me several minutes to detangle the worst of it.

"Does this hurt?" I asked, but received no answer—just a blank stare. There was no one home. I stripped off my clothes and dressed the other Persi in them, doing my best to conceal the scars from the missing garland.

It was a struggle to dress her. Her limbs were stiff, and she only responded to basic commands. I was worried about causing her pain. She was thinner than me, and I bruised her arm with my rough handling as I tried to put her into the sleeves. It was a haunting reminder of how I used to bruise easily back at The Hive.

"I'm so sorry," I whispered, feeling tears threatening to overflow. But there was no time for that. I changed into her white slip. When Senior entered the room with two guards, he found what he thought was me lying motionless on the floor. I remained still, lying in bed, as Senior approached the other Persi.

"What happened to her?" Bernard asked as he inspected the motionless figure from every angle. The floor trembled under his heavy footsteps.

"She was fine when I left," Senior said, sounding concerned as he bent down and shook the girl's shoulder. "Persi? Persi?"

With their backs turned, I seized the opportunity. With the stealth and poise of a First Nurse, I slipped out of bed, took six quick steps towards the door, and ran out into the night.

The encounter with the other Persi left me stunned. I was up against something far beyond my understanding. Kendel was right; Noah's plan to bring me to The Hive was dangerous for him and everyone. I couldn't put him or his community in harm's way. I had to find a way back to The Hive to save Myhhris on my own. Just then, the bushes nearby exploded in activity.

Lister?

I stumbled back, trying to regain my balance. But it wasn't Lister. Instead, strange night birds emerged and flew toward the moon. *Bats.* I had seen them from a distance before, but never this close.

The bats circled and flew off in The Hive's direction. I couldn't trust Lister, but the bats gave me a better idea: Piper's drone. If I could find it and fly it myself, I could return to The Hive.

With a newfound sense of determination, I set off towards the plateau where Piper had landed his drone. It was a desolate place, and the only sound was the crunch of gravel beneath my feet. As I drew closer, I could make out the shape of the vehicle. It was a sleek, metallic thing, and it looked like something out of a sci-fi movie.

I circled the vehicle, trying to remember how to open the hatch. The partial moon gave just enough light to make out a small, green button. I hoped it was the right one. The only problem was I couldn't reach it. Piper was taller, and even he had to stand on a box to press it.

After jumping up and down to no avail, I searched for something to help me reach it. I found a rotten tree stump in the brush, but it wouldn't budge. When I returned, I noticed something unexpected. A silver backpack lay near the drone. Had Noah left it there? It seemed impossible, as he didn't know of my plan.

"Piper?" I whispered. No answer. Crickets sang, and the wind whistled through the rocks.

Someone was on my side, and it was time to act. I placed the backpack on a nearby stone and stood atop it to reach the button. Just as I was about to make my first attempt, someone hit me from behind.

Hands grabbed my hair and pulled me down.

"Gotcha!" Lister exclaimed as he tackled me to the ground, his arms wrapping around me as I fell.

CHAPTER THIRTY-EIGHT

I FOUND MYSELF lying in a dark cave when I opened my eyes. "Carum?" My voice echoed with a dull and hollow tone. I rubbed my eyes and blinked several times. Through the darkness, I could see a sliver of sunlight from the cave's opening.

As my mind cleared, I remembered the heartbreaking truth—Carum was dead. A dark figure appeared before me, and I realized it was Lister. He grumbled as he saw me. "Didn't think I'd killed you, but I wouldn't be surprised if you ruined my day." He rummaged through his silver backpack, took out a box with several vials, and began counting them.

"Infusions?" I asked.

He nodded. "How else do you think I survived without food during my journey here? You broke one of them when you stepped on it."

"Dr. Whisper lied to us. We thought we were living long, healthy lives, but it's not true," I said.

Lister sneered. "Do you think I'm stupid? I know the real score. But, unlike you, I was smart enough to turn it to my advantage. Now, will ya make this easy or hard?"

"What do you mean?" I asked.

"I promised Dr. Whisper I'd bring you back when the time came. Now it's time for me to get my reward," he said.

"What if I refuse?" I asked.

"You know what will happen to Myrrhis if you don't cooperate," he replied, his tone threatening.

"Yes," I replied, my voice trembling. "Okay. When are we leaving?"

"After dark," he said.

"The sun won't hurt you. That's just another lie," I pointed out.

"We'll leave when I say we will, and now, be quiet. I'm tired."

We remained silent as the sun shone outside. It was strange how I had found the sun oppressive just a short while ago, and now I longed for its warmth. I found a dusty, gray jacket lying on the ground and put it on over my flimsy clothes. As the day brightened and the cave's darkness faded, Lister shifted farther into the shadows.

"Move deeper inside."

"It's wet."

"I don't care. Move!" He brandished the metal rod over my head.

Tired, wet, and hungry, I rested against the frigid stone and racked my brain for a way out. "It's a long walk back to The Hive."

Lister snarled. "Don't you think I know that? Once I get the points, it'll be worth it."

"There's a faster way. Much faster. We can fly."

Lister cocked his head and sneered. "In the drone?"

I nodded. "Yes."

He narrowed his eyes. "Your brother's stolen drone? So we're just going to fly off in it. Nah. We'll crash."

"No. He taught me. It's easy. There's a secret button. You press it, and...it will take us right back. No walking. Imagine the points you'd get...me *plus* a stolen drone. The last one."

Lister shook his head, but I noticed something there: greed. "Too dangerous."

"Think about it."

Lister massaged his knees. The journey had been hard on him. But, now that I'd met Noah and his community, I knew what healthy was supposed to look like. Lister's face was pale and yellow with sunken, bloodshot eyes. The rasp of mucus in his lungs filled the air when he breathed.

"Drone. Pfff." He looked at me and then counted the syringes in his pack again.

"Carum died coming here, and I almost did too. The winds come from the direction of the Free City. You must have noticed that when you walked. The wind always at your back, pushing you away?"

He spat. "There's a tunnel, you dumb bitch. We won't be strolling through The Desolation."

That was news to me. "Okay, suit yourself. A long tunnel sure sounds fun."

I waited until it got dark out. Lister stood, shaking his legs, trying to work the cramps out. My legs were wet and stiff, too, and I wanted nothing more than to be in bed. Even picking cradleberries didn't seem so bad.

"So, you know how to fly the drone?"

"Yes."

"Don't mess with me, girl. I can make things worse for you. Much worse."

"I'll show you, and you can decide. I'm sick of this place, Lister, and I'm trying to get us back as fast as possible. If you want to take the slow way, that's up to you."

After a long pause, he sighed and shrugged. "If you try anything or if your friends are around, you're dead, and your sister, too."

* * *

The silver-gray drone glimmered in the starlight, a beacon of hope.

"So we just hop on and fly away?" Lister rubbed his dirty hands together.

I nodded, trying to hide my disappointment. I'd hoped we might run into Piper and have a chance to turn the tables on Lister.

"That's right. In that direction, towards the Free Cities. You can barely make out the lights. It's several days' journey, but with this drone, it'll be worth it."

"Yeah, yeah, so you said. Prove it. Open it. Quick," Lister said with a snarl.

Lister gave me a hand up, and I got the hatch open after several attempts. "Well, now we're getting somewhere. Get in," he said, his eyes gleaming with excitement.

Once inside, Lister's presence made the cramped space feel suffocating. He prodded me with a metal rod. "Farther," he said, his tone menacing.

I felt sweat bead on my forehead. I needed to return to The Hive on my terms, not as Lister's prisoner. I had to help my sister, and I wasn't sure how I could achieve that without an element of surprise.

"Okay, let's get this thing moving," Lister said, smashing buttons with his meaty hands.

"No, wait! You'll—!" I yelled, but it was too late. Lister's thumb hit the home button, and the drone's engines whined to life. The hatch door started to close.

"Ah ha! We're headed home." A sinister smile spread across Lister's face.

I knew I had to act fast. I grabbed the metal rod and jammed it into the door just as it was closing. I slipped through the gap and tumbled into the desert, shielding myself from the wind and flying debris.

The drone disappeared into the night sky, headed towards The Free Cities. I breathed a sigh of relief, but it was short-lived.

"What happened? Noah's gone. He asked me to find you. What kinda trouble have you got yourself in now?" Piper's voice rang out. "Whoa! Wildfire, my drone. What the hell happened?"

My heart sank. "I'm sorry," I muttered and quickly explained the situation.

Piper's face was gloomy as he stared off toward The Hive. "Now they have a drone again. Persi, are you working for him?" he asked, his tone suspicious.

"No, I'm not," I replied firmly. "I'm trying to help Myrrhis. She's in trouble."

"It's too late for her, Persi," Piper said, his voice heavy with sadness.

I stood up, determination in my voice. "How can you say that? How can you know that? She's your sister too. There's a tunnel that leads back to The Hive. Are you willing to help me or not?"

Piper hesitated, but I turned and walked away before he could answer. "Persi, wait! Not that way. They're looking for you!" he called out. A few steps later, the stillness was broken by the sound of lights and voices closing in.

CHAPTER THIRTY-NINE

I DUCKED BEHIND a moss-covered rock formation. Down below, a group of men carrying silver knives shook the walkway as they marched in my direction. I'd never seen people carrying weapons before. Events had taken a new turn.

Piper crept beside me and placed his hand on my shoulder. "Don't worry," he said. "I won't let them hurt you."

"So you trust me?"

"Maybe, I dunno. Would you blame me if I didn't?"

"No, not really. I'm not sure if I trust myself sometimes."

"Go that way," he pointed to a narrow path I hadn't noticed. It followed the curve of the cliff-side and led to the dark entrance of a tunnel. "Take the first left and wait there. I'll send them in the opposite direction."

When I reached the first left, I heard shouting. Then the voices faded. Piper told me to wait, but as minute after minute passed, he didn't come. Had they caught him? I was about to continue when he arrived, sweating profusely.

"They don't trust me anymore, thanks to you. It took a while to shake 'em off. Come on." He brushed past me with a frown. "Go slow. There are a lot of ups and downs in this passage, kinda like life."

We had no light, but Piper knew the way. I stumbled and almost fell. "What made you decide to help me?" I continued to follow him down the gloomy passage.

"Look, you're my sister. I wanted to help Myhhris, too. But we're too late. Just ask Crane."

"No. It's not too late. I won't abandon her."

"Look, I'm not abandoning anyone! From the start I've tried to help you both, remember?"

"The cupcake?"

"Yeah, the cupcake and my plan for Noah to help you and Myhhris escape. I started this, so I'll help you finish it. You hafta understand something. I love Kendel. My place is The Cliffs, but I'll help you get back to The Hive if that's what you want."

The tunnel grew wider, and a gentle wind drifted in, carrying the dry, dusty smell of The Desolation.

"Do you think I'm crazy?"

"Maybe, but it runs in the family. Plus, you've run out of options, I'd say." We exited the tunnel and began to climb a ridge. It wasn't too far from the spot where I learned the truth about my age and Dr. Whisper's manipulation of time.

Piper helped me scramble up the cliff face. The stones on my garland received a signal and illuminated. My heartbeat quickened. Was Dr. Whisper tracking me now? We hadn't gone far when something on the ground caught my attention—a clump of hair.

"Don't." Piper grabbed my arm. But I shook him off. Something told me I needed to see who or what lay there. I stumbled across a graveyard of stones and discovered the body of a young girl. As I drew closer, I gasped. Her body had desiccated. Her skin was yellow and pulled taut as a drum. But this, again, was me.

"Did you know about this?" I asked.

Piper nodded. "Yep."

"What about the other Persi? The one that's still alive."

"There was another me, too. But I kinda killed him."

"You killed…yourself?"

"No, not myself. Him, it? Whatever they are. It just…happened. I'm not saying I should have."

"Who are they?"

"There are five sectors. But, of course, you know that by now."

I nodded. I'd seen The Hive from a distance. Five arms stretched from the central compound.

Piper continued. "There are five sectors divided into seven zones each. The doctor is trying different experiments in each sector, and I think there're variations between the zones too. When everyone in one sector dies, he resets it and starts over."

"I tried to talk to the other Persi. But I couldn't wake her."

"Do you think she knows more than you do?"

"Maybe not more, but different things. We could work together."

Piper's face darkened. "Mine tried to kill me. So what the hell was I supposed to do?"

A chill went up my spine. One thing I knew—if the other Persi ever attacked me, I could not bring myself to kill her, or anyone.

Piper clenched his jaw. "Dr. Whisper manipulated us. We thought we were doing good for The Hive, but he was the only person who benefited. Look at what he created."

"How did it get to that point? I feel so confused."

Piper shrugged. "How do you boil a frog?"

I grimaced. "Why would you want to boil a frog?"

"Here's something else. Are you ready? Persi, Myhrris... What do all our names have in common?"

They were just our names and meant nothing else to me.

"They're Latin forms of various foodstuffs, spices, and all that. That's what he saw us as: components of his recipe—a means to an end."

"Persi is the name of a spice?"

Noah spelled out the full name. *Persicaria odorata*. "Noah calls it coriander, I think. I forget what Myhrris' is, but Noah grows it in his spice garden. Mine is Piperis—pepper."

"Oh, that spice tingles my tongue and makes me sneeze. It suits you." I attempted to dodge Piper's playful swat, but failed. Ironic that all this time, we called ourselves various food-related items while eating itself was forbidden.

"All the doctor cares about is his goal to consume every living thing, not in his control," Piper said.

Laughter escaped my lips, and I couldn't stop. Piper looked surprised, a rare expression for him. "Do you think this is funny?" he asked.

"No, I don't. It's the most horrible thing. But I just realized that he wants to eat us," I replied, my laughter turning into shivers. "You said he wants to consume every living thing. The doctor wants to add us to his perverted recipe."

A wry smile spread across Piper's face. "Recipe X. Yeah, that's one way of looking at it."

I felt chilled to the bone and rubbed my arms to warm up. "Well, I'll give him something to chew on."

Piper shot me a sideways glance. "I'm not following," he said.

"It doesn't matter. I still don't understand why, but I know what to do. What you told me confirms it. I hope I'm not wrong."

Piper led me to a cave. "Wait here until dark. I'll help you get back to The Hive," he said before leaving.

As I settled down to wait, I realized the area was familiar. Carum and I had stopped here before. I sat in the cave until dark, but Piper never returned.

An entire day passed, and then another. I heard the sirens that signaled infusion times back in The Hive several times, drifting in the wind. Their mournful wails echoed across The Desolation like a dying bird. Once upon a time, they had sent thrills of delight through my body. Now, each time I heard them, I felt a cold, sick dread.

At dawn, a violent wind rose, and I remembered the storms I'd seen from the safety of The Hive. I tried to retreat as far into the cave as possible and covered my mouth with my sleeve, closing my eyes and trying to sleep. As the wind howled outside, I wondered if I'd ever see Piper again.

CHAPTER FORTY

FINE, BEIGE DUST exploded through the thick cloth I'd hung to block the entrance, causing my eyes to sting and my lungs to burn. I didn't know how long the storm would last, but I remembered nights back at The Hive when it seemed the storms lasted for weeks. But now, I realized that what I thought were weeks were only days or maybe even hours. This realization still gave me a headache.

My throat felt parched, and my belly was empty, but with the storm raging outside, I had no way of finding food or water. I feared Noah would conclude that I was the one who stole the spirit root and would hate me. And as for Myhrris, if Crane was right, she was lost to me forever. The thought of starving to death seemed ironic but fitting.

I lay on a dirty blue mattress but moved to the dirt floor when I caught a whiff of stale sweat. Lying in the dust didn't even bother me anymore. I closed my eyes and tried to sleep, hoping that I would starve in my sleep and not know the difference. But just as I was about to doze off, I heard a scrabbling sound that shook me from my despair.

The wind whistled through the rocks, and the sound disappeared and rose again. The cloth flap-flopped back and forth at the bottom where it had come undone, letting in dust clouds. I crawled closer to fix it, but the swirling dust blinded me. Then the material was yanked away, and I fell back in fear, coughing. When my vision cleared, I saw Kendel unwinding fabric from around her face and taking off a pair of goggles.

We remained there, looking at each other, and she led me further into the cave. "Piper told me to find you here, but I got lost. Nasty out there." She handed me a silver flask of water. The cool liquid I drank was one of the most delicious things I'd ever tasted.

Kendel crouched down beside me. "You stole the spirit root," she said, staring at me.

"I—"

"Don't lie. It's not a question."

Stubborn, I remained silent, eyes locked with hers.

Kendel drummed her fingers against her bent knee. "Look, it's your choice. Give it to me, and I'll show you the way back to The Hive."

"Or?" We continued our staring match.

"Or I'll leave, and you'll starve to death. Your choice."

If I gave her the spirit root, it would ruin my plan to save Myhrris. After a few seconds, she turned to leave. My throat constricted. I'd had a glimpse of my fate here—trapped with my thoughts—waiting to starve or die of thirst. I would be no help to my sister then, that was for sure.

"Wait! Okay."

She turned. "Well? You have five seconds before I leave." She held out her hand.

I took the spirit root from an inner pocket. "How do I know I can trust you? Do you promise you'll show me the way back to The Hive?"

Kendel nodded. "You have my word."

I handed her the root, and she stashed it in the inside pocket of her jacket. Fear gripped my gut. "Will we have to take one of those maglevs?"

"No. There's a better way. We'll leave when the wind dies down."

* * *

Kendel and I had no interest in speaking. We sat, lost in our own thoughts, waiting. Finally, after a long time, the winds slowed. "Let's go," Kendel said, standing up. I stretched my tired limbs. Carum and I had taken ages to cross the Outlands, and I was not looking forward to the punishing walk in the harsh sun or freezing nights. Plus, we'd never walked during the day.

"Are we taking the tunnel or—?" I asked as we walked.

Kendel led me to a massive pile of boulders, four times our height, scattered along a barren bluff. She scraped away some dirt and pulled open a metal hatch. A shaky wooden ladder led downwards.

"You bet. This tunnel leads right to The Hive." Kendel motioned for me to go down first. I swung my leg over the edge and descended, trying to avoid the splinters. "How much farther?" I called up to Kendel, who was blocking the light. The enclosed space made me feel claustrophobic. Kendel didn't answer. "Where does it go?" I continued down the ladder, speaking to take my mind off the tight space. I reached the bottom. It wasn't as bad as a pod, but still not great.

Kendel hopped off the ladder and raised a cloud of dust that set us both coughing. "I told you—it leads to The Hive."

"But *where* in The Hive? To the place we first met?"

"No," she said between coughs. "That's why we're not taking the maglevs. This tunnel leads right to Zone One. It will be safer. Here, we might as well change. It'll save me from carrying so much." She handed me a sanitary shield and a blue uniform. "You'll blend right in. The rest is up to you."

The smooth and sleek sanitary fabric brushed against my fingers as I changed. Wearing the uniform, I felt like the old me again, and I wasn't quite sure if I liked that. "You won't be coming with me?"

"It'll be safer to split up once we're there."

"You need to have enough points for Zone Three or be a First Nurse to wear blue," I told her.

Kendel rolled her eyes. "You think I give a crap?"

We entered a larger tunnel with plenty of room to stand. A musty breeze blew from deeper inside. Kendel turned on her flashlight and walked quickly. It was hard to keep up.

Ahead of me, Kendel swore. When I caught up, I found a massive pile of dirt and rubble blocking the tunnel. "How long will it take to dig through?"

Kendel let out a bitter laugh. "Are you serious? There's no way we can dig through all that rock. It will take several strong men with shovels a week or more."

"I don't have that long!"

"I'm sorry."

"No. You promised! You gave me your word."

Kendel turned back the way we came. "The tunnel collapsed. It's not my fault."

"You knew, didn't you? That's why you offered to help."

"I did *not* know. I keep my word."

"Well, take me back to The Hive or point me in the right direction. Can't we continue above ground?"

Kendel shook her head. "There are too many dust storms this time of year. I gave my word, not my life."

I felt my stomach drop. Now I had no hope. Losing it was even more painful than never having it in the first place. "My poor sister."

Kendel chewed her lip and looked at me. "Well, I could take you to the maglev. Yes. Of course, that's what we'll do."

"No. I won't ride in one of those things. The space is too small."

"Do you want my help or not?" Kendel asked.

I followed Kendel back up the ladder. The dust storm had cleared. The sky stretched above an inky black dotted with bright pinpricks. In the distance, the cliff and massive stone formations loomed like guarding giants. And on the other side, The Hive sprawled like a spider waiting in the desert.

"I-I don't know if I can," I stammered.

"Listen, I'll take you back to The Cliffs," Kendel said. "I won't let you die out here, but I have to be honest. You won't be free again. We'll confine you, and this time, you won't escape until we clear the tunnel. Then you'll be escorted back to The Hive."

"Return so they can stab me to death? I saw them with their knives."

Kendel sighed. "No one will stab you. They're afraid of you, and to be honest, I am too. Piper's double tried to kill him."

"He told me that. But you trust Piper! He can do anything. Go anywhere."

"Piper saved us from the drones on several occasions! It's thanks to him that the drone attacks stopped. He's proven himself to be a friend. All you've done is steal from us!" Kendel said, eyes flashing.

Her words felt like a slap in the face. "That's not fair."

Then her tone softened. "Look, I don't blame you. The doctor brainwashed you. But you have to understand our perspective, too."

"Take me to the maglev," I said.

"Are you sure?"

"Yes. I'm sure."

Kendel changed direction, and we didn't walk far before I saw another body. The storm had uncovered it, and I grabbed Kendel's arm and pointed. Frowning, she changed direction and walked towards it. As we got closer, a chill went up my spine. Something about the way the body lay there, or perhaps it was the profile, harsh against the gray-green sky.

The skin was desiccated, pulled taut over the cheeks like leather, and her eyes were gone, withered away like cradleberries in the sun. But the features—this was me—yet another Persi.

Kendel looked at me and then looked away. "Creepy."

"How many of me are there?" I asked.

Kendel walked ahead at a quicker pace. At first, she didn't respond, but eventually, she spoke. "There are five sectors in the hospital," she said. "Noah and I think there are five copies of each clone series, but we're unsure if they're alive or dead."

We trudged back to The Cliffs but avoided the central area. If Kendel had wanted to betray me, she could have, but the tension in my shoulders eased. We circled the clearing where Piper's drone had been and emerged on the other side.

Hours later, we reached a set of silver tracks and followed them, staying to the side in case a maglev train approached. The tracks ended at an enormous depot devoid of human presence. Giant robotic arms unloaded maglev hoppers and placed the cargo into a massive pipeline that crossed a deep chasm. Fog obscured the other side as if the pipeline had vanished into a cloud.

"Where does it go?" I asked.

Kendel shrugged. "Nowhere good," she said, her voice low and ominous. As we gazed into the dense fog, the hairs on my neck stood up. If all went well, soon I would return to The Hive. I couldn't shake the feeling that I was about to face my greatest challenge.

CHAPTER FORTY-ONE

DEEP IN THE valley, a maglev arrived. A robotic crane unloaded silver canisters, which were then sucked away into the pipeline and sent across the expanse—swallowed was the word that came to mind. Noah would be proud. The eerie metallic ringing sound the canisters made reverberated through my skull.

"The empty ones are returning to The Hive." Kendel pointed to a departing maglev. "Follow the edge around the cliff, and we can head down the south side where it isn't as steep."

Another maglev arrived. Canisters got loaded on and loaded off at a rapid pace. More canisters came than arrived. There were no people. Only the clanking, whirring machines and they did not register our presence.

As we circled the rocky terrain, we grew closer to the pipeline. It extended into a blank nothingness that my eyes could not pierce, no matter how hard I strained. The air smelled of electronics and a dank, earthy scent from the surrounding fog. A roaring, rushing sound traveled from somewhere far below in the mist.

"What the hell is this pipeline transporting?" I wondered out loud.

Kendel gazed across the expanse. "It's better not to know what happens beyond this island. Some say they created this chasm to keep something out."

We followed the ridge for several minutes, but Kendel raised her hand and stopped me. "Be careful on your left. The fog can deceive, and there's a long fall below. Let's go slow."

Sun pierced the gloom just long enough for me to see to the bottom. Steel wreckage and rocks were scattered along a raging river about half a mile below, explaining the persistent roar.

A whooshing sound came from the tube. Then, canisters arrived from the other side, where the robot arms loaded them onto the maglevs, ready to transport them to the Free City.

"Noah told me he lost a friend here."

Kendel nodded. "Sedrick. He was my friend too. He tried to crawl across to the other side." Kendel pointed to the giant pipeline, glancing back at me and not watching where she stepped. It happened suddenly.

"Kendel, watch out!" The ground to her left crumbled, and she fell, grabbing a rocky overhang at the last minute. I rushed to help. She hung over the chasm, legs dangling, arms straining to maintain her grip. The river and its rock and jagged pieces of steel lay waiting hundreds of feet below.

"Well, this is your golden opportunity," she grunted as she gazed up at me, eyes filled with fear.

"What are you talking about?" I grabbed her by the forearms and braced myself. Kendel scrabbled to get up with my help, but she threatened to pull us both over the edge. Finally, her feet gained traction, and she crawled onto the landing. We lay, panting, staring up at the endless white fog. Kendel had bloody scratches on her right arm, but otherwise, she was okay.

"You saved my life," she said, her eyes filled with new respect. "Crane was wrong about you." I blushed, feeling embarrassed. I'd done nothing special. What kind of person would have let her die? We stood up and continued, staying a safe distance from the edge.

As we descended the south slope, the sound of the canisters passing through the tube warbled and shifted in strange ways. Each one emitted a metallic echo that bounced off the rocks. "It sounds like singing," Kendel said.

I looked at her blankly.

"You don't know what singing is?" Kendel asked.

195

"No."

Kendel cleared her throat and made the most beautiful sound matched with rhyming words. "Oh, cliffs that rise so high and steep, a challenge for the bravest of hearts to keep, but we shall not be swayed by fear, for we are strong, and we shall persevere."

A spontaneous smile spread across my face. Kendel smiled back. "Noah's right. You have a pretty smile."

I couldn't help but smile again. "Sing more," I urged.

"Oh, okay, I'll give you the chorus. It is the best part." Kendel sang again. "With cradleberry mead, our spirits will soar, as we face each obstacle, and so much more, for we dare to confront our plight, and rise above our challenges, with all our might." She gave a slight bow. "That's Piper's favorite song," she added.

"I can see why—he sure loves cradleberry mead."

"Oh, yeah, that boy can drink." Kendel laughed.

As we approached the maglevs, I noticed something strange. One canister had fallen from the robotic arms and spilled its contents. Inside were several smaller canisters. I picked one up and saw that it was cracked, about the length of my arm, and six inches thick. A reddish substance was leaking from the crack.

I showed the canister to Kendel, who held it and turned it over. Some of the red material rubbed off on her fingers, and she sniffed it. "This smells like blood," she said.

"Why would they send dried blood?"

"Presumably, it wasn't dry at some point."

Something clicked into place—the infusions. "When Dr. Whisper detoxed us from pathogen exposure, he said our blood was being cleaned. Perhaps he sends it somewhere? This is our blood. The blood of Free Citizens."

Kendel frowned. "Nothing about that place would surprise me."

I wondered if any of my sister's blood had whooshed past as we stood here. I hoped she was okay.

Kendel pointed to the Maglevs. "Watch for *Hopper 902*. It never gets filled with canisters, and we won't get crushed."

Several maglevs came and went, but none had *Hopper 902*. When Kendel thought we might need to wait until the following day, a new maglev arrived.

Kendel pointed. "There!"

Finally, a maglev arrived with *Hopper 902*. "Do you want a compartment of your own, or should we take the same one?" Kendel asked as we rushed towards the tracks.

Either option terrified me. Cramped together with Kendel I'd have very little space. In that scenario, I'd experience The Fright. Alone…I'd be well, alone. Maybe that was for the best. No one would be there to witness me lose my mind.

"I'll be fine alone." My stomach churned, and I worried I might vomit.

Kendel smiled. "I thought so. The compartments are cramped."

We walked closer to the loading dock. The giant robotic crane loomed over us like a living creature.

"Hurry! We won't have much time."

I stalled at the hatch. Panic flooded me at the thought of entering this tiny space with no escape. Would I even make it to The Hive alive? A question burning at the back of my mind burst forth. "Kendel, what you said earlier, about me stealing and all that…is that how Noah sees me? Is that why you came instead of him?"

Kendel hesitated. "Noah left for The Hive two days ago. He went there to look for you. I'm worried about him. Now quit stalling."

She helped me in just as the hopper slid closed.

CHAPTER FORTY-TWO

WHEN THE HATCH closed, my first reaction was to stop it. Luckily, some presence of mind caused me to pull my hand back, or I might have lost several fingers. As The Fright intensified, I sat up and banged my head against the metal. This intensified my panic. It made me realize just how tiny the space was.

The maglev hummed and rocked as it hurtled toward its destination. I pounded my fists against the metal until they throbbed.

I cried out for Kendel, but it would make no difference even if she heard me. Exhausted, I lay back down, shaking. A conversation with Noah came to mind.

"All feelings pass, just like food." He'd said something like that, and then he'd laughed. *"Get it? Food passes?"*

In a flash, I understood his bad joke for the first time. A burst of laughter weakened my fear, and The Fright backed off several notches. Then, forcing myself to breathe, I repeated it over and over…*all feelings pass, just like food,* while I thought of Noah.

At some point, I drifted off to sleep. A jolt woke me as the maglev came to a stop. With a hiss, the hatch slid open, and I jumped out, relieved to feel the air on my face.

I was back in The Hive.

Kendel stepped out of the car in front of me and stretched her legs. "Well, we made it," she said before noticing the blood on my forehead. "Whoa, what happened? Your forehead is bleeding."

"It was a rough ride," I admitted. "But I survived. Now, where?"

Kendel shone her flashlight around as robotic equipment began *whirring* and *clanking* nearby. "Let's move out of the way before we get hurt," she said as the robot claws began to load and unload their mysterious cargo. She then reached into her pocket and handed me a flashlight. "Here, take this."

I shone the small light around and noticed the nest of stuffing I'd laid in when Noah found me. I stomped my feet to get the blood flowing back into my limbs. I was hungry and thirsty.

"This way," Kendel said, and I followed her down a narrow, dark passage—the same one where Lister had tried to strangle me. A damp breeze rustled my hair, and something scurried away. "A rat," I said, but Kendel didn't respond.

When we reached the end of the passage, we stopped. The smell of food drifted through the air. *Eaters.* I thought—eaters eating eggs.

A smile passed over my lips. I could tell the type of food by its smell. Noah prepared eggs in at least one hundred different ways, and I'd made them myself. It hadn't been an overwhelming success, but if you had asked me a short while ago if I'd be able to cook food, I'd have called you a liar.

We descended a ramp that led to a rusty metal staircase. Each step groaned under our weight, and we had to tread lightly, afraid the entire structure might collapse. At the bottom, we entered a large, vaulted space that I recognized as the place where I'd found Lister and Carum eating.

Kendel pointed to a silver door. "That door leads up to the kitchen," she said, taking a disk out of her pocket. In the center of the disk was a tiny garland stone. She waved the disk in front of the door, and the three red lights embedded in the surface flashed. She tried to pull the handle, but it wouldn't open. "That's odd," she said.

My stomach rumbled, and Kendel chuckled. "I'm hungry too," she said, "but I came prepared." She took out several brown packages and handed me one. "Here's some water." We drank a few sips, and she showed me how to ignite a portable stove. "Boil the rest using the stove," she said. "Cook us a package and change into your uniform while I find the other disk."

"You want me to cook for us?" I asked, surprised.

"Dump the package in the boiling water and stir. Can you handle that?" A wry smile spread across her face.

My back straightened. "Yes."

Before long, a pot of bubbling stew sat ready. The task hadn't been difficult and felt like cheating. I hummed to myself as I stirred the stew, imitating what I'd seen Noah do. However, a distant shout stopped me.

"Kendel?" I arced my flashlight back and forth and walked in the direction she'd gone. I found several hard-boiled eggs lying dirty and broken on the ground. Not far beyond them was Kendel's rucksack and a metal frying pan covered in blood.

Then I saw a larger pool of blood on the floor, and tears rose in my eyes. I stood still, wary of any threat, but the area remained silent except for the omnipresent whoosh of air and distant dripping.

Just a minute earlier, I was hungry, but the sight of blood made the thought of eating fill me with disgust. Food and eating remained confusing and inconsistent. I wanted to help Kendel, but I didn't know what had happened. I picked up her jacket and searched for the spirit root, but the pockets were empty. I noticed a small knife lying on the ground and put it in my pocket.

An odd creeping sensation traveled up my spine, and I shouted, "Who's there?"

"Stupid," I whispered to myself. If someone were there, they wouldn't reveal themselves just because I asked. If her attacker lurked elsewhere, they'd find me. My flashlight roved over the gray metal and concrete sections. Where was that silver door? After several more minutes, I found it. It lay ajar—a bright light shone through the crack. I pulled it open and entered.

A sterile white passage greeted me. Did the sanitary clerks patrol here? I glanced down, and my breath caught in my throat. Bloody footprints. *Poor Kendel.*

Tension gathered in my body like a wave. Part of me wanted to leave, run back to the maglev, and return to The Cliffs. Instead, I followed the footprints that led to a pristine white stairway. The footprints led up the steps and disappeared around a corner.

As I took a few steps into the corridor, a voice shouted from behind, "Girl!" I turned just in time to see a metal rod zoom toward my head. I tried to duck, but it was too late. The rod glanced off my forehead, and

I fell to the ground, blinded by pain.

Lister spun me over, his face contorted with rage and his forehead covered in blood. He lifted the metal rod above his head again, bringing it down, but I dodged it just in time. The rod hit the hard white surface next to my ear, and I felt a searing pain in my earlobe, but I escaped the worst.

I thrust my elbow into Lister's stomach, causing him to lose his hold. I scrambled to my feet and pulled the knife from my pocket. We stood facing each other.

"Put it down, Persi. You'll never get my points."

"Back away!" I thrust the knife toward him. Sweat stung my eyes, and my head throbbed.

He feinted toward me with the metal bar, and I dodged, trying to catch my breath. If there was any moment I needed the calm and grace of a First Nurse, it was now.

"Where's Kendel?"

"Give me the knife. I'll convince the doctor to show mercy."

I ignored him and did the first and only thing that came to mind: I took the First Position. If nothing else, it allowed me to keep him in my view. My limbs flowed gracefully, the knife pointing up and down, and I kept my eyes locked on him.

"What the hell are you doing, you crazy bitch?"

My limbs flowed, more graceful than ever, knife pointing up toward the ceiling, down, and then up again. All the while, I did not let him out of my sight. Hesitation entered his eyes, and he glanced around.

"Is he here? Is the doctor here?"

I smiled, nodded, and continued my dance, keeping my eyes locked with his, moving into Position Two's hypnotic, flowing motions.

"I have it; I have what you want. Doctor?" Lister took the spirit root from his pocket and held it in the air. Using the mesmerizing back-and-forth movements, I disguised the distance between us, which grew shorter and shorter. It put me at risk, but Lister remained bewildered by my actions and seemed to think Dr. Whisper had something to do with it.

When he looked away, I lunged and tried to grab the bar from him. He raised his hand to strike me, but my knife blocked the blow. Blood flew, and the metal bar clanged to the ground, the spirit root with it.

"No, oh, no!" He woke from his trance. His hand shot out and grabbed my knife, palm wrapped around the blade. Blood spurted. He yanked the knife from my grip. It flew from my grasp and skidded down the corridor.

"It will please the doctor that—" he gave a sudden gasp of breath and fell forward, driving me to the floor. His weight landed on my chest, and then he went still. I squirmed out from beneath him. The knife sat lodged in his neck.

My hand flew to my mouth in horror. The spirit root lay where Lister dropped it, and I grabbed it before the pool of blood reached it. Kendel limped toward me, dirty and with blood on her hands.

"Are you okay?" I asked her.

Kendel grimaced. "I sprained my ankle pretty bad, but I'm fine otherwise. Go on without me. I won't make it up all those stairs. But first—" she held out her hand. "The spirit root?"

"Kendel, I'm sorry." Weeping with fear and relief, I grabbed Lister's disc and ran up the stairs.

CHAPTER FORTY-THREE

THE STAIRWAY ASCENDED through Zones One, Two, and beyond. At first, I tried to walk at an acceptable pace, but then I remembered none of that mattered No one was there to observe me, or at least not yet. My sanitary shield crackled as it purged pathogens from my breath. At each landing, I stopped to look for an exit, and at some point, I feared this was a trap.

I reached the top, and there were no more stairs. Instead, a single, standard portal lay in front of me. I placed Lister's disc against the receptor, and unlike the nonfunctional doors in my old ward, this one slid open. The smell of delicious food filled the air, and I heard a home-cooked meal being made in the distance.

A woman in blue approached, balancing a stack of silver trays on a metal cart. She paused when she saw me. Thinking fast, I stepped out of the stairway and approached.

"Come here. You took too long with those trays," I said. "Quick, I need your help with a spill." I pointed through the doorway I had emerged from. As she took another step, I pushed her through and swiped the disc. The portal slid closed, and now the test began. Did she have a disc of her own? If she did, my plan would fail. The thought of using the knife at my ankle crossed my mind, but I dismissed it. No, I would never resort to that.

A muffled thump rose from behind the portal, but she did not re-enter. I removed the silver trays and wheeled the empty cart back, hoping to appear like I belonged. My legs shaking, I continued.

The corridor opened into the central kitchen. This place was nothing like Noah's homey kitchen. With its shiny metal and strange equipment, it looked more like a laboratory but still had everyday items such as pots, pans, and dishes. Noah wore a sanitary shield. The bee-like disinfecting molecules swirling around his head obscured his face, but I recognized him.

He was laboring in front of an enormous pot of broth, muttering a recipe to himself as he added various spices. He was as handsome as ever, with his tongue poking out into one cheek, as he often did when concentrating. Eight Sanitary Clerks I didn't recognize monitored the site from a rampart above, but no one gave me a second glance as I entered the room and wheeled the cart next to a similar one. I went straight to Noah.

"What else can I help with?" I asked, hoping he would recognize my voice. At my words, he stiffened. Maybe he was angry, and that was why he came to The Hive looking for me. Perhaps he would turn me in, and it would all be over. I faced the same issue with my sister after I ate the cupcake, and a feeling of helplessness arose. My fate lay in his hands.

"Yes," he turned to me. "Come, I'll show you what needs to be done."

He led me to a table where several bunches of bright green fresh-cut herbs lay on a pristine white cutting board. I wondered where they came from.

"Cut them in precise three-centimeter sections." Then, beneath his breath, he whispered. "How long have you been here?"

"Combine the marjoram with the oregano in a one-to-three ratio."

I chopped the herbs into tiny pieces the way Noah had taught me. "Today. Kendel helped me get here. She hurt her ankle, but she's fine."

"Do you have the spirit root?"

I was about to answer when one of Noah's helpers interrupted with a question, and he left to address the issue. A chime rang. I recognized it—a warning bell. Workers in the kitchen picked up their pace.

Grabbing a knife, my hands shook. What had Noah told me again?

Two-centimeter sections and a three-to-one ratio? Or was it three centimeters and a two-to-one ratio? I considered going to ask him, but remembered I was being watched.

"You!" Noah snapped his fingers at me. "Come help with this compote." I'd worked on a compote during my brief training. I remembered to stir neither too slowly (in which case the sugar burnt), nor too fast (in which case it would not solidify).

Noah found excuses to be close to me as he ran back and forth between various tasks. "After dinner, there will be the gathering."

The First Nurses. My heart leaped.

"You should find your sister there."

"Noah, about the spirit root—" my throat constricted. I didn't want to be dishonest with him. "I have it in my pocket."

"Noah! How much truffle oil goes on his salad?" A voice rang out over the kitchen noise. My heart went cold. Angelica? He dashed over to her, and the bustle continued. Dirty dishes arrived in tiny compartments transported from somewhere else. Clean dishes laden with food traveled in a separate compartment. More food than I had ever seen traveled on covered plates, massive serving trays, and ornate bowls.

Noah returned. "You were saying?" he whispered.

I told him everything that had happened, leaving out the part about Lister's death. I didn't want to think about it.

Noah pulled me close to him and whispered. "Why do you want the spirit root?"

"Please, trust me." I pushed him away. "And be careful. Physical contact is forbidden."

But it was too late. A guard pointed a weapon at us but, thankfully, did not fire. This weapon was unlike any safety gun I had ever seen—it was long and black.

I couldn't help but wonder what would happen if they scanned me, an eater in a zone I had no business visiting, and a former Free Citizen. Although, thanks to Dr. Whisper, my garland was illuminated with plenty of stones. The doctor's manipulation of language to trick us into believing his view of what was true and good made me nauseous.

"Go!" Noah whispered. "I'll send a signal when it's safe."

How was I going to survive without getting caught? Nevertheless, I'd told the truth, and Noah was still on my side. That was a tremendous relief.

Two options lay before me, each with its own set of dangers. If I retraced my steps, I would have to confront the woman I'd taken the sanitary shield from. I didn't want to hurt her, and I also didn't want to risk encountering Kendel after stealing the spirit root. I wasn't sure if she would be as forgiving as Noah.

Walking, not running, I entered the hall that led from the kitchen just as Angelica emerged from a broad doorway. I continued, keeping my head down and the sanitary shield set to high. Angelica walked past without a glance and returned to the kitchen. Taking advantage of the opportunity, I continued. Soon I came to a wide staircase. It led to another hall wider than any I'd ever seen, decorated with beautiful lanterns and lush blue and gold carpeting.

A bell rang, and the door at the far end slid open, revealing a room with a massive table, ornate candelabras, and beyond it, the entrance to the silver stairway that must have led to the Great Hall. Dr. Whisper had been feasting before the First Nurses celebration! This explained why the ventilation in the Great Hall was as strong as a stiff wind—he wanted to make sure we never caught a whiff of cooking food.

My eyes locked on the stairs—the sacred stairs. I hurried to them and descended. These stairs were only meant for Dr. Whisper—or rather, his digital avatar. I realized I'd never seen Dr. Whisper in the flesh, although perhaps I would soon.

The entire structure shook as I descended. It may have been built for show and not meant for human weight. It swayed, and an audible groan sounded several times.

Soon I reached the bottom. For a moment, I stopped, stunned. This was so much like my dream. I stood on stage in the Great Hall alone. The only part of my dream that was missing was Dr. Whisper.

I'd never seen this space empty. The walls were white, and the circular stage was white, too. The Great Hall was large but simple… just the vaulted ceiling and a circular stage with plenty of room surrounding it. It felt like standing in a great nothingness.

A warning siren blared. The Free Citizens would enter soon! I turned to the stairs and found them rotating and ascending from where they came. Meanwhile, the square portal on the stage floor appeared to be the entrance for the First Nurses, but I couldn't open it. Plus, I did not know where it led. Desperate, I sprinted to the edge of the stage and peered down at the daunting fifteen-foot drop. I couldn't stay on the stage, but the thought of jumping filled me with fear. I was trapped.

I eased myself over the edge until I clung by my fingers, preparing myself for the drop and hoping nothing broke. The impact jarred me from heel to head, teeth snapping against each other so hard I saw a brief, bright flash of light.

When I got up, I turned first one ankle and then the other. They ached, but I could walk fine. Then, as fast as possible, I hid by the main entrance. The crowd was so eager to enter they did not notice me shrunken to the side. Soon all eyes were on the stage, ready and waiting for the dance of the First Nurses.

I took a moment to place my hand in my inside pocket and ensure the spirit root was safe. My fingers clutched at—nothing. The root was gone. Panic set in as I realized my plan would no longer work.

CHAPTER FORTY-FOUR

MY HEART WAS pounding, but I didn't have the luxury of thinking about the spirit root. The dance had begun, and the First Nurses appeared. I saw Myrrhis among them.

To most, all the dancers looked indistinguishable, with their sanitary shields, bright stage lights, and identical blue uniforms moving in unison. However, I saw the differences that others could not. For example, poor Myrrhis had a slight limp. Even though her upgrade had fixed her foot, a subtle imprint was left—a slight delay that only I could spot.

The First Nurses danced in circles and swooped around the stage, their blue slippers whispering on the shiny white surface. After several rotations, a staircase descended from the stage and the crowd parted. The First Nurses went down to circulate among the audience. One of them came so close that I could've touched her, but I didn't. Two others separated me from Myrrhis, and I couldn't tell if she had seen me through her buzzing shield.

The dancers spun three times and turned. I knew this section of the dance well. They finished their last movements and left. Dr. Whisper's avatar was about to descend to address the crowd. I couldn't let Myrrhis out of sight, and I feared that people would notice me in my blue uniform when the dancers withdrew. So, in a split-second decision, I performed a variation of the fourth movement, floated out from my hiding place, and joined the group.

The crowd didn't even murmur—they were blinded by the lights and mesmerized by the dance. I took my place in the last row of the First Nurses and danced with them. It took all my focus and coordination to match their steps.

We slid, swooped, and shuffled, ascending the staircase and performing three wide arcs around the stage. In the process, I lost sight of Myrrhis. I directed my full attention towards keeping up with the complex and synchronized dance steps, hoping that I would fit in.

You've dreamt of this your entire life. Enjoy it. Part of me urged.

But the stakes were too high, and I couldn't relax. I also had no clue what would happen once we left the stage, as I'd never seen that part before.

We revolved like a flock of birds until we descended through the dark gap in the stage floor, separated by a curtain of bright light. I followed the other dancers and stepped into a dark corridor leading to a small lift. The lift shook as it rose, and I had a moment of rest. I spotted Myrrhis standing two rows in front of me.

I whispered her name, but my voice sounded harsh in the silence, and I regretted it. No one responded, not even Myrrhis. A computerized voice started counting down from ten, and I felt anxiety rise. The doors opened on "one," and we entered a large, ornate room where a strange sight waited.

A corpulent man reclined in a motorized chair at the end of a long wooden table. A closed-mouth smile grazed his lips. Others sat with him, their faces unfamiliar and expressions blank. *Were they alive or dead?* The table was littered with half-eaten food and dirty plates, and the smell of food lingered.

We spiraled around the area. The man opened his eyes and darted his eyes to the left. The dancers followed to the left, then he looked his eyes to the right, and again the dancers followed. Each time he did this, I almost missed a step. Finally, he stopped. All the dancers paused and froze in position.

I heard him speaking to the crowd and recognized his voice as Dr. Whisper. When I glanced over, I saw a video feed of the Assembly room with the doctor's flickering digital avatar standing onstage. He was slender and handsome but looked nothing like the man controlling it.

Walking down the white, featureless corridors, I tried to understand what I had just seen. No one I knew had ever seen Dr. Whisper in person, and this explained why. He must have created an avatar to hide the actual appearance of the person behind the holographic image.

We turned a corner, and the First Nurses entered their quarters. Myrrhis went into her room, and I snuck in behind. No one noticed or said anything. It had a single infusion pod in the center and a shower for sanitizing. My sister stripped off her clothes and headed straight for the shower.

"Myrrhis!" I whispered. At first, she didn't react, but then she paused and turned as if she had heard me from a distance. "It's me, Persi!"

Up close, I saw Myrrhis had red, crusty sores all over her face, worse than I had ever had. Her eyes rolled back and forth, unable to focus on anything. "Persi?" she said, with an odd tone in her voice, as if she were tasting the word for the first time.

"Your sister," I said, lowering the setting on my sanitary shield so she could see my face.

Ignoring me, she was about to enter the sanitizer when I asked, "Wait! Are you okay?"

She turned her gaze toward me as if she was looking through me. "I'm fine, Persi. It's infusion time. There's no room for you here."

"No more infusions, Myrrhis. I've come to rescue you," I said.

"Rescue me?" she asked.

"Get you out of here," I explained.

After a long moment of hesitation, she gave a curt nod. "I understand. We must be quick. Come with me," she said and left the room. I followed her down the now empty hall. After a few minutes, we reached a door. Myrrhis tapped her garland, and it slid open to reveal Angelica standing with a quizzical expression. I tried to raise my sanitary shield, but it was too late.

"You were right, Angelica. She returned," Myrrhis said in a deadpan voice.

"You!" Angelica shouted and raised her safety gun.

Myrrhis had betrayed me. I dodged to the left and ran down the corridor. All the doors were closed, and Angelica could search each room. They were all laid out the same way, with an infuser and sanitary shower—nowhere to hide.

With no other choice, I returned to the room where I'd seen Dr. Whisper and the strange people sitting at the dinner table. If they were still there, this would be a risky move but I had no other choice.

My time with Noah's people running up and down their walkways had left my legs strong. I felt healthier than I ever had before. I outpaced Angelica and entered the room.

The room lay abandoned, and I took my chance, scurrying to the massive table and hiding underneath. Moments later, Angelica rushed past with others close behind. The room appeared to be off-limits as no one entered. I waited, exhausted. Unable to keep my eyes open, I fell into a restless slumber.

* * *

When the morning music echoed through the hallways, I jolted awake, filled with dread. I had slept through the infusion period, and soon the halls would fill with people. What did the First Nurses do during the day?

I emerged from my hiding spot and looked around. Could I reason with Myrrhis? I couldn't stay here. That much was certain. My eyes roamed the room, taking in the entrance I'd used to enter, the lift I'd ridden with the First Nurses, and the trolleys filled with clean dishware, ready for dinner.

A delectable aroma wafted through the air, reminding me of my favorite dish—ji! I was sure it was a message from Noah. Inspiration struck. I knew how to find my way back to the kitchen. The plates traveled in and out of the openings in the wall, each equipped with a small lift connected to the kitchen. I crawled inside one, hit the button, and held my breath as the door closed. The lift ascended.

When the door opened, my heart sank. I was back in the kitchen. Several people bustled around making food, but Noah was nowhere to be seen. Dr. Whisper sat in a massive chair on wheels, surrounded by three muscular guards. Kendel stood rolling balls of ji, a look of grief on her face and eyes puffy with tears. The guards turned to me.

I pushed all the buttons at once. Then, just as the doors were about to close, one guard strode over and blocked it with his foot. He forced me out of the lift, and two men pinned me on either side.

"Hello, Persi," Dr. Whisper smirked as his chair rolled toward me. "Do you have something you'd like to give me?"

"First, I have questions for you," I said, sounding braver than I felt and hoping to delay the moment when he learned I no longer had the spirit root.

His expression changed to anger as he shouted, "You have questions for me? Search her!" The men pushed me against the wall, and I knew my time was up.

CHAPTER FORTY-FIVE

I WOKE UP to find a cloth bag over my head, body aching from rough handling. Someone yanked me to my feet and dragged me along what seemed to be a hallway. We entered a room filled with the mouth-watering aroma of tasty food.

"Noah!" I tried to shout through the suffocating cloth, but my voice was muffled. The fabric grew damp from my breathing, and I struggled for air. Then, something hit my tailbone hard, and they ripped the bag from my head, revealing a room filled with flickering candlelight.

In front of me was a silver plate set with a knife and fork, while across the table sat Dr. Whisper, his gargantuan body and bulbous nose vastly different from his avatar. But his dark, piercing eyes were all too familiar.

Beside him sat an ancient-looking woman while a row of First Nurses sat, one after the other, like human statues. My heart skipped a beat as I saw Myrrhis staring straight ahead between a man and a woman.

Dr. Whisper was the only one moving, shoveling food into his mouth and making smacking noises as he chewed with his mouth open. He gestured towards me with a finger. "A moment," he said before swallowing an enormous mouthful of ji. "Persi, my dear, welcome to dinner. I apologize for starting without you."

I tried to stand but got forced to my seat by the men behind me.

Dr. Whisper raised his hand. "Now, now. I'd like an enjoyable meal now, wouldn't you, Persi? Your friend, Noah, cooked a delectable dinner. And in such a beautiful room, wouldn't you agree?"

As I surveyed my surroundings, I realized that my earlier rush through the room hadn't allowed me to appreciate its splendor. The walls were gilded with a golden material. Or maybe it was gold? Hundreds of candles flickered in silver sconces on the walls, casting a warm and mesmerizing light. Delicate images of two beautiful angels holding long, gold instruments were painted on the ceiling.

Trumpets.

The room combined magic with beauty; however, the loathsome man sitting across from me ruined the stunning ambience. The door opened, and a shuffling figure entered.

It was Noah, but he struggled to walk because of strange, jerky movements. Veins bulged from his neck. As he approached, I saw blood around his collarbone—a *garland*. Dr. Whisper had implanted a garland into Noah!

"Serve our guest first." Dr. Whisper said with a grin.

"What did you do to him?"

Dr. Whisper frowned at Noah, then turned back to me. "He fought the neuro implant vigorously. However, it is you who perplexes me, Persi." His eyes narrowed. I felt a tingling in my garland, and a distant knocking echoed in my head. This time, I did not let him in. "You seem to be somewhat immune. It must run in your family. Remember, though, that I broke your parents, eventually."

Again I tried to get to my feet, and the men forced me down. This time, I kept struggling. I bit the man's hand as hard as I could, tasting the salty tang of blood.

"Ouch!" Dr. Whisper shouted. "I do not tolerate misbehavior." One guard raised a safety gun and pointed it at me. "Noah made a scrumptious meal, and your theatrics will ruin my feast. Stop now, or you will suffer."

"Go ahead. I've been shot before. Noah! Noah? Are you okay?" He stood near Myrrhis. "Myrrhis? Can you hear me?" A second guard pointed one of the long black guns I'd seen before.

"You'd do well to sit still and enjoy dinner unless you'd like a hole in your head."

Uncertain what the other weapon did, I stopped struggling and sat back down.

"That's better. Years ago, in the twenty-first century, I held fundraisers in this room. Some were enjoyable, but a certain unpleasant sort appeared. They asked tedious philosophical questions, forgetting that to make an omelet, you must break a few eggs. Isn't that true, Gertie?" he turned to the woman beside him and nodded. She nodded along with him, and then, horrifically, her head continued to bob back and forth as if unable to stop.

"Oh, quit nodding, you silly git. You don't have a brain left to embody." The woman stopped, and her head drooped to one side.

"Gertrude was one of my original donors. However, she lacked faith in science, so I had to help her see the truth through more forceful means." It was then that I noticed something strange; they all blinked at the same time—even Myrrhis.

"Do you understand? Now, please, eat!" Then, with a tightened jaw, Dr. Whisper turned to Noah and seemed to use his mind to force Noah into submission. "Serve our guest!" he commanded. Sweat dripped down Noah's forehead as he approached, his hand shaking. He ladled me moon soup, then stumbled away.

Dr. Whisper noticed the horror on my face and spoke. "Oh, you ain't seen nothing yet," he laughed. Myrrhis, the woman next to the doctor, and all the First Nurses echoed Dr. Whisper's horrible laughter. When he stopped and belched, they all belched in unison.

"What did you do to them?"

"Liberated," Dr. Whisper replied with a smile. "I made a bet with some colleagues to see who could achieve immortality first. While they may have succeeded before me, my method has proven superior. By transferring my consciousness into self-perpetuating clones, I will live forever. We will live forever. Recipe X is almost complete. Would you like to try the soup?" Everyone, including Dr. Whisper, lifted a spoonful and slurped it in unison.

"Delicious," they said in one voice. It was sickening to hear Myrrhis speaking with such a horrible man. But her voice, her beautiful voice, was still her own. Or was it? Perhaps she was no longer there. I covered my ears, unable to stand hearing them speak together. "Stop it!" I cried out.

Dr. Whisper scowled, still slurping soup. "Fine, fine. Why are people so narrow-minded?" he said, speaking on his own.

I remembered the mouth sores, constant fatigue, and Myrrhis' rashes. "We were never healthy. I didn't know what true health was until I left."

Soup dribbled down his chin. "You owe me your life."

"Everyone I knew in the Free Cities had something wrong with them, some chronic illness. We were all tired all the time. You poisoned us with your infusion, pretending to give us a longer life."

"Not true. You will become immortal *through* me, although not as distinct individuals. That's an inconsequential matter purely for the sake of practicality."

"What do you mean?"

"The hive mind. You'll learn about it soon."

"Your recipe benefits only you."

"Ungrateful girl! I provided everything you needed—health, meaning, purpose."

"The bears. The First Nurses?"

"In part, although the toy bears also serve a commercial function. The Nurses provided Free Citizens with a useful distraction. As for me, well, I've always fancied dancers but never had much rhythm myself," he said with a wink.

"Why didn't you join the other immortals if they achieved it first?" I asked. "Why not just leave us alone?"

My question irritated him. He slammed his fist on the table. "The others achieved immortality *without* a human body. That is no life at all! Life without the pleasures of food? Sex? What kind of recipe is that? A recipe for despair. Technology became their god, but they were duped. Science is the true religion, and the body is its temple."

The moon soup sat steaming in front of me., reminding me of Noah. It was then that I noticed it—the spirit root floating in the soup. Noah must have taken it from me in the kitchen, but he trusted me enough to give it back! I blinked away my tears and stirred some green vegetables to hide it from view.

"We cannot trust individuals to make the right choices," he said with disgust. "Humanity has proven that. The illusion of freedom is better than freedom itself," he added, laughing as his mouth transformed into a yawning maw of fleshy pink surrounding perfect white teeth.

As he laughed, inspiration struck me. I had an idea, a plan, my destiny. I took a spoonful of the moon soup and placed the spirit root in my mouth. I remained silent, not wanting to reveal my intentions.

"Noah is yours to possess if you tell me where the root is," Dr. Whisper said. "Imagine, Persi, he will be at your command. You'll feel everything he feels, and he'll only feel what you want him to. You'll own him forever."

I pretended to think it over for a moment, then I nodded and allowed a small smile to spread across my lips. "I knew you'd see reason, but I wasn't sure when," Dr. Whisper said, laughing again, mouth opened wide.

Without hesitation, I spit out the spirit root with all my strength, just like I did with the cradleberry seeds on that sunny morning with Noah. It flew across the table into Dr. Whisper's mouth, and he choked. His eyes opened wide with shock and anger as he realized what I'd done. The veins in his temples throbbed, and two of the First Nurses rose to pound on his chest.

Several seconds later, he coughed and swallowed. The guards at my side grabbed me as the entire room, including my sister, erupted in rage.

"What have you done?" they all shouted.

"I gave you what you wanted," I said. "The spirit root."

Noah, the only person not entirely under Dr. Whisper's control, moaned. Dr. Whisper swallowed hard. "Not for me to consume, you fool! To create Recipe X and solidify the hive mind!" he shouted.

He stuck his fingers down his throat and gagged several times. As I watched, the spirit root took hold of him, just as it had with me. Dr. Whisper's face trembled, and tears filled his eyes. "You don't understand what you've done," he said. "I'm the only one who can access the infuser. Without me, the infusions will cease, and—"

His eyes darted around the room as if seeking an escape. "This isn't fair. The contract must be honored! If I die, you're all doomed." His guests, those under his control, including my sister, convulsed. I ran to Myrrhis, and no one stopped me.

"It would have been superbly delicious," mumbled Dr. Whisper, his head lolling forward and back. "Recipe X was almost complete, a medical opus...." The rest of his words became incoherent.

"Myrrhis! It's me, Persi!" I grabbed her hand, but she didn't respond. Behind me, dishes shattered on the floor as Dr. Whisper's chair tipped sideways, pulling the tablecloth and his food with him.

Covered in moon soup, flowered rice, and my least favorite, peppered okra, Dr. Whisper's eyes shot to the ceiling, and saliva bubbled from his lips. Then he opened his mouth in a giant howl. When his body piked and spasmed, I buried my face in Myrrhis' shoulder. It was too horrific to watch. The next time I dared look, he lay still, his mouth gaped open and staring at the two angels.

CHAPTER FORTY-SIX

THE ENTIRE ROOM went silent. The guards were breathing shallowly while Myrrhis and the other First Nurses lay in awkward positions but were still alive. Noah stood unsteadily.

"Are you okay?" I asked.

A look of shame washed over his face. "I'll manage."

I lifted my sister's head from the table and removed the mashed potatoes from her hair. I stroked her head and tried to awaken her, but she wouldn't or couldn't respond. Noah checked Dr. Whisper and confirmed that he was dead.

Myrrhis would only respond if I told her to do something, and she would do it automatically. I wondered if she still had a brain.

We found Dr. Whisper's inner sanctum, where more of his pawns lay in various states of paralysis. Again, no one tried to stop us or even looked at us. The room had an unmade bed and smelled of sour sweat, with dance slippers filling every corner.

"There must be thousands of slippers," I said as I looked around the room. "How many years or decades...." It made me wonder how many other Persis had lived in The Hive over the years.

There was a room off the bedroom with a giant circular window facing The Cliffs. I knew this view well, as I'd seen it during my clifftop meetings with Dr. Whisper. Beyond this room was a smaller one with a control panel, where multiple screens showed rotating views of different areas in The Hive.

"Those must be the five sectors and the various zones you mentioned," Noah whispered. He still hadn't quite gotten his voice back. While most of the views were dark and silent, I recognized a few faces in one area as people left their infusion chambers, looking confused. On the wall were flashing warning lights on a silver console and a screen displaying: *All Sector Warning: Recipe X Critical Failure.* Noah and I did not know what any of the equipment did.

Outside in the halls, people wandered around in confusion. Only those directly under Dr. Whisper's control suffered severe effects after his death—for example, poor Myrrhis.

A series of musical chimes ran. I knew this sound well. Once upon a time, it was the time I looked forward to the most—the dance of the First Nurses.

* * *

Several hundred people had gathered in the Great Hall, and I stood hidden down the hallway near the stage entrance as I gathered my thoughts and nerves. I kept searching for Angelica, but she was nowhere to be seen. Nervousness filled my stomach. Noah and Kendel were with me, observing and waiting. Kendel's ankle was still healing, but she was otherwise fine.

For a long time, the crowd remained silent, but a murmur rose when the First Nurses did not enter. An air of unease filled the large room as the time for the dance passed, and nothing happened.

It felt strange to stand ready to enter the stage when I had always pictured myself with the grace of a First Nurse. Right now, I felt anything but graceful.

"Well? What are you waiting for?" Kendel asked.

"You need to tell them what happened," Noah agreed. "Right?"

"Why don't you speak to them, Noah?" I asked.

"Me? Persi, it needs to be you. You know that." Noah put a gentle hand on my shoulder.

"Kendel?" I turned to her, but she just glared at me. Despite the positive outcome, Kendel remained angry with me for taking the spirit root.

I sighed. In my dream, I had always stood on the stage alone. "What will I say to them?"

"The truth as best you can," Noah said. "They deserve the truth for once."

Hundreds of eyes widened as I entered the room, crossing through the crowd and climbing the stairs to the center of the stage. My heart was pounding in my throat, but I realized that what I was feeling was not only anxiety but also excitement.

I stood where I had watched Dr. Whisper's avatar all those years—a fake doctor, fake health, and a fake existence built on fear. In the Great Hall, I'd watched what I thought was a beautiful dance, but in reality, it was a nightmare experiment.

Questions filled my mind: would they believe me? And if they did, would they be ready to accept the truth?

"Uh, hi there, uhm—"

Great start.

I took a deep breath and began again. "Hello, everyone. I know you must be confused right now. But I want to let you know what's going on. You have been told lies for years, but that's over now."

I could see the surprise on their faces as I spoke. They were used to seeing the First Nurses or Doctor Whisper, but now, here I was, telling them what they believed was the truth was a lie.

I continued, "You need to understand that we were part of an experiment. The doctor used fear to manipulate us into believing things that weren't true."

At first, it all seemed to go well, and I congratulated myself on my communication skills. It all unraveled when I mentioned the end of the infusions. A low rumbling passed through the room. I heard snatches of words like *sabotage* and *assassinated*.

I raised my voice to make myself heard, "No, that's not what happened. We were part of an experiment, and Doctor Whisper had planned to merge our identities and kill our spirits. He had already started the process."

Then someone spoke. A man I recognized—Nurse Sammon. "Without our infusions, we will die."

I replied, "No, that's not true. Without proper sustenance, you will die. So you'll need to eat from now on, which was another thing Doctor Whisper lied to you about. Eating is not harmful. It is life-giving. Doctor Whisper ate a lot himself and hid that from you."

I hesitated, realizing how complex this concept was, but they needed to learn sooner rather than later. They had already missed one infusion, and another was just a couple of hours away.

"Eat?" Nurse Sammon whispered, his face twitching, then shouted, "Eater!" He pointed his scan gun at my garland and fired. I looked down at my garland. One stone went out. However, thanks to Dr. Whisper's gift to me, many remained lit. Not that his mattered any longer. Sammon raised his safety gun, ready to fire again.

"Stop!" I shouted, and to my surprise, he obeyed. The fact that the safety guns were still functioning gave me an idea. I looked at the rows of confused faces illuminated by the garlands, some fully lit and others much less so. Noah ran up onto the stage and grabbed my hand. "You better go. Give them time to think this through. Or maybe... maybe we should leave this place altogether?"

A chorus of whispers spread throughout the room, reminiscent of the dance of the First Nurses. "No," I said, and I took the First Position. The room quieted as I began the dance. The crowd parted as I descended the stairs and moved among them, respect and silence following me. I lost myself in the dance for a few moments, tears streaming down my face. My dream had come true, but in a much different circumstance than I had expected.

When I reached the center of the room, I stopped. I wasn't sure if my plan would work. What else might have stopped working if the infusion equipment had failed? However, the garlands seemed to have a separate circuit, a separate system.

I focused all my attention on the sensation I had felt whenever Dr. Whisper contacted me. I concentrated on the stones and let my mind shine out. I heard a knocking sound as if a hundred hands were banging on a hundred doors. My garland ignited with a bright glow, and then it happened: my mind linked and connected with all the minds in the room!

A sense of euphoria overwhelmed me. This was the connection that Dr. Whisper had fed from and wanted to make permanent using the spirit root. I envisioned Nurse Sammon dropping his safety gun, and he did. I envisioned every Free Citizen looking at me, and they did. I moved them to the left, then to the right. Each time I did it, I felt thrills of energy coursing through my body. I saw through each of their eyes and felt them all looking at me. The power intensified and coursed through my being, reminding me of the first night when Noah and I—

"Persi!" Noah's shout brought me back to reality. He was standing there, his garland glowing in resonance with mine, reminding me of the day we had eaten spirit root together, but this experience was paler and lacked something.

"What are you doing?" his voice echoed in the silent room.

"Setting them free," I whispered. I sent them images and let them into my mind. The energy I had gained dissipated as the minds, hungry for truth, absorbed my experiences and learned the truth about Dr. Whisper—at least, most of it. I blocked the last images I had of the doctor, of him dying on the floor. It was too much too soon, even for me. That would come later. A collective sob rose from the room.

Heat built around my neck. The garland seared my skin as it burned my flesh. Then, after one last burst of images, it shattered and disintegrated, falling to the floor as fine glass dust. All my stones were gone. Across the room, a similar phenomenon occurred, and the faint smell of singed flesh and electronics filled the air as people's garlands self-destructed.

CHAPTER FORTY-SEVEN

KENDEL FOUND A giant storehouse of food in Zone Six. This was a zone that no one except the First Nurses ever visited. They were too far gone for it to register. After all, Dr. Whisper even ate with them, and they did not care.

"What will you make them to eat?" I asked Noah. "This will be their first meal."

Noah smiled. "Well, I learned a lot when I made recipes for you. You were extremely fussy. Can they be any worse?"

I kissed his cheek. "I hope not. Was the other Persi the same? Did she also love ji?" Until now, I'd avoided asking about her. It made me uncomfortable to think of Noah with this other me.

Noah's face darkened. "No. She refused to eat no matter what I brought. Then, after we removed the garland, she lapsed into unconsciousness."

"She *never* ate? Not even when you gave her moon soup?"

Noah shook his head. "In fairness, I never made her moon soup. You gave me the idea for that recipe. But no, she would never eat."

"That's why you feel responsible?"

Noah nodded. "That and because I convinced her to have the garland removed."

"I thought you were in love with her."

His face broke into a smile. "She looks like you. Her voice sounded like yours. But I never got to know her the same way."

Relief washed over me, and I hurried away to help prepare what would be the first meal for most. What else but moon soup—well, my version of it. We didn't have the same ingredients that Noah had back home. When I finished a test run of the stock—the recipe is quite intricate—I gave it to Noah to taste.

We exchanged nervous glances. He tried it, and his face split into a grin. "Persi, you've learned to cook!"

"Well, just in time."

Noah, Kendel, and I began serving their first meal two hours later. "Let's serve them in the infusion rooms. Breakfast in bed—I mean in their pods. That will be easiest. They already associate the pods with healing, even if it's untrue."

Noah had no opinion. "You know them. I trust your instinct."

Kendel sighed. "My ankle still aches, but I'll do my best to help."

We hadn't counted on how much work it would be to travel from room to room, doling out soup and teaching them to use spoons. It was now day three since people had had their last infusion. Well, day three in the real world. That meant people had missed twelve infusions. People were weak…and, while they didn't understand it yet…hungry.

There were a few misunderstandings and difficulties, but in the end, all were willing to taste the soup. And after that first slurp, when the bellies awakened and the taste buds fired? As I'd discovered myself, Noah's moon soup was delicious and impossible to resist.

* * *

Rows of vegetables and fruit trees that bore red, green, and purple globes sat under a giant translucent dome that covered the topmost level. "Zone Seven. It's just like heaven."

Noah and Kendel gazed around, also in wonder.

"Is that what people said?" Noah asked.

"It was a saying I heard before, but it died out. I don't think most people believed Zone Seven existed." There was so much life here I could almost hear the plants growing. But there was also an eerie stillness. Robotic harvesters sat frozen in motion. "I need to show the

Free Citizens everything so they can make up their minds."

"Make up their minds about what?" Kendel asked.

"Whether they live here or go back to The Cliffs."

Kendel's eyebrows raised. Noah cleared his throat and scratched his chin. "Persi, I'm honored, and while you are welcome, my people would need to vote. It would take time to provide food for so many extra mouths."

My face reddened. "Of course. First, I'll call a vote to see if they would like to petition your community." I realized I spoke as if I were their leader. It was an odd feeling, and an enormous weight of responsibility descended.

That afternoon, everyone assembled in the Great Hall. It was unnecessary to tell them to do this. Even though the dance of the First Nurses had ceased many days ago, people still followed their routines.

Lining up in neat rows, they stood and watched the stage. It made my belly flutter, the whole thing. Although it had become necessary to address the crowd and nothing terrible had happened, I still felt frightened every time.

"The Hive has been your home for a long time; I understand that. However, we may not have enough resources to feed everyone here long term. Some of you might need to return to Noah's community if they will have us."

It had not been difficult to gather their attention. However, the look on their faces appeared to be extreme confusion.

"All those in favor of petitioning to live in The Cliffs with Noah and Kendel's community, raise your hand." Not a single person budged. A stab of disappointment ran through me. Well, it made sense people had known this place for their entire lives. It had been hard to leave, and I had Dr. Whisper's support.

"All those who favor staying here in The Hive and working to create something new." I expected a flood of enthusiasm. Again, nothing. People looked from one to the other, and no one reacted or did anything.

Noah told me I wasn't responsible for them. Okay, that was easy for him to say, but my action ended Dr. Whisper's control. Didn't that make me responsible?

"Please, you need to help me. What do you want?"

"What does Dr. Whisper want us to do?" A skinny woman in the front asked. Her face was gaunt. She looked terrified.

"Dr. Whisper is gone," I reminded her.

"What do you want us to want?" Nurse Sammon asked in a timid, shaky voice, his eyes wide. Not long ago, Nurse Sammon scared me—or at least the power he wielded. It felt odd to hear this question from him.

"What do I want you to want? For you to make up your own minds. Please think this through. Look in your hearts and decide what is right for each of you! Together, we'll come to some agreement and make it happen. How does that sound?"

Nurse Sammon nodded, and heads bobbed all around. My brain hurt. "Maybe I haven't given you enough information about The Cliffs to decide. Perhaps a few of you would like to visit and report back?"

Again, there was no reaction. "If anyone wants to talk to me and ask me questions…well, I'm here."

Afterward, I grabbed Noah. "The next time we call everyone together, I won't do it in the Great Hall. That's where we watched the First Nurses. It's where Dr. Whisper addressed us. It has too much baggage. I need to help people leave that behind.

"You can't force people to think for themselves. They have to want to wake up," Noah said, doubt in his voice.

Noah, Kendel, and I were working hard, harvesting from the garden and trying to feed everyone, but our hands were blistered, and we were only getting a few hours of sleep. We needed help, but the Free Citizens were not very efficient. We couldn't continue to feed this many people on our own for much longer.

CHAPTER FORTY-EIGHT

MY NEW LIFE took me from one challenge to another. Despite saving Myrrhis from Dr. Whisper, I feared I'd been too late. None of the First Nurses could function on their own. Each of them lay glassy-eyed, breathing but doing little else. People came from The Cliffs to help, and it took ten of us caring for them around the clock to feed them.

With Senior's permission, Kendel brought back spirit root, and Noah gave each of them a small amount. I was nervous about administering it as I wondered how damaged they were and if the same fate that befell Dr. Whisper would happen to them. But nothing happened, neither good nor bad.

I brought Myrrhis back to our old ward. Using soft fabrics Noah borrowed from The Cliffs, I made a bed out of her pod. It was kind of like the ones I'd grown to find comfortable. Piper and I took turns, but I spent the most time with her. Piper had been the brother we loved but didn't quite understand. He didn't know what to do with himself around her.

So I sat with her for hours, barely sleeping, and today, I stroked her hand as I gazed at the room with its bland metallic walls, three pods, and a disinfection shower. I wondered if bringing her back here was a mistake as all these rooms looked the same. Noah had wanted to take her back to The Cliffs, but I feared the change might do more harm than good.

"You're okay, Myrrhis. It's me, Persi. You're alright." I thought of what I'd learned about our names. *Myrrhis.* "We're named after spices. Isn't that crazy?" What could I do to remind her of me? Of how much I loved her? My garland was gone, and hers lay dark and inactive. When the other garlands disintegrated, the entire system ceased to function.

"Myrrhis, look at me." Her eyes turned to me, and she blinked. When spoken to, she would react, but if I left her alone, she would sit and stare at the wall for hours. Now that we were providing them with food and drink, their faces had regained some color, but I found the issue of urination and defecation challenging.

"They're like adult babies," Noah said as he entered the room, sweat on his brow and a troubled look on his face. "Completely helpless." He sat next to me and put his strong, warm hand on my knee.

I continued holding Myrrhis' hand, hoping the physical contact did not cause her distress. "Do you think she's in there, listening to me? Or did Dr. Whisper break her forever?"

Noah opened his mouth to speak, but then closed it again. Hope sparkled in his eyes, but then faded. "I don't know, but I want to get to know her," he said.

An idea struck me. "Maybe she'd like to hear one of your stories, like the ones you told me about life at The Cliffs?"

Noah blushed. "Ah, she doesn't want to hear my silly stories. Why don't you tell her yours?"

"I have no stories, and my garland is gone," I said. But I'd experienced so much to get to this point. Perhaps Noah was right.

After Noah left, I helped Myhrris recline on the pod bed and lay beside her. I leaned my lips close to her ear and spoke in a whisper. "A chocolate cupcake changed my life. Back then, I had no idea that such a delightful thing existed. The Hive was the only world I knew."

When I finished my tale, I drifted off to sleep. Movement jolted me awake. Myhrris stirred beside me, and when I opened my eyes, she was gazing right at me.

"Persi," she muttered. "That's the most unbelievable story I've ever heard... I don't believe a single word of it. What are you doing lying in my pod?"

Not caring whether she believed my story, I wrapped my arms around her and hugged her tight. "You're back."

CHAPTER FORTY-NINE

SEVERAL POTS BUBBLED on the giant stove. Sweat gathered on my upper lip as I monitored the savory donuts until they browned to perfection. Tonight, Crane, Senior, a few others from The Cliffs were visiting, and I suggested we welcome them with dinner. Noah wrapped his arms around me from behind and grabbed a donut.

"Hey!" I slapped his hand. "The sauce isn't ready yet...plus that was a perfect specimen."

"Mmm, delicious," he spoke with a full mouth. "They all look perfect."

After two hours of preparation, we finally finished the banquet room. I walked around the large space, lighting candles as I went. This was Noah's idea, and I was under the protective gaze of the two angels as I worked.

Initially, I planned to burn the entire room after Dr. Whisper's body had been removed, but Noah convinced me it might set The Hive on fire. He also felt that Dr. Whisper's body deserved respect, and I agreed.

However, Noah was hesitant about having dinner in the room at first. His eyes grew distant at the suggestion. When Dr. Whisper took control of Noah's body and tried to break his mind, it changed something in him. I hoped he would heal—that we would all heal.

* * *

I lit the final candle and surveyed the room. The golden accents on the four columns cast shimmering reflections. A perfumed smoky scent filled the air, soon to be replaced by the aroma of delicious food. To calm my nerves, I poured myself a small glass of red wine. The taste of fermented grape enlivened my tongue.

Crane, Senior, and others from The Cliffs would soon join us, along with Nurse Sammon and a few brave Free Citizens. It didn't surprise me that more Free Citizens didn't want to come. Anything outside of their routine often filled them with near-crippling anxiety. I worried that Nurse Sammon only agreed to attend because I asked him to. I had to clarify that he wouldn't lose points if he didn't come and that the decision was his.

Eating was one hurdle we had mainly overcome. We needed to convince them they no longer had to worry about being scanned for random violations or leaving their designated zones, as there were no longer any restrictions.

When it came time for dinner, I was so hungry I forgot my nerves—well, almost. I sat next to Myhhris. "You've taken to eating much faster than I did," I commented as she tucked into one of the savory donuts. Myhhris shrugged. "I do what I'm told, and you told me to eat."

My fork froze in midair and I turned to look at her.

"Please tell me she's joking." Noah sat to my left.

"Are you joking?" I asked Myhrris.

"If you want me to be," she said, face blank.

My appetite disappeared as quick as it had come. Then, Myhhris smiled and poked me in the ribs. "Yes, I'm joking."

Crane, Senior, and several others from The Cliffs faced us across the table. Mercy had declined the invitation, and I felt a pang of disappointment as I'd hoped to put aside our differences. Kendel and Piper sat together at the end of the table, inseparable.

Everyone appeared to be taken aback by the room's grandeur, with Kendel whispering and pointing at the intricate moldings. Petrof and Effie sat with their mouths dropped open, gawking. The towering domed ceiling and the flickering candlelight added to the magical atmosphere, making conversation seem almost unnecessary. I noticed Crane had not yet tried the savory donuts, and when she finally took a bite, I took a large sip of wine and braced myself.

She chewed for a moment, then turned to Noah with a smile. "These are incredible, as always, Noah."

"Well, I do my best," Noah said with a modest shrug. Had he forgotten that I had made the donuts all on my own, with no help from him or anyone else? I was about to nudge him with my foot, but he beat me to it and smacked his forehead. "I'm such a fool. Persi made the donuts. I had no part in it whatsoever."

Crane then turned to me. "Who would have thought that the girl who wouldn't eat would become the girl who can create such delicate flavors?" she said after finishing another golden brown donut. My heart filled with pride. All this time, I thought I would redeem myself through dancing, but it was through donuts.

The conversation became lively as the night went on, and the wine flowed. Senior explained they couldn't integrate all the Free Citizens at once. Crane chimed in, "However, you, Noah, Myrrhis, and a few others can come with us. We'll rotate people from The Cliffs to help." She waited for my response, her expression unreadable. The Cliffs felt more like home than anywhere else, but it was because of me that the lives of the Free Citizens had changed. Leaving would feel like abandoning them.

"People know and trust me here. I'll stay at The Hive until the last Free Citizen is settled here or at The Cliffs," I said, placing my hand on Noah's arm. "Noah, I'll miss you, but we can—"

He grabbed my hand and kissed it. "I'm not going anywhere. If you stay, then I stay."

"But we've all missed your cooking, Noah. I'm unsure how long we can wait for your return." Senior appeared to be joking—well, half joking.

Noah grinned. "Consider that fire under everyone's butt to help us get all these people independent."

Crane nodded. "We owe you our thanks, Persi," she said. Her words felt begrudging but heartfelt. "Noah told us what happened with the spirit root. How did you know it would work?"

"Mother—" Noah raised his hand.

"No, it's okay," I said. "When I took the spirit root the first time, something or someone told me that was what I needed to do. It also came from a dream. To be honest, I wasn't sure it would work. I'm grateful that it did."

Crane nodded, and the conversation moved on to other topics. Midway through dinner, Noah rang his spoon against the glass to get everyone's attention. All eyes turned to him, and we had spoken about this earlier. He had told me it was customary for hosts to make a toast to their guests, and I should be the one to do it.

My hand trembled as I held up my glass. The red wine looked as dark as blood in the candlelight. "A toast to unexpected pleasures," I said, glancing at Crane. An amused smile spread across her face. "And to our guests from The Cliffs," I nodded at the crew, "and to the Free Citizens, for whom eating is still rather new." Nurse Sammon, another man, and three women smiled shyly, and I noted they had not yet touched their meals. There was still work to do.

"Noah and I struggled with whether we should have dinner here tonight. Dr. Whisper used to address the Free Citizens from here while he ate, although you never saw him in person, just his avatar. By celebrating and eating with you, I hope we can leave those ghosts behind and look towards what I hope will be a delicious future."

The entire table clapped and pounded their knives on the table. After dinner, we had one of my favorite desserts, cradleberry pie. "You must have hidden the berries from me! I never even saw you make it."

"Petrof brought them," Noah said.

"I remember you mentioned how much you enjoyed picking them," Petrof said with a bark of a laugh.

Holding my fingers to the flickering light, I examined them. "Yes. They're still slightly purple."

After dessert, there was music, which led to more drinking. Kendel and Piper sang together while the entire table clapped. Piper jumped up on the table and knocked over a vase of flowers. The Free Citizens gasped in wonder as the music's tempo increased.

Crane approach from behind. "May I have this dance?" she whispered.

We moved to the center of the room. She took First Position, and traditionally, I should have followed. Instead, I took Third.

Her face broke open into the biggest smile I'd ever seen her make. "What beautiful harmony," she said, and we continued like that. I matched her Fourth with the Second Position, and we moved about the room.

Noah joined us, and we broke into fits of laughter when I tried to teach him First Position, and he fell on his butt. Wine, food, and dance flowed well into the night, and a warm glow of happiness filled my belly. Despite the certainty of countless challenges ahead, both seen and unseen, I'd never felt more content.

<< >>

Continue reading to be the first to hear about Book 2 in the *Awakened Series*!

Hey there! I have a quick question: did *Recipe X* make your mouth water and leave you feeling satisfied?

If you loved it, then I would be so grateful if you could do me a solid and leave a review. Your review will help other readers out there find my work and enjoy it as much as you did. Remember, sharing is caring!

Your feedback means everything to me, and I am eagerly looking forward to hearing your thoughts. So, please don't hesitate to share your opinions and spread the deliciousness.

Thank you in advance. You're awesome!

Join my V.I.P. list! Get a FREE Book plus be the first to learn about Book 2 in *The Awakened* Series, receive advance review copies and other good stuff!

Join my V.I.P. List
www.mskaminsky.com

Other Books By M.S. Kaminsky

The Mermaid Curse Series
Amazon #1 Bestselling Series
Heart pounding with plenty of twists and turns, bestselling author M.S. Kaminsky takes you on a suspenseful fantasy adventure you won't forget...

Alabaster Island
Winner of the New York Author Project contest in YA Fiction.
Now available as an Audio Book - FREE with an Audible trial!

The Atlantis Twins: Book 1
"Not many books surprise me like this one did."

The Atlantis Song - Book 2
"Epic Mermaid Fantasy Rages On!"

The Atlantis Queens - Book 3
"I love, love, love this series! Read these! And then share the wealth!"

Merman Rising: A Standalone Mermaid Curse Book

Deep in the ocean evil stirs, corruption reigns and the only escape is up.

Other Books By M.S. Kaminsky

Thunder's Rhyme

A violent past. An ill-fated mission. A love that refuses to die.

The Last Wolf

A sixteen-year-old shifter who is the last of her kind. A school for magical creatures on the brink of catastrophe. Learn who to trust fast or it's extinction, baby.